PSYCHO PATH II

PSYCHO PATH II

Psychotic Break

J.C. TOLLIVER

AuthorHouse™ LLC
1663 Liberty Drive
Bloomington, IN 47403
www.authorhouse.com
Phone: 1-800-839-8640

Published by AuthorHouse 05/08/2014

ISBN: 978-1-4969-0473-7 (sc)
ISBN: 978-1-4969-0472-0 (e)

PREFACE

Charlie, Chase's best friend, knew he had to think fast about what he was going to do with her body but he just wanted a little more time with her while she was dead. She was his first victim. He did not mean to kill her, but she left him no choice once she had seen his face and could identify him. He did not want to have sex with a dead woman that was not what he was about. He was about causing terror. What he did want to do was lie next to her until her body had become cold. She started to get stiff. He savored the coldness. It was like the coldness he felt in his heart. He thought his heart was made of ice. He held her hand and he told her how beautiful she was. He told her nice things. Things that he could never tell a live woman and mean them. He wanted to keep something of hers to remind him of how special she was to him. He decided that he would keep a lock of her beautiful hair as a memento. He did not like the word trophy, at least not for her. She was his first victim, therefore special. He rolled her over to her back. He made two small ponytails on the back of her hair underneath, and then he cut the locks of hair. He didn't know why he felt like he had to hide the spot where the hair was cut from because she would be unrecognizable soon, once the water and creatures of the river took what it would. He cut a lock for himself and one for Chase. He wanted to share something of this first experience of killing a woman with his best friend. He turned her back over on her back. He brushed her long, brown hair down over her shoulders. He pushed her tongue back into her mouth. He shut her mouth. He did not close her eyes until the very last. He could see himself in her glossy dead eyes and he was so happy that he was the last person she ever saw.

He felt immortal now somehow, now that he got her prized virginity and that he would forever be the light in her eyes. He lay with her for a long time after, just staring into her eyes and reliving the intimate experience that they both had shared together.

DEDICATION

Psycho Path II, my second novel is dedicated to my loving husband, who always sees me through to the end. I also dedicate this new novel to all of my amazing new fans.

Into The Darkness

The darkness comes, the darkness goes,
you only see what I want to show.
I could be your neighbor, friend, pastor, lover,
you will never know, I'm under cover.
If you get too close, and I'm out of control
I'll use your body and take your soul.
I travel the streets under the cloak of night,
I will get you if you are in my sights.
My life goes on, I'll kill and kill,
until death overcomes me, and I'm still.

J.C. Tolliver

"PSYCHO PATH II"

"Psychotic Break"

"PART I"

Caleb and Molly decided to call Caleb, Jr. Chase. It was much easier not to get Caleb Jr. and Sr. mixed up when you were talking to one of them. They asked Chase if that would be okay with him. He replied, "Yes, I like that name better anyway."

Caleb and Chase got back to the house from the barn. They wiped the mud off of their feet on the back mat. Molly knew Chase and she knew right away that something was wrong. He was looking down and shuffling his feet back and forth with his arms crossed in front of him. He did not even look her in the eyes, he just said", Night Mom." she said, Goodnight Chase". Chase turned and headed upstairs to his room to get ready for bed. Caleb told his son "Good night" then he sat down at the kitchen table and Molly sat down next to him. She urgently said, "I just got Katie in bed, before you walked in the door. She is probably still awake, if you want to go and tell her goodnight." He replied, "Yes, I'll go and kiss her goodnight. Caleb walked into Katie's bedroom and knelt next to her toddler bed. She was the sweetest little thing that Caleb had ever seen. Caleb thought she was really smart for her ripe old age of two. She smiled at him, this always melted his heart. She pleaded with a look he could not resist, "Daddy, book, pleaseeee". Caleb said, "Okay honey, a short story". She gave him another big smile. By the time, he was finished reading, she was fast asleep. He did not know you could love a child as much as he loved her. Of course, he loved Chase, however, Chase did not make it easy for him to love. It had been a couple of years since Chase wanted to be tucked into his bed, now he did not even like anyone in his room, especially his sister. Chase was not affectionate either. He really did not like for anyone to touch him. He did allow his mother to hug him sometimes. He never hugged her back. He never kissed anyone or showed much emotion. Caleb and Molly were very proud of him though, especially of how smart he was. Chase was so much smarter than most kids his age. Caleb was back to the kitchen in a few minutes. He sat back down at the kitchen table and Molly sat down on the chair next to his. Caleb took her hands in his. Caleb had a grim expression on his face. Molly nervously said, "Okay, Caleb, spill it, what's going on?" He looked her in the eyes and whispered, "Molly, we have a problem on our hands. We have to get some help for Chase. Molly said anxiously, "Caleb, your scaring me, please tell me what is wrong." He told her the whole story about how much Chase enjoyed slaughtering the hog and loved the smell of the blood. He told her about finding Chase behind the barn. He was stabbing the tiny kittens with a vengeance and seemed to be in a trance-like state. He told Molly that Chase seemed to be really enjoying stabbing the little white kittens. With this, Molly got a horrified look on her face. Finally, he told Molly how much it scared him when Chase looked at him, just like Henry, Caleb's brother use to do, with those steel blue eyes. He surprised Molly by bringing up his brother Henry. He mentioned Chases real lack of any emotion except anger and rage. Molly never really noticed that. Molly sat there quietly and did not interrupt the whole time

Caleb was talking. When he was finished, he looked at her and asked, "Well?" Molly said, "I thought it was just me, when I saw so many of Henry's facial expressions on Chase's face, now I know it was not just me. What should we do Caleb?" He replied, "We have to get him some help. He needs to see a shrink doctor for kids. I will get to work on that tomorrow. while you are at work." Molly asked, "I don't know if he needs help just because his facial expressions are a lot like Henry's were. Do you really think that is the route we should take? I mean, maybe it is just some kind of a phase he is going through. Maybe it is normal little boy behavior. maybe we are overreacting?" Caleb replied emphatically, "No, no we're not over reacting Molly. Trust me on this, this is what Chase needs. It is not just Chase's facial expressions; it's also his love for blood and torture. I do not think it is just his personality not to show emotion. I think it is more likely that he does not have any, or has very little. When was the last time you have heard him laugh or even seen him even smile? He may be a psychopath, just like my brother Henry. I will call and find him a shrink tomorrow while you are at work and Katie is taking her nap. No one needs to know about our business." Molly told him, "I don't want him getting bullied at school because he went to a shrink". Caleb looked surprised as he said, "Molly, he's only in kindergarten. How much bullying could go on in kindergarten? Besides, no one else has to know." Molly thought about it for a few minutes and quietly said, "Okay, Caleb, if you feel that strongly that this is what he needs, that is what we will do."

The next morning, Caleb got Molly off to work, Chase on the school bus and put Katie in front of the television, watching cartoons. He got the phone directory out. He looked up pediatric psychologist. He felt like Chase would like talking to a woman, instead of a man, at his tender age of five. Caleb wanted someone young, smart, and up-to-date on the newest treatments for children. He found two female doctors that he thought would fit, and who had offices in the next town. He looked up their bios. He read what the other patients had to say about the both of them. Finally, he chose a Doctor named Doctor Nancy Clark. Caleb thought, "A nice simple name". He called to make an appointment. Even though it was Thursday; he was hoping to get in to see her this week. The receptionist came on the line and asked, "Can you hold please?" She put him on hold before he even had a chance to respond. When she came back on the line, Caleb told her how rude that he thought she was. She apologized profusely for it. Her name was Angie. Angie was able to get Chase an appointment for the following Tuesday, which Caleb thought was great. "Just my wife and I are coming for this first visit, to meet Dr. Clark and to see if we think she would be a good fit for our son Chase. Molly worked four hours a day for an interior decorator, whose shop was 40 miles away. There really was not much use for a decorator here in the country. She and Caleb did not need the money, but that is what Molly loved doing, so Caleb wanted her to be happy. Molly was always redecorating one of the rooms in the old farmhouse. When they first got married, they turned the two rooms in the basement into a master suite. Molly had a huge bathroom and huge walk in closet put in. The only thing she did not like about down there was there were only two, very small windows. Caleb had the windows made as large as construction would allow. Molly liked to have the natural light. In one corner of the suite was a small kitchenette with microwave and refrigerator. They had a large flat screen hung up on the wall across from the king sized bed. The small room off of the other room, where Caleb's Mother used to send him for punishment, sometimes for days at a time, was completely filled in and walled over. That was also, where Caleb's Mother was buried for a short period of time. Now the room was gone and no one ever had to go in there again. They only place that the little dark room existed now was in Caleb's memory. Now that it was gone, Caleb did not mind having their bedroom in the basement. As a matter-of-fact, it looked better than the rest of the house. Molly decorated everything in soft blues and yellows which gave it a calm appearance.

Katie occupied Caleb and Henry's old room upstairs and Chase occupied his Grandmother's old room. Molly had let both children help in the decorating of their rooms. Katie's room was pink and very girly and Chase's room was black and red. The front room on the first floor, that had been Hillary, Calebs sisters room when she was a baby, was now a guest room where Hillary stayed when she wanted to sleep over. Molly got home around noon, just in time to eat lunch with Katie and Caleb. When she got home, Katie was just waking up from her nap. Molly went to the kitchen, where Caleb was making her a glass of ice tea, just the way she liked it. She said, "Thanks Honey". Caleb was very good at spoiling Molly. He did everything for her, including cooking sometimes. He still liked cooking and was a much better cook than Molly. Molly did not want for anything. Caleb could afford to give her whatever she wanted. She only wanted what they already had. The farm, the peace and quiet. She shopped but not as much as most women. She shopped more for Caleb and the two children than she did for herself. They sat down at the kitchen table and Caleb told Molly all about his search for a shrink and that he found one. He told Molly as much about Dr. Clark as he had read on-line. He had even copied all of the Dr.'s reviews for Molly to read. He told her their appointment was next Tuesday. The first appointment was for them to meet the doctor. Chase would be in school and Molly said she would call one of her friends to come and watch Katie. Molly still looked skeptical. They both decided beforehand that they would go ahead and make Chase an appointment while they were there if they really liked Dr. Clark. Katie had a monitor in her room, Molly, and Caleb could hear that Katie was up. She was two now and was sleeping in a toddler bed and could get up if she wanted. Unlike most toddlers, Katie loved her bed. Molly had painted little lambs all over it and put her name on the end piece of the bed She did get up, ran down the steps, then down the hall to the kitchen, and jumped in Molly's lap. Katie was all smiles. Katie was such a beautiful little girl. She had red/gold ringlets of hair, big green eyes; and a beautiful, little smile. She was the apple of her father's eye, a real "Daddy's Girl".

That evening, Molly made spaghetti and meatballs, along with cheesecake for dessert after dinner. It was Chase's favorite dinner. When they all sat down to eat,

Chase asked, "What are we celebrating?" Molly replied, "Nothing, I just felt like cooking, that's all". Chase knew that his mother really hated cooking and he knew that something was up. He did not talk much through diner. He knew his mother knew what he had done to the kittens and he did not want to talk about it. This seemed like a celebration dinner to him and he could not figure out what they would be celebrating. He was afraid that if he started talking, she would talk about him and the kittens. He did not feel remorseful that he had killed three of the kittens and he hated cats. He did not feel any shame either, as a matter-of-fact, he did not feel anything but satisfied, but still, he did not want to talk about it with his mother. He would love to go back out there after dinner. He would kill another kitten, but he knew that his father was keeping a close eye on him. He knew he would not get away with it. He so loved killing those cats and watching the lights go out of their eyes and their little bodies go limp. He liked to hold their bloody little bodies after he killed them; he liked to feel them go from warm to cold. He liked to feel them starting to get stiff. He killed any small animal he could find on the farm. He was really, really pissed off that his father took away his favorite knife. His father had told him he was too young to carry a knife. It would be years before he seriously thought about killing a person. When Chase was finished with dinner, Caleb told him, "Chase, go upstairs and do your homework." Chase's parents were surprised that a kindergartner would have homework. Chase thought it was just stupid work, for stupid people. Chase already knew how to read better than a lot of adults. "You could do some reading and when we get the dinner dishes cleaned up, your mother and I would like to talk to you about something." Chase thought, "Oh no, here we go." He knew that something was going on. He knew that his mother did not fix his favorite meal for nothing. He could feel the tension in the air. It took Caleb and Molly about a half hour to clean up the kitchen. They got Katie settled in front of the television. They called Chase to come downstairs, so they could talk to him. It seemed to take forever for Chase to come downstairs. They all three went in and sat down at the kitchen table to talk. Molly looked at Chase sweetly and said, "Chase, first of all, I want you to know that I am not angry or disappointed with you for what happened with the kittens. We know it is unnatural to want to hurt an animal. Your father and I want you to go and talk to this nice woman. Her name is Dr. Clark. She will help you figure out why you killed the kittens and why you enjoyed it so much."

Chase thought. "Oh God, it's worse than I thought, she knows that I liked killing the kittens." His face turned bright red with anger as he said, "Okay, Mother, whatever you and Dad think I should do, I'll do it." Caleb thought, "Just like Henry, he always had the right answers." Caleb told Chase that he and his mother were going to go to the first appointment, just to meet the doctor and to see if they thought she would be a good fit. Chase said, "Okay, Dad, but I'm not sick. I do not even have a fever." Caleb said, "It's not that kind of a Dr. Chase. It is just a Dr. that all you do is talk to her". Molly told Chase that if they liked this doctor, that they would be making another appointment for him. Chase hung his head and all he had to say was, "Okay". He knew it would not make a difference what he said at this point, because their mind was made up that he was going to this Doctor. He decided that he had no choice but to do what his parents wanted.

It was Tuesday before they knew it. Molly got Chase off to school and one of her friends just got here to look after Katie. When they got in their car to leave, Molly looked at Caleb and said, "Do you still think we are doing the right thing?" Caleb replied, "Yes, I do. I think if someone had given my brother Henry a chance, he would have turned out a lot better and not been so evil and mean."

Dr. Clark was located fifty miles away, so it would be a long ride for the both of them. They left their house at 8:00. It would take them about an hour and a half to get there and then they had to register. Caleb and Molly got to the doctor's office on time and filled out the appropriate paperwork. After waiting another half hour, they were finally called back to meet with the doctor in her office. Angie showed them the way to her office and told them to have a seat. There were two seats positioned in front of a very large desk with a leather top. Another smaller room could be seen behind this one and it looked like a schoolroom, with puzzles, crayons, markers, dry erase boards, etc. Everything in this office looked very expensive, from the art on the walls all the way down to the thick, blue carpet. They both sat down in the two chairs facing the desk. They held hands. They were both scared to death for Chase and Molly still was not sure they were doing the right thing. They looked at Dr. Nancy Clark's many diplomas that hung on the walls. Everything in this office, from the walls to her desk were in order and perfectly straight. A few minutes later, Angie walked in and offered Caleb and Molly something to drink, they refused. Then Angie told them, "Please, make yourselves comfortable". Then she left the room, shutting the door behind her. It was not long before a beautiful, well-dressed, young brunette walked into the room. She smiled warmly at the both of them. She introduced herself as "Dr. Clark". She smiled, "You must be Chase's parents." They both said, "Yes" in unison. Dr. Clark asked, "Well, what kinds of problems is Chase having?" Caleb spoke first, "He is obsessed with blood and killing and he has killed small animals. When he is killing them, he goes into a trance-like state of rage. Focusing only on what he is doing. He feels no remorse or hardly any other emotions, including love." Molly spoke up, "He doesn't even like to be hugged or touched. He is only five, not some kind of animal, he is just different. Molly was trying to take up for her son a little bit. Dr. Clark said, "I see. Does he have any other siblings at home?" The question surprised Molly. She said, "Yes, he has a two year old sister, why?" Dr. Clark replied, "Have you ever noticed Chase being mean to her?" Caleb said, "Yes, he is always pushing her and yanking her hair, really anything he thinks he can do and get away with." Dr. Clark said, "I see." Then Caleb piped up and said, "He is a hermit most of the time. He does not like to go outside. He is very introverted. The other day I had to slaughter and process a hog and that is the first time in a long time that he has gone outside, except for school." Molly looked at Caleb like, "Don't say so much". Dr. Clark said, "I would have to talk to him for a few visits of course, before I gave him a diagnosis. Molly asked, "Will you tell us what he says or talks about while he is in here?" Dr. Clark said, "No, I can't do that, it would ruin his trust in me and then he would not talk about anything. The only things that I can discuss with you, would be anything I think that would be harmful to him. For instance, if he told me he was playing with knives or that sort of thing." Molly said, "I understand." If the both of you feel comfortable with me, why don't we go ahead and make an appointment for Chase to come in and see me?" Molly and Caleb both agreed that they would make an appointment with Dr. Clark for Chase. On the way out, they stopped at the receptionist office and made an appointment for Chase for three days from today. They shook hands with Dr. Clark, and then left the building. Molly looked at Caleb and said, "Well, what do you think of Dr. Clark?" He answered, "I like her a lot. She seems very nice." Molly said, "She made a good first impression on me also, but we will have to see how it goes."

Molly and Caleb were both quiet on the way home. Finally Molly said, "Caleb, how come we didn't see this ourselves, we didn't even know it was coming?" Caleb said, Because he knew how to hide it well. It is hard to tell with kids anyway, what they are thinking. It is especially hard with Chase because he is so much smarter than your average kid. He is a lot smarter than the kids are in his class. The one thing that he cannot hide is the expression on his face or when his eyes light up. Those are things you cannot hide at that young of an age. You can tell when he likes something; he can't hide that from us." Molly said, "I thought he was always a happy little boy, always well behaved. He does what he was told. I guess I did not look hard enough at his face to see what he was feeling about things." Caleb said, "You still might not have caught anything. Chase may be like Henry was and not have any feelings." Molly gasped, "That's a terrible thing to say about our son!" Caleb said, "Calm down Molly, I know this is hard. I lived with Henry all my life so I was probably more in tune with that kind of behavior. No matter what it is, Molly, it's not our fault."

For the next few days, Molly watched Chase very carefully. She wanted to make sure that she noticed any little thing different about him, but she didn't." Tomorrow was Friday, the day of Chase's first appointment with Dr. Clark. Molly and Caleb were both planning on going with him.

When it was time for bed, Molly stuck her head in Chase's bedroom to say, "goodnight". Chase, looking grumpy, said, "I don't know why I have to go and talk to that stupid Dr. tomorrow, I am fine Mom, really." She looked at him sympathetically, "I know you are fine. Sometimes it helps to talk to someone other than your Mom and Dad." Chase said, "Is she going to give me a shot?" "No honey, she just wants to talk to you, that is all." Chase's brows furrowed and he seemed to be concentrating, he asked, "What is she going to talk to me about?" Molly said, "I don't know, but it's not a test or anything to worry about, okay?" She was doing her best to reassure him. He said, "Okay, night Mom".

"Night son, I love you." He said an automatic, "I love you to".

On the way to Dr. Clark's office the next morning, Chase was fidgety. Molly said, "Chase, why don't you play one of your video games that you brought along?" He got his video game out of the bag his mother carried everywhere. He started playing it but he could not concentrate on the game. He was nervous about going to the Dr., especially when he was not even sick. It seemed like it took forever for them to get to the doctors office. He said, "Mom, how long do I have to be here?" She answered, "About forty five minutes I think."

They walked up to the waiting room and hadn't been waiting long, when a little boy, about eight years old, came bouncing out of the Doctors office. When the little boy saw Chase, he stopped for just a second and they looked at each other and said, "Hi" at the same time. When the other little boy left, Dr. Clark came out of her office. She bent down to be eye level with Chase. She introduced herself. she said, "You must be Chase" He said, "Yes, my name is Chase." She said "Okay, Chase, let us go into my office. I think you'll like it in there." Chase got up and followed her in. He thought she was very pretty. He did not know why, he thought she would be old or something. The Dr. told him to have a seat over in the corner where there were a table and two chairs. She asked him about his school and about his friends at school. He said he really did not have any good friends at school. He hated school. He said the kids made fun of him because he liked to read and he did not like baseball or any sports. Some of the kids in his class played baseball and soccer but he never had the desire to play. He said he was the only kid in school that did not look forward to recess. When they did go out for recess, he sat by himself on the corner of the playground and read one of his books. He told the Dr. that he likes to be alone because he was so much smarter than the rest of those kids were. Dr. Clark said it was not unusual for a boy of five not to have any friends yet. He talked about a particular boy in his class that was always pushing and pinching him and making fun of his glasses, especially on the bus ride to and from school. The boy called him a little kindergarten nerd and talked about how the boy embarrassed and bullied him all the time in school and on the bus. Dr. Clark noted how angry and animated Chase got when talking about the bully. She said, "Okay, let's calm down. Would you like to draw some pictures?" He said, "No, drawing and coloring is for little girls." She said, "Okay, do you know how to write?" He responded, "Of course I do." She said, "Would you like to write down some things then, you speak very well for your age." "She could tell that he liked the compliment because his face turned a little bit red. He said, "What do you want me to write about. I could write about a lot of stuff." She said, "Do you know what a journal is?" He replied, "No." She said, "It's a book that you write in every day, about what you did on that day and how you are feeling. It is sort of homework assignment, but not hard. No one will ever read it but me, especially your parents. I promise." Chase said, "Okay, I can do that." She handed him a notebook and she said, "This is it, you have to write only honest and true things about how you feel about something." He said, "Okay". She said, Would you like to help me put a puzzle together today?" He said, "Sure, I guess so." She got the puzzle out and they spread the pieces on the table. It was a 100-piece puzzle, appropriate for his age and intelligence. They spread the pieces on the table face up, Chase did a quick scan of the table and he said, "Two of the pieces are missing. I do not like to do a puzzle that has missing pieces because you can never finish it." She said, "Are you sure they are missing. You didn't count them." "I'm sure, that's all I know". Dr. Clark did not count on how extraordinarily smart that Chase was. He did not even belong in a kindergarten class. No wonder he seemed bored; he was not being challenged in school. She said, "Oh, I'm sorry about the puzzle Chase, I didn't know, I will throw it away." He said, "No, don't throw it away just because it is missing a couple of pieces. Most kids do not ever get half way through a puzzle like this anyway. You do not always throw something away because it is damaged. That's what my Dad says." "Okay, Chase, that's a good idea, I won't throw it away." They spent the rest of the forty-five minutes talking about Chase's family. The Dr. asked how he got along with his little sister. Chase told the Dr. that he did not like his sister very much. She was always getting into his stuff. When their time was up, Chase actually looked a little bit disappointed. She thought that his first visit went extremely well. She said, "I will see you next week Chase, and don't forget to write in your journal every day and bring it with you when you come so I can read it." On the way out the door, he said, "Okay, good-bye Dr. Clark". Molly and Caleb thought it was a good sign that Chase was smiling because he did not smile very often. This first visit must have gone well.

The next week that Chase went back to see Dr. Clark, she had him draw some pictures of his family. He did not like coloring pictures but he would draw some for her. Chase drew his sister Katie without a head, with blood spurting out. The rest of his family looked normal for a 5yr. Old drawing. Dr. Clark asked Chase why he would draw such a picture of his sister with her head cut off. He simply said, "That's just what I'd like to happen to her. She bugs me all the time and she and goes in my room. I just do not want her to touch my stuff anymore that is all. Dr. Clark said, "There are better ways of handling things than through violence." Chase replied, "I know." She asked him if he liked to kill things like bugs or something and then his face got animated when he told her the story of killing the kittens. He lied to her and told her that he just killed one of them, and it was an accident, but he did like seeing and smelling the blood of the kitten. He thought that other kids liked it also. He did not yet know that was abnormal behavior. Dr. Clark said, "We will work on those thoughts." That confused Chase.

Sometimes he would see the other boy from school in Dr. Clark's reception area. They started talking in addition, became best friends. Chase had not yet had a best friend, but he really liked this kid, Charlie. He and Charlie were even starting to hang out together in school. Chase told Molly and Caleb about his new friend and wanted to know if his friend could come over for dinner and have a sleep over so that they could play their video games. They both said, "Sure, they were glad to see Chase have a friend. Chases friend Charlie came over to the house the following Saturday. They all sat down to dinner and Molly noticed that Charlie had no table manners what so ever. He reached across the table to get whatever he wanted. Molly had also heard Charlie use a cuss word while they were in Chase's room when they thought that no one else was listening. Charlie was three years older than Chase. Molly thought that there may be too much of an age difference for them to be friends. She would discuss this with Caleb later on tonight. The boys stayed in Chase's room. They played video games all night.

The next morning, about five in the morning, Molly heard Katie screaming at the top of her lungs. Molly jumped up to go and see what was wrong. She found Chase and Charlie in Katie's room. Charlie had Katie over his lap and he was giving her a spanking. Molly said, "Charlie, stop it right now! What is going on in here? Why are you all up so early this morning?" Chase said they were playing. They were pretending that Katie was their slave and when she did not do something right, she would get a spanking". Molly said, "whose idea was it to play this game?" Charlie said, "It was my idea, I've played it before". Molly said, "It's a horrible game. Now, the both of you apologize to Katie, right away. Both boys hung their heads and murmured "sorry". Molly said, "All of you go back to bed and quit playing. It's not even light out yet."

Growing up, Chase and Charlie continued to be friends. Now, even though Chase was thirteen, Charlie was sixteen; the age gap did not seem to matter to them. Both of them had stayed out of trouble for the last few years except for the one night when Chase talked his parents into letting Charlie spend the night again. Caleb did not want Chase to hang around Charlie but he was overruled by Molly. Molly said it would be okay for Charlie to spend the night because he had only spent the night once, years ago and the boys were older now. She told the boys that they better behave themselves this time.

After dark and after everyone else had gone to bed; Charlie and Chase were out sitting behind one of the small outbuildings. A barn that was used to store hay. They were smoking cigarettes and drinking rum that Charlie had brought over from his parents liquor cabinet. Both of Charlie's parents smoked and he just took a pack out of one of their cartons. His parents never missed the cigarettes or the liquor. Since the boys were not used to drinking, it did not take very long for the both of them to get drunk. Chase did not like smoking, it made him cough but he smoked one anyway, to be cool like Charlie. Charlie laid his lit cigarette down on the dry ground for just a moment, or so it seemed that way to him, and the building just caught fire. The building was full of dry hay to feed the animals. As it went up in flames, both boys were laughing. It went up in flames pretty quickly. Molly and Caleb had smelled smoke from their two small basements windows. They both got up to investigate. They went around the whole house and didn't find anything. Molly lightly knocked on Chase's door and did not get an answer. She opened the door. The room was empty. Molly looked worriedly at Caleb and said, "The boys aren't in here". Caleb replied, "Let's look outside, maybe they are on the back porch. When Molly and Caleb got back down to the kitchen, the smell of smoke was even stronger. Katie had also been awaken by the smell of smoke. She got up and found her parents looking out the back door. Katie asked, "What is going on Mother?" They all went out the back door to look for the boys and that is when they saw that the hay barn was burning. There was no point in calling the Fire Department the outbuilding would burn down in a few short minutes. They all rushed out to the barn and on the other side of the barn, they found Chase and Charlie. The boys were sitting in the grass at a safe distance from the fire, pointing at the fire and laughing like two crazy people, drunk on their ass. Caleb and Molly led them back to the house and up to Chase's room to sleep it off. They would deal with the boys in the morning. The outbuilding had burned to the ground. All of Caleb's hard work in rolling and stacking the hay had been for nothing. Caleb and Molly knew the boys were lucky to be alive. If they would have been inside that barn, they both would be dead right now.

The next morning, Caleb and Molly both lectured the boys until they were all talked out. The boys hung their heads and appeared to be truly sorry, which they were not of course. Molly told Chase that he was grounded for three weeks, and that meant from his room where all of his cool stuff was. Chase jumped up and shouted, "You can't do that!" Caleb stood up and told Chase "She can do whatever she wants and I suggest you follow the rules or she will make it that much harder on you. You know you deserve whatever you get. She told Charlie that it was time for him to go and that she would be calling his parents to tell them what he had done. She asked them to come and pick him up from their house. Charlie said, "Go ahead, they won't care anyway". Charlie walked out the door to wait on the front porch for one of his parents. Molly placed a call to his parents, telling them what Charlie had done. His father said, "Is this going to cost me money?" Molly replied, "No, it was an old building, one we just used for storage anyway. Molly could hear Charlie's mother in the background saying, "What did Charlie do now?" Her husband handed her the phone. She said, "What did Charlie do this time?" Molly told her and she also told her that Chase was grounded for three weeks. Charlie's mother replied, "Okay, thanks for calling." and she hung up. Charlie was right his parents did not care about what he did.

One evening while Chase and Charlie were sitting in McDonald's, and were waiting for their food. Charlie was brooding. Chase said, "What's wrong?" Charlie said, "I've had my driver's license for three months now, and my Dad will not let me drive his car. He said I would have to get a job and buy my own car, just as he did when he was young. He's an asshole." Chase thought, "Wow, that takes nerve to call your father that". Charlie looked at Chase and said, "I have an idea, why don't we just steal a car?" Caleb said, "Are you crazy?" They both laughed at that. Charlie said, "Common, why not. We could take it for a ride and then just leave it somewhere nearby. No one would ever know who it was. We could ride in to Cincinnati and see what is going on. You know it's a dead place around here." Chase thought about it for a minute and then said, "Okay, why not? Do you know how to steal a car?" Charlie said, "It's easy. You just look for the car that someone left the keys in, which you know around here that happens all the time. How about the football coach's car, he always leaves his keys in his car and leaves it unlocked." Chase didn't want to look like a little sissy, like some kids at school told him he was, so he said, "Let's go."

After school, they walked around to the side of the building where the faculty parked. They spotted the coach's car. They both walked on either side of it and peered in to see if the keys were in it. They were and the doors were unlocked. Charlie had a big smile on his face as he said, "You ready?" Chase said, "Yes, let's do this". They both hopped into the car quickly, Charlie started the car up and they backed out of the parking lot without anyone seeing them. They both started laughing, it was such a rush. They got on the highway a few blocks from school and headed towards downtown Cincinnati. They got off on the 5th Street exit. After turning off the exit, Charlie ran smack dab into a Metro bus. Both boys were thrown into the windshield and the whole front of the car was smashed. They did little damage to the bus and thankfully, there were no passengers inside. An ambulance came to the scene and took both boys to the nearest hospital.

When they got to the hospital, they rushed Charlie off right away. Charlie was the most seriously injured. A police officer told Chase that they were going to call their parents. Usually kids are upset when you tell them that you are going to call their parents, but Chase did not seem to care one way or another. Chase gave the officer both his and Charlie's home numbers. The officer called their parents.

Molly was in the kitchen and Caleb was in the living room watching television. Katie happened to be staying with one of her girlfriends tonight. Molly answered the phone, and Caleb heard her say, "Oh My God! Is he all right? We will be there right away." Caleb rushed in the kitchen and asked, "Molly, what is it?" She said, "Common, we have to go to Christ hospital in Cincinnati; Chase has been in a car accident." Caleb said, "Is it serious?" Molly said, "I don't know, they just said to come to the hospital, our son was in an automobile accident. Let's go, hurry." Caleb grabbed his car keys off of the kitchen counter and they headed out the door.

Once on the road, and driving a little too fast, Molly said, "He was probably with that boy Charlie. Chase told me that Charlie just got his driver's license." Caleb said, "Probably, you know I don't like that kid and I told Chase to stay away from him, that he was nothing but trouble." Molly said, "That boy's parents are never home and they let Charlie do whatever he wants. I do not care for Charlie either. There is just something cold about him that I don't like, but on the other hand, he is Chases only friend since Chase was in kindergarten." Caleb said, "I know, but that still doesn't make it a good thing." It took them forty-five minutes to get to the hospital, the way that Caleb was driving. They walked into the emergency room and asked the person behind the desk, who they thought was a nurse, where their son was. Molly told her that their son was brought in some time ago from an automobile accident. The nurse behind the desk said he was in exam room two but that she needed them to fill out some paperwork. Chase needed to go to surgery for a broken leg. Molly said, "Does he have any life threatening injuries?" The nurse said, "No, just a broken leg. He was lucky because they hit a Metro bus in downtown Cincinnati." Molly said, "Oh My God!" She and Caleb rushed over to exam room two. Chase was sitting up in bed with an IV in his left arm. Molly ran over and hugged him hard, which he did not return. Caleb said, "Chase, what the hell happened? What were you doing with Charlie in downtown Cincinnati?" Chase said that they were bored, so they took the coach's car for a little spin, because the coach always leaves his keys in his car." Caleb said, "What? Do you mean to tell me that you and Charlie stole the coach's car?" Chase answered "Yes." without any emotion at all. In the meantime, the coach had called the police to report his car stolen. Charlie and I did not mean to have the car out long. We were going to bring it back. Now, Charlie and I have to go to juvenile court. Doesn't that really suck?" Caleb was getting angrier by the minute. Molly touched his arm so that he would calm down. "Chase, you know you can't just go around stealing from other people. Whose idea was this anyway?" Caleb already knew it had to be Charlie's idea, but Chase said, "It was all my idea. Since Charlie got his driver's license, I wanted to go somewhere out of this hick town." Molly knew that

Chase way lying to protect his friend, his only friend. Caleb knew it also. The nurse came in with some papers for Molly and Caleb to sign, granting the hospital permission to operate on Chases broken leg. Chase was angry and started yelling, "I don't want any fucking surgery, and my leg will be fine!" Caleb said, "You are a minor and have no say in the decisions we make concerning you". Chase yelled again, "I don't want any fucking surgery on my leg! Molly or Caleb either one had ever heard Chase say a cuss word in his life, and now to be yelling the main one, felt like he had been using it for long time. Molly said, "That's nonsense Chase, you are having your leg fixed, so get used to it. The nurse came in and gave Chase a pre-op shot in his IV. A few seconds later, Chase was calm and feeling just fine. The hospital transporter took him to surgery and gave Molly and Caleb a beeper and told them to go and wait in the surgical waiting room. While they waited in the surgical waiting room, they met Charlie's parents also sitting there. Molly and Caleb had never really met them, but had only seen them when they picked Charlie up from somewhere. Molly introduced them, then she said, "I feel like I already know you, even though we have never met face to face." Charlie's Mother just said, "Oh, Hi". Molly asked, "Is Charlie going to be okay, did he get hurt very badly?" Charlie's Mother said, "He has a lacerated liver and damage to one of his kidney's but he's going to be fine. Charlie's father said, "This is going to cost us a lot of money because our health care does not cover everything. He admitted that he did not have Charlie's insurance paid yet. That is why he would not let Charlie drive his car, and Charlie knew that. Charlie's parents never asked about Chase. They did not even ask if he had been injured in the accident. Charlie's mother said that Charlie has been seeing Dr. Clark for years now, but he never seems any better. Molly looked at Caleb and said, "We really have not noticed any big changes in Chase either. Molly's pager beeped. Chase was out of surgery.

The coach had reported his car stolen. When Chase's parents found out that the car the boys had stolen was the coach's car, they called the coach right away. They told the coach that they would be more than happy to pay for damages to his car and asked him to please not press charges against the boys for stealing it. They told the coach that was the first time they had ever been in trouble and they did not want their son to have a juvenile record. The coach was angry, however, he said, "Okay, as long as you pay for any damages."

It was not long after the phone call that the police knocked on the coach's door and told him that they found his car and what happened. The coach said he did not want to press charges against the boys, that he forgot that he told them they could take it anytime they needed it. The coach said he knew those boys and he didn't want to press charges as long as their parents covered the damages to his car.

Chase went home from the hospital, two days after his surgery, Molly waited on him hand and foot. Chase never said, "Please or thank you." to his mother for anything, he just expected it. Molly and Caleb both talked to him and told him how lucky he was that the coach did not press charges. Caleb told Chase that he did not want to hear of him ever being around Charlie again. Chase knew that was never going to happen so he just said, "Okay Dad".

Chase was now considered one of the "Bad Asses" at school since he stole the coach's car. Chase really liked the change. He was not bullied for once.

Chase turned sixteen and got his driver's license, just like most kids his age. For his sixteenth birthday, his father gave him one of his old cars that he had fixed up and Chase said that he loved it. His father showed him how to check the oil, change a tire, and anything else that he might need to know about maintenance for his car. He went over to Charlie's house to show him his new car and to show him that he could drive now. Charlie was now nineteen. He had graduated last year and had been a couch potato ever since the accident, Charlie didn't seem excited for Chase, he just said, "Oh, that's cool". Chase was disappointed in Charlie's attitude because he was excited about driving. Chase thought that Charlie was just jealous, which he was. Charlie's father had never given him a car or anything else that he could remember.

Chase was glad to be driving because there were a couple of girls at school that he wanted to ask out. There was a special girl at school; her name was Miranda. They called her Mini for short. Chase decided to get up enough nerve to ask her out for the following Friday or Saturday night. On Monday, Chase saw her standing by her locker in the hall. He thought, "It's now or never." He just walked right up to her before he lost his nerve and said, "Hey Mini, ya doin anything on Friday night?" She answered, "Yes, I promised my Grandma that I would come and help her with some things." Chase said, "How about Saturday night?" Mini looked at him and said, "Yes, I'm free on Saturday, why?" She was not going to make it easy on him. Chase responded with, "Can I pick you up and take you out for pizza or something?" Mini said, "Yes". She told Chase to pick her up at six on Third Street. Chase could not believe she said "yes". He told her, "Okay, see you Saturday". He was elated. The first time he ever ask a girl out and she accepted.

That evening while Chase and his family were eating dinner, he told his parents, "I have to go out shopping for a little while after dinner." Both of his parents and Katie looked at him as if he had finally lost his mind. Chase knew they would be surprised and thought, "I might as well get this over with." Chase said, "I have a date with a girl named Mini on Saturday and I want to get some new jeans. Please, do not make a big deal out of this. It is just a date. Katie said, "Awwww, it's your first date." He said, "Shut up stupid." Molly looked at the both of them and said, "That's enough. Chase, tell us about this new girl." Caleb piped in with, "Okay, everyone leave Chase alone. End of discussion." Chase looked at his dad gratefully for saving him and Caleb just gave him a slight nod.

Chase tried to kiss Mini on their first date and she did not like that he tried and she told him so. She did not let him kiss her until their third date. Chase told her she was too uptight. They had been dating for three weeks now and Chase felt like he should be getting more from Mini. Chase did not have feelings like most people but he had observed kids at his high school who were dating and he learned what to do from them. He held Mini's hand, opened doors for her, kissed her on the cheek, and put his arm around her. He knew all the right moves. He could not understand why Mini would not have sex with him. It was not from his lack of trying. He had heard other guys talk about how they got laid by their girlfriends and he thought it was Mini's problem, not his. He would keep trying, at least a little while longer.

They had been going out for about a month, and Mini had still not given it up to Chase, he was starting to get really angry with her. They sat at a table at the local Pizzeria. Charlie walked in and Mini did not like Charlie in the least; he was just plain weird and gross. Mini got up and told Chase she was going to the restroom. Charlie sat down where Mini had been sitting. Chase noticed that Charlie was really built and asked if he had been working out. Charlie said, "Oh, just a little bit while I'm still trying to find a job". Charlie did not go right into college like the rest of his class at school. His parents could not afford it. His father told him that he had to get a job and save some money if he wanted to go.

Charlie envied Chase because Mini was a really cute girl. Charlie said, "Chase, have you tapped that yet? Chase said, "No, of course not. She won't even let me cop a feel." Charlie said, "I have an idea." Chase moaned, "Oh Brother! Not another one of your foolproof plans, is it Charlie?' Charlie said, "No, of course not. My parents went away on vacation for two weeks and I have the house to myself. we could take Mini there and do whatever we want with her. We could keep her for a few days at my house". "Chase replied, "The first person they will look at is me." Charlie said, "We will wear a mask, she won't even know who we are". Mini was making her way back to the table and Charlie said, "Chase, we will talk about this later. Come by my house after your date." To Mini, he said, "Later Honey". Mini looked at Caleb and said, "He is such an idiot; I don't know why you even hang out with him". Chase said, "He's been my friend since I was in kindergarten".

When Chase dropped Mini off at her house, he decided that he would stop over at Charlie's and see what was up. Charlie was sitting on his couch watching television and drinking beer. Charlie said, "You want one?" Chase said, "No, don't touch that stuff. It messes with my head and I do not like that." Charlie said, "Did you think about what we talked about? Chase said, "Yeah, but not Mini. It has to be someone else, someone we do not even know". Chase said, "I'm on spring break next week, that's when we will do it, but there has to be rules." Charlie said, "What kind of rules?" Chase said, "I want to have fun with whoever we take, I don't want to permanently hurt them and then when we are finished; we simply let her go." Charlie said, "Hey, I don't want to really hurt anyone, just have a little fun. I got a couple of date rape drugs that we could give her so she will not remember a thing". Chase said, "How are we going to choose who it will be?" Charlie said, "I don't know. We could just take someone off the street." Chase said, "No, that would be too risky, they would remember the car." We will have to meet someone and drug her before we take her in the car so she will not remember. We could take her from a park." Charlie said, I will get one of those cute, little puppies from the shelter. Girls always come over and talk to guys who have a cute puppy. We could offer her a drink with the drug in it." Chase said, "That's a good idea but she has to be alone, not with anyone else hanging around and we will have to have the car close." Charlie said, "How are you going to get out of the house for a few days? Your parents hate me and you know they won't let you come over here." Chase said, "That's easy, I will just do something to make my dad angry, which is easy to do and then I will let it escalate until he throws me out. When this is all over, I will go back and plead for forgiveness. Mom will make him let me come home." Charlie said, "Okay, when do you want to do it?" Chase said, "How about on Monday? On a weekday, there will not be many people at the park. I will come over on Sunday night and we will go get the dog and go to the park on Monday. What are we going to do to the girl?" Charlie said, "We're going to fuck her until we go blind". Chase said, "sounds like a plan to me." On his way out, Chase said, "I'll see you on Sunday. I will bring my white cane." He laughed at his own joke all the way to his car.

On his drive home, Chase thought about how much alike he and Charlie were. They both thought alike, they were both really smart and they both had pretty much the same psychological problems. Chase thought that Charlie was loose cannon. His ideas were smart but he did not want to do enough preparation to make sure he had covered all of his bases. Chase would sit and think about every possible scenario and Charlie always wanted to charge right in. Charlie knew he was smart and he thought that he was a lot smarter than the police or anyone else, except Chase. He knew he was not smarter than Chase and that really pissed him off sometimes. Other than that, they thought pretty much the same, they liked the same things, they were not afraid to tell each other what they liked because they knew the other one would not think them strange or weird. Most of all, they both liked anything to do with pain, torture, and killing. They talked about it. It made them feel powerful to hold something's life in their hands. It gave them a real rush. They both killed small animals together. then wiped the blood on each other. It was kind of their ritual. That is probably what they would do with the puppy. They both had talked about killing a person someday. That would be the ultimate rush, but Chase did not know if that was something, they would ever do. If he did ever kill someone, he did not know if he would ever want to stop. He did not know if one person would be enough. He did not think so. He thought that killing was in his blood.

Chase wondered if his late uncle Henry ever killed anyone. His father never said and he would not say even if he knew. Chase did not relish spending the rest of his life in prison. Of course, Charlie was starting to believe that he was too smart to get caught at it anyway, and Chase was smart enough to know that was dangerous thinking. The police were not as stupid as Charlie thought. He believed they could not catch anybody, and that kind of thinking ended you up in prison. Chase respected the authorities, and besides, his aunt Hillary and he have always been kind of close and so he would always have a free lawyer. Chase knew he was just bored. Bored with everything, school, his family, the farm, his life. He needed this to make himself feel like he was alive. Charlie was a lot like Chase although not quite as smart as Chase was, and that was okay because he was better looking; at least that is what he told Chase all the time. Charlie was a big boy at 190lbs. with a lot more muscle. He was blonde with blue eyes and very good-looking. He could get just about any girl or woman he wanted. The problem was that plain old sex was just boring to him. Chase would settle for plain old sex, especially since he was a virgin. Charlie liked it rough and most women did not go for that kind of thing. He liked to degrade woman, put them in their place. His own father had always been sexist and treated his mother as if she was his slave. Charlie thought that was the way it should be. He just has not found the right woman yet. Chase was not sexist, he felt equally superior over men and women.

When Chase got home that night, his father was still up. Caleb said, “You’re getting in kind of late, aren’t you? It is two in the morning. Chase’s Dad knew that nothing good went on at two in the morning. Caleb asked, “What have you been doing?” Chase said, “Mini and I went for pizza and then we went back to her house. Her parents were home and we just sat out on her front porch talking. I did not realize how late it was getting. Sorry, Dad.” Caleb said, That is okay, I have lost track of time myself before. Especially in the company of a pretty girl." Chase thought, "I'm not really lying because he and Mini were going to go out again the next night. Caleb asked, "Chase, how's the car running?" Chase said, "She's running great Dad. I baby her just like you said. Night." Chase went on up to bed. Chase had a hard time sleeping that night, thinking about what he and Charlie were planning to do.

It was exciting to think about and it also made him really horny. He beat off to the thought of torturing some girl and finally knowing what real sex felt like. He also knew that he would try again with Mini the next night.

The next evening, around six, Chase picked Mini up for a dinner date. They went to a local steak house for dinner and towards the end of their meal, Mini asked, "What's the matter Chase, you have been so quiet all night?" He said, "Oh, I'm okay, just a lot on my mind lately." He knew that their school prom was coming up. He had never had any desire to go to any of his proms since he had been in high school and did not now, but he knew that Mini was waiting for him to ask her to go with him. When they finished dinner, Chase asked Mini, "Would you like to go to the park for a while?" Chase knew the spot at the park where high school kids went to make out. Mini said, "Sure, I guess so." The park was only a few miles away. Chase pulled into a spot and turned off the car engine. It was a beautiful May day and warm outside. The days were getting longer and it was still light out at seven o'clock. He put his arm around Mini and pulled her close. He kissed her a long, passionate kiss. They kept kissing and both of them were breathing hard. Chase slipped his hand up under Mini's shirt and cupped her breast. She had nice, full breast, probably a C cup. He wanted her so badly. He wanted any female badly. He had had a brilliant idea at dinner of how to get Mini to give it up. Mini said, "Stop Chase, you know I won't go all the way with you so please, stop trying." Chase was a little angry. He said, "Mini, we have been going out for a long time now and you know I love you. If you loved me like you say you do, you would want me to have all of you." She answered, "Chase, you know I am saving myself for the right person, and I don't know yet if it is you." Chase would tell Mini what she wanted to hear. Chase asked Mini to the prom, and of course she said, "yes". Chase really did not want to go to prom. He was socially awkward and he could not dance. He knew that Mini really wanted to go and she had hinted to him that if he took her to prom that she might let him touch her or something. He told her that he would, but he knew that he would never go to prom. He was just hoping if he told her that he would take her, she might see how serious he was and she might give it up to him. She did not, and they did not go out again.

Chase and his Dad had not been getting along very well lately. Chase was using more and more cuss words around the house and Molly even caught him smoking out by the barn. He would have to think of something that would make his father so angry that he would throw him out of the house on Sunday.

Up until Sunday, Chase did everything he could to aggravate his father. He used more cuss words around the house, smoked on the front porch and listened to his parents speeches all weekend however, he just rolled his eyes at them. Now it was Sunday morning and Chase knew exactly what buttons to push with his Dad. His dad was always spoiling that little brat, Katie. He would do anything for her and let her do anything she wanted. Katie was a smart girl also and got straight A's in school. His parents were so proud of her. Later that evening, before dinner, when Chase knew everyone would be in the house, getting ready to eat, Chase went into Katie's room. She said, "Chase, what are you doing in here?" He said, "Remember that CD I let you borrow?" She said, "Yes, so?" He said, "I want it back now." She said she did not know where it was at this exact moment. She told Chase to get out of her room. Chase was truly angry with her for her attitude toward him. They had not grown up close, like most brothers and sisters. As a matter of fact, they hardly ever talked to each other. Chase made sure that he left the door to Katie's room open. He jumped up, his face red and he grabbed Katie around the throat and started choking her. He let her get a scream out first that would alert his parents. He choked her good, until she started turning blue. He yelled, "I'll kill you, you little bitch!" Molly and Caleb ran into Katie's room and Caleb pulled him off of Katie. Caleb, said, "What in the hell do you think you are doing Chase? You could have killed your own sister!" Chase screamed at his Father, "I don't care, I hate her anyway. She's just a fucking bitch!" His father grabbed him by the back of the shirt and dragged him downstairs and out the back door. His father said, "Chase, if you want to be angry with someone, let it be with me, not your sister. You could have killed her!" Chase said, "I don't care, I hate her anyway. I hate all of you the same! I am tired of living on this fucking pig farm and I'm tired of you trying to run my life all the time." Chase lit a cigarette and started to walk toward the back door, where his Mother was watching thru the screen door. Chase turned around to his father and said, "I hate you most of all. You are just a big hick that lives on this dirty pig farm, you don't know anything." At that, his father's face turned red and he punched Chase right in the jaw. Chase punched him back, all 120lbs. of him, as hard as he could. They both went at it, rolling on the ground. Molly tried to break up the fight but Chase, breathing hard, said, "Stay out of this bitch." Caleb delivered a last punch that landed Chase on the ground in pain. He looked down at his son and said, "Get your ass out of my house. No one talks to me and your mother like that or tries to hurt Katie. Pack your shit and leave." Molly grabbed Caleb by the arm. She said, "No Caleb, you can't kick him out. He is only 16, and you know that he has mental problems. Dr. Clark said to expect episodes like this, remember?" Dr. Clark had indeed put Chase on anti psychotics but he did not take them half the time. Chase got back in his dad's face and said, "Fine, I'll leave, I don't want to live on a fucking pig farm anyway!" Chase went inside and slammed the screen door as hard as he could before going upstairs. He could hear his mother downstairs, pleading with Caleb not to let him go like this. She said, "Caleb, you know our son is sick and I know he has not been taking his medications, as he is should. Please do not let him leave like this." His father said, "No, let him find out how hard it is to make it on your own. I do not want him here. He is a danger to you and Katie. He almost killed Katie and there is no telling what his limits are. Don't worry about him Molly, he will be okay." Caleb thought to himself, "At least I didn't throw him in the dark room like my mother did to me."

Killing made Chase feel powerful and in control, and that was an awesome feeling. He also loved slaughtering the hogs. He especially loved the iron rich smell of blood. Chase knew that he was not normal, not your average person. He sometimes wished he could be like other people, really grossed out by the things that he thought were great. Sometimes he wished he really cared about or loved someone, he just did not. He knew how much his mother loved him; she showed it all the time. Mostly he did not care, however, there were those rare incidents when he did wish he could return her love. He did not consider himself some kind of monster as most people would, he just thought that was how he was made, and he accepted it. Chase also knew that others could not accept the way he was, like his family. He felt he had to hide things from them. Out of all of the people he knew and all of the people in his family, his father knew him the best. Katie knew him pretty well, but she did not understand the way his mind worked like his father did. Chase knew that it was because of his long deceased uncle Henry, his father's brother. Chase thought that his late uncle Henry must have been a psychopath also by the way his father talked about him. Chase had heard his father talking to his mother about his uncle Henry many times when he thought that Chase was not listening. He had heard his father refer to his brother Henry as a psychopath but never talked about anything bad that Henry had done, or at least nothing that was all that bad.

Not every psychopath was a killer, liked torture or got off on causing others pain. Even though there is no cure, some people can be somewhat controlled by medication. Chase thought that medication never really did much for him, that is why he did not take it most of the time. Caleb dealt with Henry all his life and so he could understand him better than anyone could, even though Chase did not like being compared to anyone. The very first time he and his father had dressed a hog, when Chase was little, he still remembered thinking that his father was going to throw up, and again when he saw the kittens. Chase really just did not care what his father thought of him. Ever since Chase had dressed their first hog together, Chase had thought his father weak.

Molly went upstairs and into Chase's room. She said, "Chase, please don't leave angry. You just upset your father. He really doesn't want you to leave." Chase said, "Too bad, that's exactly what I am going to do." Molly tried to hug him but he would not let her. She tucked a wad of bills into his shirt pocket and said, "Here, for whatever you need it for." Chase did not say "Thanks"; he did not say anything at all. He walked down the stairs with his bag in hand and went out the front door, slamming it as hard as he could. He left for Charlie's house. Chase was smiling the whole time. That was easy, except his jaw hurt from where his father punched him

When Chase got to Charlie's house, he just went in and started yelling, "Charlie, are you here?" Charlie yelled back, "I'm down here, in the basement." When Chase got down to the basement, Charlie said, "Did everything go alright?" Chase replied, "Yeah, I got my dad angry enough to throw me out. I can go back when we are finished here and beg for forgiveness and he will let me back in the house. What are you doing down here anyway?" Charlie said, "Come on back here to this second basement room and I'll show you." They both walked to the back room. Charlie had put a twin mattress on an old iron bed frame, with handcuffs attached to it. There was a support pole in the middle of the room, With ropes tied loosely to it and a CD player over in the corner. Chase said, "Wow, you have been busy." Charlie said, "Yep, we are ready to go. Do you still want to do this?" Chase said, "Of course I do or I would not be here. Where is the rohypnol?" Charlie said, "It's up in my room. I have two little vials of it. Chase asked, "Where do you get something like rohypnol?" Charlie replied, "Don't worry about it, I have my sources. We will put the first one in some lemonade, to offer to the girl we pick out." Charlie had been with a lot of women but Chase never had sex yet. Chase was starting to get excited all over again, just thinking about what they would do to the girl.

The next morning, Chase and Charlie went down to the local animal shelter and found a very cute puppy. They purchased him, stopped, and bought him a leash at the local grocery store. They also bought some snacks and container of lemonade. It was noon and time to go to the park. They had a blanket in the back of Charlie's car and a blind fold and handcuffs for the girl they chose. On the way to the park, Charlie asked Chase, "What kind of girl do you like?" "I like tall blondes with big tits." Charlie Said, "Me to!" They got to the park and they walked around all afternoon, trying to get a girl's attention, however, none of them ever came over to look at the puppy. It was getting late, it was starting to get dark out; they decided to head on back to Charlie's house. When they got back to Charlie's, they were both hungry and made themselves a sandwich. Chase said, "Charlie, I think we need a new plan. This one is not working. Charlie replied, "Well then, think of a new plan with that brilliant mind of yours.

When Chase left, Molly could not even finish dinner, all she did was cry and cry. She was angry with Caleb for kicking out their only son. Caleb said "he deserved what he got. "Anyway, he would be back." Kids always came back. He told Molly, "I won't have any kid in my house that behaves like that or talks to us like that." Molly said, "He's just going through a rebellious stage right now, you know that. You know that Dr. Clark warned us that something like this might happen around the age of 15 or 16. Remember when she had us come to her office for a conference and what she told us Caleb?" Caleb, replied, "Yes, but don't forget, she also wanted us to have him locked up somewhere." Caleb remembered that day in Dr. Clark's office very well. She told him and Molly that Chases final diagnosis was psychopath, or as they call it now, Antisocial Personality Disorder.

It is the same disorder that serial killers have. Periods of rage, killing or doing harm to an animal or a person for sexual gratification, feeling no remorse for his actions. These were only a few of the horrible traits that this disease was associated. Molly had asked, "Is there a cure for this disorder?"

Dr. Clark said, "No, but we can keep his rages under control with medication. Dr. Clark also told Caleb and Molly that Chase should be locked up somewhere because some of the things that he old her he wanted to do were too disturbing to even hear." Molly and Caleb both thought about it however, they did not want their only son locked up for the rest of his life when he had not done anything. Dr. Clark said she would only treat Chase until he was eighteen because she was a pediatric psychologist. Dr. Clark thought to herself, "That time won't come soon enough." She was afraid of Chase. He had grabbed her arm and squeezed it a couple of times now. She fully believed that he would kill someone one day and she did not want it to be her."

Katie was fourteen now and a very good student. She never got into trouble for anything. She hated to admit it to herself, but she was glad that Chase was gone. He was so unpredictable, that she kept her door locked at night. Her parents were just now seeing the Chase that she had known all her life. She knew that all kids acted differently around their parents, but Chase was just plain evil. She did not want to be around him. She did feel a little bad for her parents though, especially for her mother. She and Chase had a good mother that would do anything for either one of them. Katie did not want her parents hurt by her evil brother. She was not stupid; she knew that something was up with Chase. He orchestrated this whole evening so that he would get thrown out of the house because there was something special he wanted to do, or somewhere special he wanted to go. She did not know why her parents could not see that, except maybe they liked to believe their children are the best. She has heard her parents talk about Chase and she knows that he is on a lot of psych medication. Her mother usually gave into Chase, whatever he wanted, like a car because she he would hound her about it until she finally gave in. Katie thought that Chase was on the brink of madness and maybe he was. She just hoped that he never came back. Katie went downstairs to comfort her mother. She thought that was what she was supposed to do.

Chase and Charlie went out on Charlie's front driveway to shoot some hoops by the light from the garage. Charlie asked Chase how he got his parents to let him come over here and he told them. Charlie Said, "I guess being crazy does have some advantages." and they both laughed. They played some videos and then decided to go out and get some pizza. When they got to the pizza parlor, Charlie said, "Are we going to try the park again tomorrow?" Chase said, "No, I have something else in mind, I'll tell you about it later, I'm still thinking about it". Charlie replied, "Are we going to need the dog anymore?" Chase said, "No." and they both started laughing. They knew that they were going to get to kill at least something tonight.

That night while they were just sitting around watching television, Charlie asked, "Are you ready to tell me about the new plan yet?" Chase said, "Yes, just hold onto your seat because it's a big one. I am still working it out in my head but I will tell you the basics so that we can get started." Charlie got excited because he knew that Chase was excited and for Chase to be excited about something, it must be pretty good. Chase looked at Charlie and said, "Who is the one woman that we both have in common, that we both want to kill sometimes?" Charlie jumped up and said, "Oh My God, Dr. Clark? That's freaking awesome! What made you think of her?" "She has just really been getting on my nerves lately. She told my parents that they should lock me away because one day I would end up killing someone. Little did she know it would be her. I hate that bitch." Charlie said, "How are we going to kidnap her? We don't even know where she will be this week." Chase replied, "We aren't going to kidnap her for a very long time. We are going to scare her for a long time first. It will be more satisfying. that way. "Charlie looked disappointed as he said", I don't know if scaring somebody is my thing." Chase said, "Oh, rest assured, my good friend, we will kill her. You can count on that." They both started laughing. Chase said, the first thing we are going to do is make phone calls to her this week and tell her something like I am watching you and I want you to suck my dick" You know, that sort of thing. Charlie said, "She will recognize our voices; she has only been talking to us both for years". Chase said that tomorrow they would go down to one of the shops in town and find one of those voice machines that you talk into. Chase said, "I think those things sound even scarier, don't you?" Charlie still was unconvinced about this whole plan. He wanted to kill someone now, not weeks down the road. Charlie said, "Chase, we can do your plan but I want to go out and get a girl tonight. I don't think I can wait." "Charlie, do what you think you have to do but I am not in on that one. Too many loose ends, we should have planned it better and I don't want to go to prison." Charlie said, "Oh Chase, you are such a worry wart and so damn dramatic. Well, this opportunity does not come along very often, that my parents are gone on vacation and I have the basement set up for a woman. I have decided that tomorrow is the time. I will tell you all about it later Chase." Chase said, "Okay you can tell me all about it in a couple of days or when you turn her loose. Charlie, you are going to turn her loose aren't you?" "Of course I am, I'm not stupid Chase." Chase said, "I never thought for a minute that you were Charlie. I just think that you could do better planning on this one." Charlie said, "Where will you go tomorrow night since your parents threw you out?" Chase said, "It's no big deal, they will let me back in. No worries." On Chase's way out the door the next morning, he yelled back at Charlie, "Good Luck tomorrow night, and be careful!" Charlie yelled back, "That's my middle name." Chase knew that Charlie would go through with kidnapping a woman tonight and he also knew that there was a real good possibility that Charlie would kill her. Chase knew that he was smart but Chase also knew that Charlie could not control himself sometimes, at least not like Chase could. Chase practiced patience and self-control because he knew that could make the difference between getting caught at what you did. No, Chase thought, "I can't be a part of this but I am jealous that he will be the first one of us to take a woman." Charlie was his only friend so he hoped that he was wrong, that Charlie would not get caught.

When Chase smoked and left, Charlie was sitting on the couch wondering if he really wanted to do this kidnapping, and sexual torture. It was a long prison sentence if he got caught. He would be very careful. He knew that he would go through with this sooner or later. Now, with the house to himself, was the perfect opportunity. He was only nineteen, so he could not go to a bar to meet a woman. He would go to the laundry mat uptown, near the University of Cincinnati. There should be some pretty female students in there. He put handcuffs, duct tape, blindfold, and a board and anything else he thought he might need in his trunk. He put a bunch of dirty clothes into a basket and put it in his back seat. On the way to the laundry mat, he stopped at one of the university stores, bought a large football jersey, and removed the tags. He went to the laundry mat and stayed in his car. He had his laundry basket full of laundry sitting on his trunk, as if he was getting ready to go in and do laundry. It was almost dark outside and this was a good. He was getting more nervous by the minute. His hands were sweating on the steering wheel. He was breathing hard and fast. He couldn't believe he was really going to do this. He didn't have some grand plan like Chase would have had but thought that he had thought this out completely. He waited for a long while and finally a great looking girl came out of the laundry mat with her laundry basket and was heading toward her car. Her car was only two cars down from where Charlie parked his. When she got close to her car door, he yelled, "Hey, How ya doin?" She said, "Okay". He picked up the university football jersey from his basket, and he asked the girl if he could show it to her because he had a stain on it and he did not know how to get the stain out or even how to wash it.

She threw her basket in the back seat, turned around, and said, "Sure, let's see it". He came over with the shirt and she was standing with her driver's side door open, reaching in the car for something. As she was bent over, Charlie hit her on the head with a board that he had wrapped up in his shirt. She passed out immediately. He had knocked her out cold. In the dark, he did not stand very close to her, he was sure she had not seen his face well enough to identify him. He was careful not to touch her car to leave a fingerprint. She was a small girl, so he picked her up and quickly carried her over to his car and put her in the trunk. There was no inside trunk release on his old car so he wasn't worried about her escaping. Once he got her in, he quickly blindfolded and handcuffed her hands behind her back. Luckily, this place was deserted tonight. He got back into the driver's seat and headed towards his home.

Charlie pulled into the garage and closed the door. Oh My God! He could not believe that he really did this, kidnapped a woman! This was going to be great. She was his now, to do with as he wished without fear of being interrupted. The girl was unconscious in the trunk. He lifted the trunk lid carefully to make sure the girl was still unconscious. He was scared for a split second that he had killed her. He felt for a pulse to make sure that she was still alive, that he did not hit her too hard. She was still very much alive. He picked her up and took her down to the basement and placed her on the iron twin bed. He removed the cuffs from behind her back and he cuffed her hands to the top of the bed frame and then he spread her legs and cuffed her ankles to the bottom of the bed frame so she lay all spread out. She was a beautiful girl. She was at least twenty, long brown, silky hair, almost to her waist. She had full lips with just a hint of lipstick on and beautiful, clear skin that was obviously browned from a tanning bed. Most importantly, she had a rockin body. She must be one of the college Co-eds. She probably belonged to an uppity sorority. Her Daddy probably paid for her college education. He had placed a hood over her head so that she could not see him. She was waking up. He would remove the hood from her head when she was fully awake so that he would be able to see the fear in her eyes, which was the whole point of kidnapping her in the first place. He could tell when she was finally fully awake by the way she struggled against the restraints and screamed. Charlie got down near her ear and he whispered, "If I remove the hood, will you stop screaming? Just shake your head yes or no. She shook her head yes. He said, "That's a good girl. He put a black hood on himself before he slowly removed the hood from her head. She looked at him and he could see the fear in her eyes. He said, "That's a good girl, nice, and quiet." She said, "Please mister, let me go. I will not tell anyone, I swear." He said, "You won't tell anyone anyway." She started crying hysterically then and she begged him, "Mister, please don't kill me, pleaseeee." He slapped her hard across the face and told her to shut the fuck up. He left the imprint of his hand on her cheek. He liked that. He wondered if he should call Chase and let him join in the fun since he had never even been laid, but then he decided, no, since Chase would not help him tonight. He bailed on him because he had his own stupid ideas. After he slapped the girl, she shut up and was just crying softly. He said, "Do you see this hood over my head?" She said, "Yes". He told her, "If you pull it off, or if it accidentally comes off and you see my face, then I will have to kill you. Do you understand?" She nodded. He said, "Answer me, do you understand?" She said, "Yes, I understand." He said, "Good because I don't want to have to kill you but I will if I think it's necessary". He pulled off all of his clothes and she could see that he had a hard on. He noticed her looking at it. He said, "Have you ever had sex before?" She looked terrified and she pleaded with him, "No, I'm a virgin. Please don't rape me mister, anything but that. I have been saving myself for marriage. I'll give you a blow job if you want or anything else you want but please don't rape me. Think of all the trouble you will be in if you do. I'll do anything else for you and I swear I won't tell a soul." He smiled and said, "So, I get the prize." He walked over to the table near the bed and picked up one of his big knifes and twirled it around in his hand. The more terrified she got the more it turned him on. He slowly cut her clothes off, working until she was completely naked. She was shaved in all the right places. She was beautiful. She looked to the table to the right of her and saw that he had all kinds of gadgets laid out on that table. She said, "Please, please don't hurt me. I'll do whatever you want, but please don't hurt me." He said, "You will do whatever I want anyway." She started crying again and it was getting on his nerves. He yelled, "Shut the fuck up I said!" She shut up but still had tears running down her face soaking the sides of her hair and the pillow. She was also noticeably shaking from head to toe. He went over to the table. He picked up something else. They were steel nipple clamps. He leaned over to put them on her breasts and she jumped when he first touched her. She screamed after he put the first one on, "Please mister, that hurts, please take it off." He put the duct tape back on her mouth even with her shaking her head back and forth. He was tired of her endless pleading. He just wanted to be able to see the terror in her eyes. She cried. He ran the tip of his knife down her stomach to the top of her pubis, barely making a mark. He said. did you lie to me? You better tell me now." She shook her head "no"; she did not lie to him. He walked back over to the table, put some lubricant on, and then came back to her. He climbed on top of her as she tried to wiggle away. He rammed himself into her hard. She screamed behind the tape. He told her to shut up. He pounded away at her until he came and he was spent. He said, "Good girl, you did not lie to me. He could see the evidence of the small amount of blood on the sheet. "He undid her hands and feet and made her turn over. She was lying completely on her stomach now. He shoved a large dildo up her ass and she screamed again. He played with her ass and made little cuts on it with his knife. He loved asses and he loved cutting on them. This is pretty much how the next two days went. He had used all of his toys and knives on her at least twice. She constantly cried and begged to be turned lose. He expected nothing less. He only fed her some crackers but gave her water and let her up to go to the bathroom. When she tried to get up, she could hardly stand. She looked weak and Charlie loved that because he was the one to make her look that way. On the third day, Charlie was bored with these games. He had cut her every place he could without making any cuts that would kill her. All of the cuts were shallow. He now had to think about whether he was going to kill her or not. If he was not going to, he had to find a way to turn her loose. He could give her the date rape drug and just drop her off near her neighborhood. Then he decided. If he killed her, the pleasure would be short lived. He would get more pleasure out of the fact of her remembering what he did to her and her telling someone else. Her picture had already been on the news and they had already been looking for her. Yes, he decided, that is what he wanted to do. He would let her go. He may even contact her at a later date and remind her of what a good time they had, just to scare her and it would turn him on to hear the fear in her voice. Charlie told her to get up and get dressed and he got dressed also. He made her a drink of Coke with the drug in it. He told her to drink it and when she came to, she would be near where her car was. She would not remember a thing. She was afraid that if she drank the drink, that he would kill her. She knew where his weapons were at all times. She was not too far from his big knife. She took the glass. She took a big mouthful and she immediately spit it all at him, while trying to get to the knife. When she spit the coke at him, he fell backwards, his hood coming off. He jumped up and she had the knife in her hand. He easily overpowered her. He screamed at her in a sudden rage, "I told you not to let my hood come off. You have seen me and now I will have to kill you!" She started screaming. He threw the knife down, pulled her over to the bed, and straddled her. He put his hands around her slim throat and slowly squeezed. Her eyes were bulging and her tongue was hanging out. Her face was turning a shade of blue/purple. He took his slow, sweet time squeezing the life out of her. After all, this was his first human kill. He had to kill her, so he wanted to enjoy it to the fullest. He watched her eyes until they looked glazed over. He knew she was gone. He thought, "Oh My God, I finally did it, I actually killed someone! Oh My God, what a rush that was! It is something I will never forget as long as I live. He guessed it was like sex, you never forgot the first one. He was glad that she saw his face, so now it was all her fault. He had to do it. Had he not warned her from the very beginning not to let his hood fall off? He knew he had to think fast on what he was going to do with her body but he just wanted a little more time with her while she was dead. He did not want to have sex with a dead woman, that was not what he was about. He was about causing terror. What he did want to do was to lie next to her until her body had become cold. She started to get stiff. He savored the coldness. It was like the coldness he felt in his heart. He thought his heart was made of ice. He held her hand and he told her how beautiful she was. He told her nice things. Things that he could never tell a live woman and mean them. He told her she would be going to a better place and that she should be happy that he helped send her there. Those are supposed to be words of comfort to families who have lost someone. Charlie really believed that you did not go anywhere when you died you just ceased to exist. He wanted to keep something of hers to remind him of how special she was to him. He decided that he would keep a lock of her beautiful hair. He rolled her over. He made two small ponytails in the back of her hair underneath, then he cut it. He didn't know why he felt like he had to hide the spot where the hair was cut from because she would be unrecognizable soon, once decomposition set in. He cut one for himself and one for Chase. He wanted to share something of this experience with his best friend. He turned her back over on her back then brushed her long, brown hair down over her shoulders. He pushed her tongue back into her mouth. He shut her mouth. He did not close her eyes until the very last. He could see himself in her dead eyes and he was so happy that he was the last person she ever saw. He felt immortal now somehow, now that he got her prized virginity and that he would forever be the light in her eyes. He lay with her for a long time after, just staring into her eyes and reliving the experience that they both had shared together.

He took the lock of hair up to his room; he put it hair in an envelope and sealed it. He stuck the envelope in one of his favorite books, Psycho. He wondered if he ever got caught if someone would write a book about him. He knew neither one of his parents would ever look in this book. He gently wrapped her up in the sheets and moisture proof mattress pad she had been lying on and wrapped her in plastic bags. He tied bungees around her and attached enough of his gym weights to the bungees to keep her down in the water. He decided that he would drive down to the river. There were several places along the Ohio river that you could go without anyone seeing you. He would have to drive very carefully as to not get stopped by the police for a traffic violation. The police always wanted to check your trunk. He put her in his trunk and drove her to a secluded spot. He got her out of the trunk and he waded into the river as far as he could go. He dropped her in the water and watched as she slowly sank. It was a good thing that he had been working out because she was heavy in the bags with weights. She sank like the weights he had tied to her. It would be a long time, if ever, before anyone ever found her. She would be fish bait now, and after the river took what it would, there would be nothing left of her.

Charlie drove home and he felt good about what he had done this week. It was the ultimate rush for him, however, he knew it would not be the last time he killed someone; it was just too much of a high. He and Chase had talked about killing someone many, many times and they both agreed that once they started, they probably would never stop. Charlie felt good; he got to be the first, before Chase, to kill someone. He would tell Chase all about it. He kind of doubted that when it came down to it, Chase could kill someone, not by himself anyway. A killing plan would never be perfect enough for Chase. He would forever be going over the "What if's". He would be so focused on all of the things that could go wrong that that alone would prevent him from the final act of killing a human.

When Charlie got home and pulled into the garage and shut the door, he went into the laundry room and got some cleaning supplies and cleaned the trunk of the car. Next, he went down to the basement and cleaned everything he thought the girl could have touched or anywhere where she had been. He cleaned his toys with bleach then put them in a safe place. When he was satisfied that all was back to normal; he sat down on the couch and called his best friend Chase, to tell him to come over so he could tell him all about it. Chase answered his phone and said, "Hey what's up?" Charlie said, "I did it." Chase knew what he meant by that right away. He said, "I'll be right over".

When Chase got there, and Charlie let him in, he could tell how excited Charlie was. Charlie told him the whole story from start to finish. Chase said, "That's unbelievable! You could have called me." Charlie said, "I know, it was kind of a weird thing, a first time thing, a virgin killing you know, but I do have something for you. Charlie gave him the lock of hair he had cut from the dead girl's head. Chase took it from Charlie and appeared to be very grateful but in truth, he would dispose of it as soon as possible when he left here. He did not want to have any evidence of the killing. Chase said, "Are you planning on doing it again?" Charlie said, "Absolutely". Chase said, "Did you really have to kill her? I mean, you could have threatened her or something." Charlie said, "You know I couldn't do that, I would have been caught for sure." Chase did not mind the killing, as a matter of fact, that is the perfect end to violence and torture. He did not like the killing for the fact that there was more of a chance to get caught. Chase said, "How was it to kill someone? To have control over their death?" Charlie answered, "It was the biggest rush I have ever had in my whole life. I choked her and I watched her eyes until the light went out of them. Power over life and death is a lot of power." Chase said, "One day I will get to experience it for myself. I am so glad that you got to fulfill your dream and that it was so satisfying. Let us hope that no one discovers her for a really long, long time. Charlie asked how it was at home, how he got his dad to let him come back. Chase said, "I just went home and told them how sorry I was for all of the trouble I caused and that I would never, ever do anything like that again if they would just please let me come back. And of course I threw in, "I know I missed a couple of my doses of medication, but I will be more careful about taking it." Of course, his mother hugged him. She told him that everything would be okay. His father just said, "Take your medication and if you need help with anything, just come, and talk to me son." Chase promised that he would. He even said that he thought that he should try to see Dr. Clark twice a week for a while instead of once a week. They thought that was a great idea. Katie saw right through him and she just rolled her eyes at how gullible her parents were Chase did start seeing Dr. Clark twice a week, on Tuesdays and Thursdays. The Dr. spent the whole visit asking him how he felt about certain things and he spent the whole visit staring at her legs and butt. Of course, she noticed, and had noticed that for a long time. She was glad that most of her patients were children. She knew that Chase knew and understood his diagnosis. He had the same frame of mind as a serial killer and that would never change no matter how much therapy he received but the medication he was on was supposed to keep him from acting on his fantasies. Today, she asked Chase what he had been thinking about lately. He told her, "I've been thinking what it would feel like to kill someone." She said, "With your diagnosis, I'm not surprised that is what you think about. It is how you act on that thought that separates you from a murderer. These conversations always made her uneasy, especially when he looked at her with those steel blue eyes. Sometimes she saw those eyes in her nightmares. Even though Chase just turned 18, she told Chase that she was going to talk to his parents and tell them that, the end of the month would be his last visit here. He needed to see a psychiatrist for an adult. Chase looked at her and said, "Why, Dr. Clark, I thought you loved me". She said, "Sorry Chase, but no". That put Chase in a terrible mood. He made a mental note to call her in a couple of days with his voice disguised and scare her a little. We will see if she feels so smart then.

A couple of days later, Chase sat in his car after school, he wondered what the good Dr. was doing. He decided to dial Dr. Cl ark's home phone number that he stole from the receptionist desk when she had to get up and leave for a minute. Dr. Clark answered on the second ring with "Hello". Chase used the voice projector, which made him sound like a robot. "He said, "Hey gorgeous, I've been watching you. I know where you live and I watch you in your house." then he hung up the phone. He called her for the next 10days, always from a different phone. He would say things like, "I'm coming for you." or, "I can't wait to see you tonight." The last time he called, she didn't hang up on him but instead said, "Who is this and what do you want?" He said, "I want you, I want all of you and then I want you dead". Then he hung up the phone. She was hard to scare but he was doing a pretty good job of it. She thought she was so much smarter than he was, he would show her that she was not that smart. He decided to take off of school tomorrow, since he knew that Dr. Clark would be at work and he would go to her house and try to get in. He just wanted to mess a few things up and scare her even more. When he got home that afternoon, Molly said, "Dr. Clark called and said that it was time that the two of you parted ways since you are almost a grown up. She suggested you see another Dr. his name is Dr. Epstein. She left his number and said you should call and make an appointment with him. Chase said, "Oh, I don't know. I am used to talking to Dr. Clark, I do not know if I would like someone new. Molly said, "I know, but you have to see someone so that you stay on the right medication". He said, "Okay, I'll give him a call. He got Dr. Epstein number from Molly and dialed it. A female voice answered the phone. He made an appointment for the following week, on Thursday. That made Molly happy. Now she would not have to worry about Chase going off the deep end again. Caleb came in the back door and said, "Thank goodness, I'm finished with the farm for today." Chase said, "Hey Dad, I have to go out for a while but I'll be home for dinner." Caleb answered, "Where do you have to go this late in the afternoon?" Chase said, "I have to go down to the library for a while. I have a big term paper that I have to finish for school and I can't find the information that I need on my computer." Caleb and Molly knew little about computers and believed Chase when he said he couldn't find the information he was looking for. Caleb said, "Okay, be sure you are home for dinner". Chase answered, "Okay, see you later".

Chase got in his car. He called Charlie and asked, "Charlie, can you meet me somewhere?" Charlie said, "Where?" Chase gave him the address of Dr. Cl ark's house. He told him to meet him up the street from there at about 5:00 pm, just to look for his car. Charlie said, "Okay, I'll be there. Chase loved having a best friend, but sometimes he thought that Charlie was a loose cannon and that he would be responsible for getting the both of them caught at something one of these days.

Charlie had cruised down Dr. Clark's street. He thought, "This must be where all of the rich bitches lived. The houses looked like mansions." He knew that Dr. Clark was single and he wondered why she would live in such a big house all by herself. When he had driven around the block for the second time, he saw Chase parked alongside one of the connecting roads and he pulled up behind him. He got out of his car and went to sit in Chase's car. Charlie said, "Hey man, what are we doing here?" Chase said, "We are going to break into Dr. Clarks home. I know that she is at work now. She will have an alarm system on. We will have to disconnect it and I do not know how to do that but I know that you do." Charlie said, "Yeah, this should be fun. Why are you breaking into her house? When you know she isn't there?" Chase said, "I am taking it slowly, scaring her a little. I just wanted to go in. I want to move some of her things around so that she will know I had been there. Chase said, "Here, put this workers jump suit on.

We will pretend to be delivering this package, which Charlie saw in the back seat. Chase said, "We will knock on the front door first, to make it look normal and when no one answers, which she will not, we will go around the back. In the back there are a lot of trees and only one neighbor back there who shouldn't be able to see the good doctors house." Charlie said, "Okay, then I can see what kind of security she has and if I can get in." They put the suits on and got the package and rang Dr. Clark front doorbell. They did not expect anyone to answer. When they went to step around the back someone opened the front door. Chase thought fast and said, "Is this the Schwartz residence? The woman said, "No, sorry, it's not, this is Dr. Cl ark's residence and I am her house cleaner. Sorry, don't know anybody by that name." Chase said, "That's okay, thanks for your help." Chase was disappointed. They would not get inside Dr. Clarks today. While Chase was talking to the house cleaner, Charlie was able to walk around a little, like he was looking for another house, and he checked out Dr. Cl ark's security. They walked back towards the car. Charlie said, "We are going to have to stake out this house, to determine when the maid is there." Chase said, "No, I have a better idea. I saw the name on the house cleaner's shirt, it said, "The Cleaning Experts. I will call them and pretend to be Dr. Clark husband and see if I can find out the information that we need." Charlie said, "That's brilliant man, that's why I like hanging out with you so much." When they got a couple of streets over, Chase pulled over and looked up the cleaning company's phone number on his phone, and got their number. He called them, and when they answered he said, "Hello, my name is Roger

Clark; I am Dr. Nancy Cl ark's husband. I wanted to surprise my wife on her birthday next week, with a few people over." Chase knew the doctors birthday, social security number, telephone number, and just about every other thing about her. After sitting in her office for the last ten years, he was able to find out all kinds of stuff from paperwork, that she left lying around. She also used one of those big desk calendars and she wrote stuff down on it all the time. He went on, "I need to know our maid's schedule at our house next week so I can decide what day to have it." The woman said, "Can you please confirm your address and telephone number?" Chase gave it to her, then she asked, "Can you confirm your wife's birth date and social security number please?" Chase was ready with those also. The woman on the line said, "I'll be back in just a moment, will you please hold?" Chase said, "Yes", as if he really had a choice. Finally the woman came back on the line and said, "The maid is scheduled at your residence, next Monday, Wednesday and Friday." Chase said, "Thanks so much." and hung up the Phone. Chase said to Charlie, we need to stake out the house for a few days, just to see what's going on in the neighborhood, who the busy body is, there is always someone who knows everything about what is going on in a neighborhood, then I might pay her a visit while you are disconnecting the alarm system. Do you think you can disarm the system?" Charlie said, "Of course I can it's a piece of cake. She has the normal, the doors, and windows alarmed, they are easy to turn off. The thing you want to worry about when you are breaking into a house is if they have a people eating dog or not. Dogs are much worse than any security alarm." Chase said, I never thought of that, good thinking." Charlie liked the compliment coming from his smart friend.

Chase and Charlie cased the house for the next few days. Charlie, in the daytime while Chase was in school and Chase at night, when he was supposed to be at the library. They each took notes about what was going on in the neighborhood. By Saturday, they thought that they knew the neighborhood pretty well and they compared notes. Apparently, a woman across the street and five houses down was the busy body of the street. She was out every evening, watering her flowers and talking to all of the neighbors, she talked to each of them that dared to come her way, until the person was obviously trying to walk away. After comparing the rest of their notes, Charlie and Chase knew that Dr. Clark lived alone and did not have a dog. They would pick a day next week for Charlie to disarm the alarm, and while he was doing that, Chase would pretend to be a life insurance salesperson and visit the busy body down the street and keep her from looking up the street at the doctors house. Chase had Charlie draw him a diagram and show him how to disarm the alarm just in case he could not get a hold of Charlie when he was ready to go in.

When Chase got home that night, Caleb asked him. "Where you been every night this week son?" Chase said, "At the library, I have a big term paper due the end of next week." Caleb, Sr. said, "Oh yeah, what's it about?" Chase thought fast and said, "Well, I can't decide between two subjects and so I am researching both of them until I finally decide which one." Caleb said, "That's great, what are the two subjects?" Chase said, "The first subject is about serial killers of the 20th century and the second one is about the abuse of mind altering drugs." Caleb said, "Those are some really heavy subjects" Chase replied, "I know, I think it is interesting." Caleb said, "Seems you forgot about the appointment with your new Dr." Chase said, "Oh No, I'm so sorry Dad, I just got so involved in my school project." His dad said, "Well, you can't fault a kid for that. Make sure that you make it to your appointment next week." Chase said, "I will Dad, I promise."

Chase went to his room and shut the door. He knew he would have to go to his appointment with his new Dr. next week. He had to keep his parents happy. He did not want a new Dr. but he was so glad not to go and see that bitch, Clark again, to talk about his feelings, sex, and how he felt about girls. Actually, he hated girls his own age. They were so stupid, always playing with their hair, wearing lots of makeup, laughing and giggling all the time. He preferred older woman's company, but at sixteen, that was hard to find an older woman who even wanted to talk to him. Although, there was one woman, a friend of Molly's, who was in her yoga class. Chase had been calling his mother Molly for the last couple of years. His father did not like it at all but Molly said it was okay, she really did not care. The woman was only twenty years old. He really liked her; she was different from the rest of them. She had long, blonde hair and green eyes. She was a very small woman, not much bigger than his sister, Katie, but she had big boobs, which Chase fantasized about. Chase wondered if his dad ever fantasized about her or any of the other women. He and his Dad never talked about such things. They surely never talked about sex, women or relationships. Caleb had told Molly that Chase could learn all about that kind of stuff in high school, just like he did.

When Amy was at the house, she was always very quiet, gently laughing at the other woman's jokes. Molly would usually invite her yoga friends over after class and they would sit and drink wine, talk about movies, books, and of course, sex. Chase noted that Amy never participated in these discussions and that intrigued Chase. Amy was younger than the rest of the women and probably did not have much in common with them besides yoga. She liked Chase; he was at her intellectual level, smart and he was interesting. Chase could talk about anything, not like most people at sixteen. She had not talked much to him directly but had listened in on conversations he was having with everyone else. A week later, on Tuesday, it was the day of Chase's appointment with his new Dr., Dr. Epstein. This Dr. was in the same building as Dr. Clark. His appointment was at four o'clock, after school. He sat in the doctors waiting room for almost twenty minutes before the Dr.'s secretary came out and told him to come on back to Dr. Epstein's office. Chase thought, "Well, let's get this over with". He walked into Dr. Epstein's office and the Dr. introduced himself and shook hands with Chase.

The man was a lot harder to look at than Dr. Clark was. He was short, fat, and balding. What could he possibly tell this old man. His thinking was probably very old fashioned. He asked Chase to have a seat in front of his desk. The Dr. sat down and looked at Chase. He said, "I understand you have been under the care of Dr. Clark since you were five years old." Chase said, "Everything is in my big folder, you should have prepared more to see a new patient." The Dr. said, "Look, don't fuck with me kid. I have treated psychopaths since I was twenty-five years old and now I am fifty-five. I know you better than you know yourself. My job is to keep you from killing anyone or committing any other crimes against someone else. It is also my job to keep you out of jail and mental institutions. What do you want me to do for you, what do you expect?" Chase started to pay attention to the Dr. after he said the word fuck. Chase said, "Don't try to act cool, like you're my age. Don't pretend to know what I am thinking about, because you do not really know. The only thing I want from you is the medication I am supposed to be on, and probably will not take, and to leave me the hell alone. I only came here so my parents will shut up about me still needing medication and treatment. Keep giving me prescriptions and don't expect me to come in here every week." The Dr. said, "You want me to lie to your parents about you being here and still charge them for your visits, is that correct?" Chase replied, "Yes, that's pretty much it Doc." The Dr. said, "You know Chase, I'm a pretty smart Dr. and have been doing this for thirty years, you know, I may be able to help you." Chase said, "No, as a Dr. you should know that a psychopath cannot be cured. If you are as smart as you say you are then you should already know that, so how do you think you can help me?" The Dr. looked Chase in the eye and he said, "You are probably fantasizing about killing some beautiful girl right now, am I wrong?" Chase replied, "No, you are not wrong." The Dr. continued, "The medication we give you should help with your rages, but will not help with your wanting to torture and kill a person. The only thing I can help you with is to talk to you about those thoughts. I can teach you how to redirect them into something positive." Chase said, "No thanks, Doc. I have been that route with Dr. Clark already and the more we talk about it the more I fantasize about killing someone". The Dr. was annoyed as he told Chase, "You know, I could have you locked up at the hospital for being a threat to yourself or others. If I really thought, you were ready to go out and kill someone, that is exactly what I would do without hesitation." Chase was getting angry now as he replied, "I guess that is your job, and your choice but that still doesn't change who I am or what I think about." The Dr. said, "What have you been thinking about this past week?" Chase responded with, "I think about blood and how good the iron rich blood smells, tastes, and the rich red color of it. I think about how it looks running out of someone or something that I have just stuck with a knife. I think about looking into eyes and watching them slowly die. I think about watching the light go out of the eyes and then lastly, I think about a body turning cold and stiff in my hands. That is what I pretty much think about Doc." The Dr. said, "What if I could help you redirect those thoughts and turn them into something more safe and normal?" Chase said, "Cut the bullshit Dr. Are you going to give me my prescription or not, your time is up." The Dr. answered back, "Yes, but I will expect you back here again next week. I do not care if you just sit in the reception area, but I will not lie to your parents about you not being here. I get paid either way because someone else will just take your spot. Look Chase, I have to admit to you that deep down, I really do not give a shit about you, I am just trying to do my job. If you don't want my help, and as long as I think you are not dangerous, you can leave." Chase was impressed with the Dr. saying exactly what he felt and he did not sugar coat it. Chase had calmed down a little bit and replied, "Okay Doc, I'll come in and see you next week." Dr. Epstein said, "Check in with the receptionist on your way out. See you next week." When Chase got home, Molly asked him "So, how did you like Dr. Epstein?" Chase thought about the visit with Dr. Epstein on his way home. It sure was a lot different from talking to and intimidating Dr. Clark. He decided that he liked him and that maybe he would talk to him next week. Even if he couldn't help him, he was someone neutral to talk to about his thoughts.

Chase was almost seventeen. He had not had sex yet, like a lot of the guys in his high school who brag about it all the time, like, "I knocked off a piece last night, I got laid, and she sucked my dick last night, etc., etc. Chase did not believe half of the stories that he heard from the other guys in the gym lockers and showers. They were all supposed to take showers after gym class, but Chase never did. He didn't want other guys checking him out and making fun of him because of his small penis, which he knew that they would because they have done that to other guys. Every school had their bullies and they used to bully Chase, until they found out that he stole the coach's car. Now they thought that he was just a quiet "Bad Ass". They pretty much left him alone now.

It was Molly's yoga night tonight and Chase would hang around to see if Amy showed up afterward with the other women. They would sometimes come back here, but they were coming back here more often. They liked to cook new, low fat recipes together. Chase sat on his bed, playing video games on his television. His Dad knocked on his door and Chase said, "Come In." Caleb walked over and sat down on his bed and Said, "What are you playing?" Chase said, "It's just a game." Chase did not know why but he was so irritated that his father even came into his room. This was Chase's private domain and he did not like for anyone else to come in here.

Caleb and Chase did not really have anything in common and they did not have a very good relationship. Chase felt he could not talk to his dad about anything because then his dad would just go off and lecture him on whatever it was, instead of talking to him. Chase knew that his father never really knew his own father. He guessed that his dad never really had a role model to go by or anyone to show him what a father was supposed to do. Even his uncle Henry had been younger than his father. Chase guessed his father was doing the best he could at raising a son. Chase thought that his parents were so old fashioned in their thinking, as most young adults did. He wanted his dad to leave so he said, "Whatcha want dad?" Caleb said, "I need a little help outside, splitting some wood." Even though they did not use wood heat anymore, they had a new furnace, his dad still liked to burn wood in the Buck stove. Chase hated the outdoors, especially working out there. He did not like to sweat and he did not like bugs. Chase did not tell his dad "no" because it made his dad angry. His dad always said you do not live anywhere for free; you have to work. You have to share the responsibilities. For fear of having to hear that speech again, Chase said, "Okay, Dad, I'll be out in a minute, let me change clothes." His dad smiled at him and said, "Okay, son." His dad left the room and Chase changed his clothes. He hoped that they were through in time for him to come in and take a shower and change in case Amy came over tonight.

Chase had cut and split wood with his dad many times. They had split and stacked about a half a cord of wood when his dad said, "Okay, I think that will do for a while. Thanks son for the help." Chase said, "No problem Dad". They never talked about anything very much. His dad said, "How's your car running? Are you checking the oil like I told you?" "Of course. I keep it in great shape." His dad said, "have you seen Mini for a while Chase? I've never seen you take her out in your car yet." Chase said, "No, and no other girlfriend. There just isn't anyone else I am interested in." Caleb said, "I've been noticing how you look at your mother's friend, Amy, when she is here. I know you are sweet on her but she is way too old for you son." Molly and Caleb had talked about the way that Chase and Amy looked at each other and she did not like it much either. She agreed that Amy, at age 20, was way too old for Chase and did not like the added responsibility of her having a three-year-old child. Chase said, "Was I that obvious? I guess you cannot help whom you are attracted. Besides, I do not think she even took a second look at me." His dad said, "Steer clear son, she's too old and your mother said that she has a little boy that is three years old". Chase said, "Oh, yeah, I hate little kids, they are so annoying". Caleb smiled at this and said, "So you're planning on never having any?" Chase said, "Yep, that's right, but I guess if they come with the woman you want, then you have to take the whole package." Caleb frowned then. His dad said, "Let's go, and wash up for dinner". Mom made us some vegetable soup and homemade bread for dinner." Chase said, "Where is Katie tonight?" His dad said, "She's at friends, having a sleep over." They both went in, took showers, changed clothes, and then met in the kitchen for dinner. While they were eating dinner, the house phone rang, and Caleb answered. It was Charlie, looking for Chase. His dad handed him the phone and listened in to what his son was saying, even though he was trying to talk quietly. Chase said, "Okay, I'll be there soon". Chase hung up and sat back down at the table. His Dad said, "I told you not to be hang-in around that boy Charlie didn't I?" Chase said, "Dad, I'm old enough to pick my own friends, and besides, Charlie is not a little boy any more. He is a grown man and a lot more mature than he used to be." Caleb said, "I don't care how old he is, I told you not to be around him, and I meant it Chase. You deliberately went against what I told you not to do. You are a really smart boy Chase, but you do not have the experience that I do with people and I am telling you, Charlie is bad news and to stay away from him." Chase said, "He's been my friend for the last umpteen years. I'm just not going to give up my best friend." They were both getting angry. They were both starting to yell instead of talk. Caleb said, "Give me your car keys, you're not going anywhere". Chase said, "No, they are my car keys, you gave me the car, remember?" If there was one thing that his dad hated, it was a smart mouth. He said, "I' would have never talked that disrespectfully to my mother. You talk like a spoiled, little brat and I said; Give me your car keys." Chase said, "No." Caleb slammed his big hand down on the table, stood up, and said, "I said give me the keys and give them to me now Chase." Chase said, "No, I have to go somewhere tonight." Caleb said, "No, not tonight you don't. Give them." Chase harshly replied, "No." Caleb took a step towards his son and he punched him right on his jaw and Chase fell over. When Chase got up, he threw an unsuspecting punch at his dad and caught him by surprise. Caleb grabbed his son around his throat and started to squeeze. Chases' eyes got huge and he was trying to break his dad's hold but could not. After Caleb had about strangled his son to death, he let him drop to the floor. Chase was trying to get his last breath and he could not speak. Caleb said, "I'll give you one more chance Chase to hand over your car keys." Chase reached in his pocket and gave his dad his keys. He thought it was not worth his own dad killing him over. Chase finally said, "I will at least have to call him back and tell him I am not coming over. His father said, clean up this mess before your mother and her friends get here, and do not talk back to me ever again boy. You may get away with this shit with your mother, but it does not work with me Chase. I know what you are about, I had a brother just like you." His dad went to his room to watch television.

Chase called Charlie, when he found his voice. He said, "I can't make it tonight Charlie, something's come up. My dad, you know. I know you are tired, just go on home and we will continue later. See ya, bye."

Chase went back up to his room. He was hoping his Mother's friend Amy would come over. that would put him in a much better mood. Chase's mother's friends, including Amy, did come back to the house around seven that night. Amy smiled at Chase when she came in and Chase smiled back. Chase had his and his father's mess cleaned up by then. Amy was wearing a little makeup. She was looking especially great tonight. Chase took his video games and played them on the big television in the main living room so that he could see Amy in the kitchen. A little while later, Amy came out and sat on the couch with Chase and said What are you playing?" He told her and she said, "Can I play with you?" Chase thought, "Boy, that's an understatement". "Of course you can Amy."

She smiled as she took the controller to the game. Of course, Chase's ego would not let him lose, however, he tried not to win it by much. When the game was over, he said, "You're really good at this game Amy. What other games do you like?" She said, "I love to play chess." Chase was surprised by this. He did not know many women who played chess. She said, "I will challenge you to a game if you'd like to play?" He said, "Sure, I love chess also." Chase set the chessboard up on the coffee table and they sat on the floor on cushions, They flipped a coin to see who was going first. They made casual conversation as they played, and then Chase said, "My Dad tells me that you have a little boy." She said, "Yes, he is the light of my life." Chase said, "That's nice." Molly entered the living room and said, "Oh, there you are Amy; I wondered where you had gotten off to." Amy said, "Oh, sorry, I wondered in here and then challenged your son here, to a game of chess." Molly looked at the board, "It doesn't look like any pieces have been moved yet." Chase said, "We've only been playing for about twenty minutes". "At that rate, you'll be playing all night." His mother said, "Well, hurry up with that game; I need Amy in the kitchen". Amy said, "Okay, we won't be long." as she winked at Chase. He liked her conspiratorial attitude. When his mother left the room, the game went very quickly and Amy beat him badly at chess. Chase was amazed. He said, "I've never seen anyone play this game that well in my life". She said, "I use to be state champion." Chase was duly impressed. He said, "Okay, the next time you come over, you owe me a rematch". She responded with, "I'd love to." She gave him her sweetest smile and went back into the kitchen.

All of his mother's friends were leaving and Caleb came out to say "Hello" and he went over to the couch where Chase was sitting and sat down next to him. He said, "I wanted to apologize to you for losing my temper earlier and choking you." Neither one of them said anything and Molly walked into the room and sat down on the couch with them. She said to Chase "Looks like you and Amy had a good time tonight playing games." Chase's dad just looked at him and didn't say anything. He said, "Yeah, she really kicked my ass in chess." His dad said, "Watch your mouth Chase, especially around your mother."

Chase wanted to change the subject. He did not want to discuss Amy with his parents. "Mom I am going to take Mini to the prom. Caleb looked at him funny and said, "Oh, I thought you and Mini quit dating?" Molly's face lit up and she said, "That's nonsense Caleb, he likes Mini a lot. So you ask Mini to the prom. We will have to rent you a tux, rent a limo, find a florist, have a corsages made, and make reservations at a nice restaurant for you!" Chase said, "Slow down Mom. First of all, guys do not wear tuxes to prom anymore; they wear a suit jacket and maybe cool gym shoes. They do not rent limos. They all try to carpool and then they get together and decorate the car they are going in. In addition, girls do not wear corsages anymore." Molly's face fell. She said, "Well, don't the girls even get dressed up anymore?" He answered, "They wear a nice dress, but not a formal one". Molly and Caleb both thought that was great but Caleb wondered why Chase had not mentioned it earlier. This is the first social event Chase has ever attended. They thought that maybe he was improving.

All three of them were still sitting on the couch twenty minutes later, when a news flash went across the television screen. It was a banner at the top of the screen that said, "Suspect in the case of missing college female student, Becky Strauss arrested. Watch channel nine news at eleven." Chase knew that she was the girl that Charlie had kidnapped and killed. He just sat there stunned and looking at the screen. Molly looked at him and said, "Son, what's wrong, you're as white as a ghost." He said, "Nothing's wrong, I'm just a little tired is all." They all watched the news and the announcer kept saying, "Breaking story when we come back from commercial." He had said that like three more times until the actual story came on. "Oh My God!" Chase jumped up and went closer to the television screen. They showed two police officer's leading Charlie out of his house in a pair of handcuffs. Charlie held his head down so no one could see who it was. "They all three said at the same time. Oh My God!" The reporter came on in the foreground and said, "Charles Thomas, arrested this evening for the kidnapping and possible murder of female college student Rebecca Strauss. He is only a suspect at this time. More on this story on our noon news tomorrow. The clip showed Rebecca's parents and siblings crying, from gratitude for finding out what happened. After the story, all three of them sat on the couch and did not say anything. Finally, Caleb said, "Chase, that's why I told you to stay away from that boy. It's a real good thing that you did not go over to his house tonight like you wanted to. Do you know anything about this?" Chase responded with, "No, Of course I don't. If I did, I would have called the authorities. I have to call Aunt Hillary and tell her what is going on." Maybe she could help him. Caleb said, "No, don't bother Hillary; Charlie is probably guilty as hell". That is why I did not want you hang-in around him. I knew he was no good from the first day I met him." Chase got up and went to his room".

Chase just sat on his bed. He could not believe what was happening. He knew how careful that Charlie had been. He could not think of anything that they found that pointed to him. He quickly got on his computer then went to the internet news. He did not find much more than he had heard on the television. Chase did not want to go to Charlie's house, his parents were there and he could talk to them but he did not want to be linked to Charlie in any public way, especially with the plans that he had for Dr. Clark. He decided, despite what his father said, he was going to call aunt Hillary. He called her home phone number. She answered on the second ring. She said, "Hey Chase, how's it going?" He told her the news story he had just heard. She said, "Oh My God! Chase, do you think he did something to that girl?" Chase said, "No, not in a million years. He has his mental problems, just like I do, and he may have even thought about doing something, but he never would have gone through with anything like that. Charlie is just too timid and too afraid of the authorities to do something like that. Aunt Hillary, you have to help him!" He decided to pull the pity card. "He is my best friend for the last ten years and his parents really do not care much about him. I am really all he has. The only person who really cares about him." Of course, he did not really care about Charlie at all. He was just someone to talk with. They liked to hang out. He told him not to do anything like that, especially without him. Sometimes, Charlie was not too smart, but he needed his help in kidnapping the good Dr. A partner in crime. He needed someone to roll over on if he were caught kidnapping the Dr. Finally, Hillary said, "Okay Chase, I'll go and see him, but just as a personal favor to you and then I will call you back." "Oh thank you aunt Hillary, you are the best aunt a guy could have. Oh, and aunt

Hillary? Call me on my cell, Dad did not want me to call you and get you involved. He never liked Charlie and always thought that Charlie was a bad influence on me." She said, "Gotcha. Can you give me Charlie's parents phone number? I will probably have to be okayed by them to see him." He gave it to her and she hung up. Chase had a feeling that this was going to be a long night. He hung up the phone. Chase went over every detail that Charlie told him, in his mind and still could not figure out what mistake Charlie had made.

Hillary called Charlie's parents and told them who she was and that she was a lawyer. She wanted to know if she could go and see Charlie. Charlie's Father said, "Are you going to represent him?" She said, "Only if it's okay with Charlie." He said, "What are your fee's going to cost me?" She said, "It's pro Bono. My nephew is Chase, Charlie's best friend and he asked me to take the case." Charlie's father was all for it now that he knew that it would not cost him anything. He said, "Sure, you can be his lawyer Ms. Thomas." She went downtown to the jail where they were processing Charlie. She signed in as his counsel. They let her go back in one of their little interview rooms to wait for Charlie to finish processing. After about twenty minutes, two male officers, one on each side of Charlie brought him in. He was shackled at the wrist and ankles. They told him to have a seat across from Hillary. They asked Hillary if she felt comfortable being in this room alone with Charlie. She said "yes". They also said that they would be right outside the doors if Hillary needed anything. Just yell and they would hear her. She said, "Fine". Charlie was bent over the table as if he was trying to curl up in a ball. She said, "I don't know if you ever met me, but I am Chase's aunt Hillary." Charlie said, "He talks about you all the time. You are his favorite aunt." She smiled and she said Charlie, did you kidnap that girl?" He said, "No, she went for a ride with me to get a pizza and then we had to stop at the store to get some more fabric softener that she needed and then we went back to the laundry mat to finish our wash and eat some pizza. We both left at different times and did our own thing. That was the last I saw of the girl. I do not even know why I am here or what kind of evidence that they think they have to charge me with." Hillary said, "After looking at the paperwork, you are the prime suspect of the missing girl, Rebecca, a co-ed at the University of Cincinnati. Hillary said, "Charlie, I know you are upset, but we need to sort through this okay?" He said, "Okay". Hillary could tell that he was scared to death as she would be if the roles were reversed. She said, "The paperwork here says that the circumstances surrounding the arrest were delayed because it took several days of going through red tape and then several more days of enhancing a photo. They have you talking to this girl next to her car holding something like a shirt, then the film cuts out and it shows you standing behind your car, at the trunk, with the girl's legs hanging out, then it shows you leaving the parking lot in that same car. It also showed the license plate, which they had blown up so that they could see it clearly. You were the last person to see her. That is pretty incriminating evidence. They are right now, as we speak, going to a judge to get an order to search your house and your car. "Oh God!" Charlie was turning white. Hillary knew that he had done something to the girl, she just did not know what it was yet. Hillary said, "Charlie, look at me. if you had that girl in your trunk or in your house, the police will find out through DNA testing. You have to tell me exactly what happened and you have to tell me the truth. If you do not, the police will crack you wide open sooner or later with their interrogation, with proof that you cannot deny. Charlie put his face in his hands. Hillary did not say anything for a few minutes; she just let the whole thing sink in. Finally, Charlie looked at her and said, "If I tell you everything, tell you the truth, will you still represent me?" She said, "Yes, I promised Chase that I would be your counsel." Charlie spilled the whole story to her, leaving out some of the more gruesome parts. He told Hillary that he killed the girl in self-defense, because she was trying to kill him with a knife. He hid the body because he knew no one would believe his story. Hillary asked him, "Where is the girl?" Charlie said, "She's at the bottom of the Ohio River." Hillary was stunned. She did not think that Charlie had it in him to do something like this, but then again, she really did not know him very well. She said, "Okay Charlie, that is good that you told me the truth. It is really bad that you dumped the body. You could be convicted of murder in the first degree. It was premeditated, was it not? He said, "Yes. I am sick. I tried to control it, I have been seeing psychologist since I was in kindergarten, and have been on medication since I was a little boy. I did not really mean for any of it to happen. Hillary said, "For the amount of time that you have been in therapy and the amount of medications that you were on, we will have to go with a "temporary insanity" defense. Hillary went home and made some coffee and wrote up her temporary insanity defense, with a copy for the prosecution. She knew the prosecutor well. She thought that she could speed things along with him.

It was only four days later and she received paperwork from the prosecutor's office. A deal that if Charlie would plead guilty on all counts, he would do 25yrs. or less in a maximum security prison and he would have mandatory visits with one of the prison psychiatrist, but the prosecution wanted to know where Charlie dumped the body before making any kind of deal. Hillary went to see Charlie in the interview room again.

She went over what the deal was from the prosecution. He got hysterical, saying, "I can't do that kind of time. I'm already going crazy, I wouldn't be able to handle it, I'm telling you, I can't, and I can't take that deal. Hillary said, "If you don't take the deal, you're looking at life in prison with no chance of parole or death by lethal injection if the jury finds you not insane at the time of the crime." He looked to Hillary pleadingly and said, "I trust you Hillary, what should I do?" She said, I would advise you to take the deal." He said, "What if we go with self-defense?" Hillary said, "No, that won't fly, the jury would never believe self-defense, since you kidnapped and raped her." Charlie said "Okay, Ms. Hillary, let me think about it for a couple of days and then I'll decide." She said, "Okay Charlie, but don't take too long or the prosecutor could resend the deal." Hillary stood up and shook Charlie's hand. She said, "I'll call you in a couple of days to see what you have decided." He did not say anything, just sat there. All he could think about was that he could not do that kind of time. He also thought about the fact that his parents had not even been here to see him once.

The next day, an officer came and got Charlie, telling him he had a visitor. Visitors were searched and checked for any kind of contraband before being allowed to see anyone. Charlie went to the visiting room where you talked to your visitor through glass on a phone. Charlie thought that it was Chase coming to see him. His only friend he ever had. When he walked in, it was not Chase but it was his mother. She had tears in her eyes. He could never remember seeing his mother cry before. He sat down and slowly picked up the phone. He looked her in the eye and said, “Mother”. She said, “Charlie, I can’t believe this is happening. I have paid for your therapy most of your life, and this is how you repay me.” Charlie replied, “I thought you were taking care of me because it was your responsibility, not because you thought I would owe you.” She said, “Don’t get smart with me boy. I have to know something. Did you really kill that girl and did you do it in our house?” Charlie looked her straight in the eye and he said, “Yes, mother, I killed her, right down in our basement.” She did not look surprised as she replied, “I knew you did it, I knew it. You are nothing more than the evil spawn of Satan himself. I am ashamed to call you my son. I hope you get what is coming to you and I will pray for Rebecca’s family.” He replied, “Mother, you are nothing more than a hypercritical bitch, who never even wanted me in the first place, you never loved me; you never cared about what was going on with me as long as you looked good to all of your friends. So, I just have one more thing to say to you.” She rolled her eyes at him, "What is it Charlie?" He said, "Fuck off Mother". He then dropped the phone and turned to wait for the officer to escort him back to jail. At least he had the pleasure of seeing his mother's face go white for once, and he really enjoyed telling her what he had been thinking about her for years. He wished he had told her these things a long, long, time ago. He felt pleasure in telling her but he also felt a sense of loss, like someone close to him had died. He did not feel bad about it because he had never felt remorse for anything he had done, including killing, so he was not sure, how that felt. At that moment, leaving the visitor's room, he had made up his mind what he was going to tell Hillary.

Chase did not go to see Charlie in jail, but it was okay because he was sure that Charlie knew why. One day when he kidnapped Dr. Clark, he did not want to be associated with someone who had done the same thing. Chase thought it was really bad that Charlie got caught the way he did. He did not really have a plan like himself, he half-asses everything. He should have cased the laundry mat and then he would have known about the security cameras. Chase thought that he would never be that stupid.

Chase thought about raping a woman. Nothing like trying to rape a woman and not knowing how to do it. He never has had sex. He would have to remedy that. He would ask out one of the girls in school with the worst reputation and see if he could get her to give it up. If that did not work, he would ask out one of the ugliest girls in school, sweet talk her and try to get her to give it up. That was his main focus right now, getting laid. Funny how he was thinking about getting laid, while his "best friend" was in jail for murder. Chase was sure that Charlie would get laid plenty in prison. He just had one of those pretty faces that everyone loved and he was ripped. He also knew that his aunt Hillary was a great lawyer and if she thought he had a chance at all of getting out of jail; she would help him do it.

Charlie sent a message to Hillary the next day that he needed to talk to her. She got to the jail that evening and Charlie was taken into the interview room. Hillary took a seat at the small table and then Charlie sat down opposite her. The officer reminded them that he would be right outside the door. Hillary looked at Charlie and said, "Have you made a decision?" His hands were folded in his lap as he looked down and whispered, "Yes. I have decided to take the prosecutor's deal. I cannot take them to the girl's body but I can show them where I put her in the river." Hillary wasn't surprised that he took the deal, she knew he was a smart guy. "I think that is a very wise decision and I will relay the message to the prosecution, what you have said about where the girl's body was placed." Hillary asked if Chase had been to see him. Charlie said, "No, but he has his reasons. My mother was here yesterday evening and it did not go well. She never loved me and now she hates me because I killed that girl. Whatever happened to unconditional love anyway?" Hillary felt sorry for him, but only slightly, he was a killer after all.

They ended their meeting by Hillary telling Charlie that he needed to sign a paper stating he would accept the deal. Hillary told Charlie that he would be going into court in a few days to plead guilty. Charlie hung his head, as he left the room, shackled, with the officer. Hillary would have to explain to the prosecutor about the girl's body and how, with the currents, it probably wasn't in the same place that Charlie had sunk her. The prosecution would be happy that Charlie took the deal, because they hated prosecuting people with mental disabilities.

It was the following week, on a Thursday that Charlie was called into courtroom number five. Hillary was there with him. They all sat down at the appropriate tables until the Bailiff announced, "All rise". The Judge walked in, a female judge. Charlie was asked to stand up and when the judge asked, "How do you plead in the case of the kidnapping, raping and killing of college coed Rebecca Strauss?" Charlie hesitated for just a moment and you could hear a pin drop in the courtroom. Charlie looked the judge straight in the eyes and said, "Guilty, your honor, on all counts". The courtroom erupted with acceptance of Charlie's plea. The judge banged her gavel on her desk and said, "All quiet" until the courtroom was quiet once again. The judge asked Charlie to sit down. The judge asked the prosecution, "Have all parties involved accepted this plea bargain?" The prosecutor stood and said, "We do your Honor." The judge then said, "We will return to court in one week from today for the sentencing of the plaintiff. Court dismissed." Again, the bailiff said "All rise." while the judge stood up and returned to the judge's chambers. Charlie had looked around and did not see his mother but saw his father sitting in the back.

When Charlie looked at him, his father looked back and gave a nod that told him he was glad that Charlie admitted to what he had done. His father looked sad; he had always told Charlie that this is where he would end up one day. Charlie's father came to visit him later that evening. They both picked up the phone and Charlie's father said, "Son, you did the right thing for that girl's parents in owning what you've done." Charlie said, "Thanks Dad, I think so to." His father then said, "I'm sorry that things didn't go well when your mother visited. She told me all about it. I know that the two of you never got along very well, but she does love you, in her own way." Charlie said, "Whatever, I don't want to talk about Mother." His father said, "Let me know if there is anything you need and I will get it here for you." Charlie said, "It is okay Dad, you do not have to pretend that we get along any better than Mother and I do." His father said, "I do love you, you were always just a hard kid to love. You never talked about anything with your mother and me, only to Dr. Clark. I did not know you had so much going on up there in that head. Dr. Clark could never talk to us about you, now we understand just how sick you are Charlie. I do love you and I'll be here for you during the sentencing phase and afterward s, if you need anything." His father had tears in his eyes as he spoke. Charlie said, "Well, you knew me pretty well Dad, and you don't have to cry or worry about me, and you really do not have to pretend that you care about me any more than Mother does. This is where I was probably destined to end up anyway." Charlie hung up the visitor's phone and signaled for the officer that he was ready to go back to his cell.

Next Thursday seemed to come around pretty fast. Charlie was led into court and he saw his father sitting in the back again. The Bailiff announced, "All Rise!" The judge came in and sat down on her bench. The Bailiff announced, "Please be seated." The judge asked Charlie to stand during sentencing. The judge read over all of the charges and then said, "Charlie for the crimes against Rebecca Strauss, I hereby sentence you to fifteen years, with a chance of parole after ten, in the maximum-security state prison, where you will voluntarily continue to undergo treatment for your mental illnesses. The court room suddenly became very noisy with shouts from Rebecca's family that the sentencing was unfair and that Charlie deserved to die. The judge banged her gavel and said, "Order in the court." Everyone quieted. The judge then asked for the victims' statements to Charlie. She asked Charlie to sit back down. The judge said, "Now we will hear the victim's statements." A small pretty woman was walking up to the podium to speak. She introduced herself as Rebecca's mother. She slightly turned and looked Charlie in the eye. She was crying as she tried to speak. "I believe that the sentence you received was too light to fit the crime for killing my beautiful daughter. You have changed our lives forever. Rebecca was an honor student, with her whole life ahead of her but then, you had to go and take that life away. She started crying harder. She asked Charlie, "Why? Why, did you kill my beautiful daughter? You deserve to be put to death for killing her, an eye for an eye. You are an evil, evil man and I hope that one day you will rot in hell for what you have done. Rebecca was my only child, the light of my life. I loved her more than life itself and you took that away from me for a few hours of your disgusting fun. You . . ." She got too upset to go on. Person after person got up. They were all related to Rebecca and each one of them said how they felt about what Charlie had done. Charlie tried to feel bad for each and every one of them, but that was life and they just had to get over it. They probably spoiled the little bitch anyway. Now they were free of her and they should be thanking him instead. He felt no remorse for killing the girl. Rebecca's father was sitting close to Charlie. The Father jumped up when everyone had his or her say, he pulled out a small firearm and shot Charlie at point blank range. He was going for Charlie's head, since he knew that they had probably put a vest on Charlie, however, he missed and shot him in the throat. Her father was tackled to the ground by the officers and hauled off to jail. They called an ambulance for Charlie right away. When Charlie was shot, blood started spurting out everywhere, especially on Hillary, since she was standing next to him. They all knew how tight the security was here and were amazed that Rebecca's father had managed to bring in a firearm. The whole section of Rebecca's friends and family were cheering for Rebecca's Father. Charlie could barely hear them in his state of semi-consciousness. The last thing that Charlie remembered was the smell of blood that he loved so much.

Charlie's next memory was waking up in the hospital. A nurse had come in his room and was glad that he was awake. She said that he had been asleep for four days. Charlie could not believe it, "Where had those days gone?" Slowly, his day in court was all coming back to him. While a nurse took his vital signs, he looked up and saw something white running through a tube. He tried to speak but only a whisper came out. Finally, he was able to whisper, "What is that?" She said it was his food. The tube went directly into his stomach. Since he was shot in the throat, this is how he got his nutrition until his throat healed. She also told him that he had a tracheotomy, a tube in his throat that led directly to his lungs so that he could breathe. He lay in that hospital bed, feeling regret that Rebecca's Father had not killed him. It would be better than where he was going. Who knows? maybe Rebecca's father would end up being his cellmate.

"PART II"

Chase was studying to be an engineer. He thought about going to mortuary college but his parents would not hear of it, besides, there is not much money in that unless you owned your own funeral home. It would be fun to play with the dead bodies and do the embalming. Once he got his engineering out of the way, he may still go to mortuary college. His parents could not complain then, because he would already have his engineering degree to fall back on.

As Chase sat in his apartment, close to his college, The University of Cincinnati, he thought about Charlie. He had been in prison for three years now. Wow, what a waste of a good mind. Chase had received a couple of letters from Charlie and it seemed he was fairing pretty well in there. He belonged to one of the many gangs in prison and anytime there was someone who needed to be taught a lesson, they let Charlie do the dirty work. He was in his element there, with the stabbings and the blood. Charlie did say that he missed having sex with women. He was the bitch of his gang leader and he got special privileges. He did not mind having sex with another man, it did not mean he was gay or anything it was just sex. Any port in the storm kind of thing. They never did find Rebecca's body and it never turned up.

Chase got his apartment when he was eighteen. He talked his father into paying for it because the dorms were horrible and they lived too far away for him to commute. As soon as he was settled into his apartment, he called Amy. He really liked Amy but she was just about to the end of her usefulness to him. She could not teach him anymore about sex than she already had, and she was starting to bore Chase with her endless, chatter. He and Amy had been seeing each other since the night of their first chess game at his parents' house. They both kept this from his parents because they knew Chase's parents would not approve and would give him a hard time about seeing Amy. He would break it off with her soon. He wanted someone new.

Amy did not know anything about his mental illnesses, his psychotic thoughts. Lately, he had been hearing just one voice. The voice he thought was God's. Sometimes he would answer the voice he heard. Someone close to him would say, "Who are you talking to?" He'd answer, "Oh nobody, just talking to myself." He was also starting to experience some horrible headaches that would keep him down for a couple of days. Today was one of those days, when he heard a knock on the door. It was Amy. She was just starting to drop by more and more lately. Her ex-husband was trying to get her back and when she needed an escape from him, she would come here, where no one knew where she was. Chase opened the door and asked, "What's wrong?" She said, "It's my ex. He told me that if I didn't come back to him, he would take my son away from me." Chase said, "He can't even try it unless there is a proven, good reason, so I wouldn't let it get to me if I were you." She said, "He won't leave me alone. He is calling, texting, or e-mailing. I got a restraining order against him today and when he found out, his temper went through the roof." Chase asked, looking a little worried, "Does he know that you are here?" She said, "No, I kept circling around the block, to make sure I wasn't followed. I need a drink." Chase said, "I'll fix you one". He kept some whiskey in the apartment, just for moments like this, however, he never drank. When he did drink, he would hear the voices in his head even more and he was also worried about what he would reveal. He was really getting tired of all of Amy's drama, especially today, with the headache he had. Maybe a booty call with Amy would fix that.

Chase knew what Amy needed, knew why she came here in the first place. She needed a release of tension and she liked it rough, just like he did. Chase did give her credit for being such a good teacher. The first time they had sex was at her house, after her husband had left her the first time. She texted him one night to "Stop by her house, her son was asleep". Of course, he would, and he would make some lame excuse to his parents for getting home so late from his part-time job as a tutor. He tutored high school kids in history and math for extra money. This usually paid his car insurance and gas to get him around. He knew what Amy wanted. He had noticed her watching him with a smoldering looking in her eyes many times while she was at his house visiting with his mother. When he got to Amy's house, it was about 10:30. She was watching for him and let him in right away before he could ring the bell and wake her son up. She practically jerked him into the house. She grabbed him and kissed him. He dropped his keys and a few roses that he had brought to her on the floor and returned her kiss fervently. He had a lot of practice honing his kissing skills on Mini. Lord knows they spent many hours kissing and doing nothing else, since she was saving herself for the "right guy". Amy started pulling off his clothes and he became a little self-conscious. He had never been naked in front of a female before and he always thought it would be on his time, not a girl's or a woman in Amy's case. Of course, he did not protest. He had been waiting for this moment for a long time. Amy removed her clothes, hardly stopping their kissing while she did. They stumbled over their clothing and the furniture getting to be bedroom. Amy pushed him down upon the bed. He jumped up, grabbed her by the arms, and pushed her down instead. They continued kissing. They started feeling each other up. He whispered in her ear, "This is my first time; you'll have to show me what you like." She showed him all right. She told him, "Don't worry honey, just do what feels natural". Before he knew it, he was inside her. He thought that she felt better than anything he had ever felt in his whole life and he told her so. He could not believe he was finally inside a real woman. He was a little clumsy. He came almost as soon as he entered her. She smiled at him because she knew that, at his age, it would not take long for him to be ready again. She showed him how to go down on her and how and where to lick her. She showed him many things over the next few months. They were sexually compatible. They both liked it rough. He was a little surprised by this because he thought all women liked it long and sweet. Not Amy, the rougher the better. She seemed to feel the need to be punished for reasons unknown, however, he was glad to accommodate her. She loved to be spanked and tied up. Their "private meetings" went on for months and they were both so happy when Chase finally got his own place. It was a place where Amy knew that no one else could find her. With Chase she could let loose and be herself without risk of judgment. She knew Chase would give her what she craved without question. After Amy finished her drink and calmed down a little, Chase grabbed her and bent her over the kitchen table. He reached up under her skirt and tore her thong panties off. She was hot and ready. She needed this release to calm her down. Chase held her down with one hand on her back and he fucked her hard and rough until they both came. They were both half-dressed and sitting on the couch, when someone started pounding on the apartment door. Chase heard a man say, "Amy, come out, I know you are in there." She said, "Go away and leave me alone. I have a restraining order and I will call the police if you don't leave now." He broke the door by kicking it in. He quickly grabbed Chase by the throat as he said, "So, this is the little Twerp you've been fucking." Amy yelled, "Leave him alone!" She grabbed her phone to call the police. Chase, like his Dad, always carried a knife. He was also pretty good at using it. He reached in his pocket, grabbed his knife, and swung it at the distraught man. It connected with the man's face and made a large gash. The man screamed and let go of Chase. There was blood pouring out everywhere. When he let go of Chase, Chase stabbed him in the chest. He died right there on the living room floor. Amy started screaming, "Why did you do that? He was my son's father!" Chase yelled, "It was self-defense, he was trying to kill me, or didn't you notice that? I thought you said that no one followed you here?" She was crying and bent over her ex-husband when the police showed up. Chase told the police that Amy had a restraining order and he had to kill the man in self-defense. He showed the cops his throat, where there were red lines and bruising starting. The police said that Chase would have to go to the hospital to get checked out and then come down to the station to fill out a report. They called him an ambulance. Before the ambulance got there; Chase called his parents to tell them what happened. He did not tell them anything about Amy except that she had just stopped over and her husband followed her there. Next, he called his aunt Hillary. Hillary told him not to talk to anyone until she got down to the station. Hillary did all of the necessary paperwork. Amy's ex's death would be investigated but it was clearly a case of self-defense. Hillary told him not to worry about it but to stay away from Amy. Amy ended up staying away from him. She was not a stupid girl, she was afraid of Chase with good reason. Now, she knew what Chase was capable of doing. She could not believe how he could so callously stab someone who was clearly distraught, in the chest with the intent to kill them. Chase did not even look upset in the least after he had just taken someone's life. She knew her ex well enough to know that he would not have really killed Chase. He just wanted to scare him so he would stay away from her. Amy hated her ex-husband but she did not wish him dead. Amy liked Chase but that was as far as it went. She couldn't understand how Chase could kill someone so callously and not even seem to be upset in the least. For hers and her son's safety, she would never see Chase again. Chase was good with that.

Chase's parents had met him at the hospital. Molly hugged her son and told him, "It's okay son, I know you did not have a choice or the man would have killed you." Chase's father said, "Are you sure it was necessary to kill the man?" Chase's father knew him better than Chase thought he did.

When Chase finally made it home later that night, he fixed himself a drink. He hardly ever drank but tonight he felt he needed one. He sat down on the sofa to think about the events of the day. He had really killed someone, he could hardly believe it. He had never thought that if he ever took a life or the first one he did take, it would be like this. Everything happened so fast. There was no enjoyment in taking the man's life. He was pissed that his first kill, his virgin kill, had happened this way. Well, when he finally killed Dr. Clark or any woman, he would consider that his first kill. A kill that was planned. A kill that was slow and involved torture and sex. He thought that he would feel something after stabbing the man, but he did not feel anything. He did remember how it felt to push the knife into the man's chest. It actually took a lot of strength to push the knife in all the way to the hilt because he was a large man. Chase would never forget the look on the man's face as he stabbed him. A look of total surprise. The man died so fast, he did not have time to take it all in.

Chase still thought about killing Dr. Clark all the time. She was his obsession. He thought that he would probably never go through with it, after what happened with Charlie, but planning her death was still on his mind. He fantasized about having her tied up and having sex with her, torturing her and making her pay for every stupid thing she ever said to him, or asks him and especially for telling his parents that he should be locked up. Chase knew, in the end, that if he did not think it was safe to kill Dr. Clark, then surely, he would find someone else to kill, maybe two or three people, maybe even a whole family.

Chase graduated engineering college when he was twenty-two. He had a great job but was now going to mortuary college, part time. Even part time, it would not take him long to finish. He absolutely loved mortuary college and dealing with the dead. He knew that this is what he wanted to do for the rest of his life. Chase's parents were not excited about Chase's new found love of mortuary science. They just could not understand the attraction there, but then again,

Chase was not your normal person. Chase like dead people a little too much. He liked draining their blood; it reminded him of dressing a hog.

Chase was getting ready to graduate mortician school and already had a couple of interviews lined up for a job. There were not a lot of jobs out there for morticians. Most graduates were really lucky if they could get on at one of the major funeral homes in the city. Chase felt lucky to at least have a couple of interviews. It might help him that he did graduate at the top of his class, again.

Chase had a few girlfriends in mortuary college, only to have sex with them. Sex with some of the girls was so unexciting, he could not even perform. They sure did not measure up to Amy in the sex department. The girls were all just a little too sweet. He had no connection to them personally. He rarely dated the same girl twice.

There was one girl that he went to mortuary college with and he had been seeing for a few months. Her name was Megan. They got along very well. Their sense of each others moods was incredible, but most of all, they had the same kind of sexual appetite. Megan liked it rough, just as much as Amy had but Megan was even more satisfying because it seemed her heart was in it even though she liked it rough. Chase could dish it out, and Megan could return the favor. Not too often now, but Megan still stops by every now and then, when she needs a booty call. She said that other men were just too nice when it came to sex.

He had moved to a new apartment when he started mortuary college. Now he was an engineer and a mortician. His mother came to his graduation from mortician school, but his father did not. His father thought that was the stupidest thing he had ever heard of. Why would anyone, especially someone as smart as Chase, who had an engineering degree, want to be a mortician?

He made good money, enough to take care of him. He didn't go back home to the farm to see his family very often. Molly did call him about three times a week. The only person that he even slightly cared about was Molly, his mother. He and his father never got along, after Chase reached puberty. All they did was argue. He and his younger sister, Katie, never got along either. There was too much of an age difference, besides, he knew that Katie hated him. Growing up, Katie was always gone to a friends house, cheer leading practice, etc. She always threw it up to him that he really did not have any friends. Besides, she was a girl and he did not like girlie things. Chase knew she had never forgiven him for what he had done to her precious bird. She also had never forgiven him and Charlie for coming into her room the night that Charlie first spent the night with him. From then on, Katie kept her door locked whenever she was in her room, even in the daytime. Even though he had sent Katie invitations to his graduations, engineering and mortuary college, she never responded. Katie had gone on to nursing school and he had not even been invited to her graduation. He had not seen her in a few years except on Christmas and then they just tolerated each other.

"PART III"

Despite his parents' wishes, Chase landed a job as a mortician at a local funeral home. The funeral home did not let him do too much right away, he was just supposed to watch and learn. He did not like dealing with the deceased's family at all. He tried to sound caring and concerned with the customers that had a deceased love one, but he really was not. He just wanted to be around the dead bodies, not having to interact with the customers. Oh well, that was part of his job.

Chase had been working at the funeral parlor for about six weeks now, the probation period of six weeks was up, now he would be able to embalm someone and be responsible for the whole place. The owner of the funeral home made all of the new morticians work the night shift.

That very first night he worked at the funeral home, it was quiet, which let the voices in his head sound louder. The voice told him, "Kill the Dr. and you can embalm her." He answered himself, "That's the plan."

The ambulance service brought in an old woman from a nearby nursing home. The family arrived shortly after. They had been sitting at her bedside for the last week, waiting for her to die. Chase did the best job he could with the family, as far as helping them pick out a coffin and do the paperwork. When they were all finished with their purchases, Chase took the deceased Granddaughter's hand and said, "I'm so sorry for your loss. We will treat your grandmother with the utmost respect and dignity, so please do not worry about a thing, we will take care of all of the arrangements." The woman that said she was the dead woman's Granddaughter asked Chase if he could remove her grandmother's rings for her. He said, "Sure". She smiled at him and seemed to like him a lot. Chase could hardly wait for the family to leave so that he could tend to Granny.

Finally, an hour later, the family left and there was no one else here but him and Granny. He put Granny on a gurney and took her to the back service elevator. He put her on the elevator and took her to the basement, where there were two embalming rooms. He picked the smaller of the two rooms because there would be less to clean afterward. He rolled the gurney alongside the cold, metal table and slid Granny onto it. All seventy pounds of her. He put the gurney out in the hall while he prepared the embalming room. When he went back into the room where Granny was, he got excited, his very first embalming! He studied the woman's body for a while, noting all of the things that he had learned from the bodies at the mortuary college. He knew why a dead person was so cold, blue, and stiff. Rigor mortise had already set in, since the woman had been dead for about six hours, but it would dissipate, because rigor mortise only lasted for forty to sixty hours after death. The first thing that Chase did was to cut off her clothes. She really was quite a looker, still at the age of seventy. Next, he removed her glasses and her dentures. He checked her whole body for any other kinds of prosthesis and he loved the cold feel of her body. He messaged her joints, neck, arms, and legs and shoulders so that some movement was restored to them. He heard that familiar voice in his head say, "Fuck her man, and fuck her now. You know you want to." Chase said aloud, "Shut up! That is one thing that is even too deviant for me. I would never fuck a dead person. What kind of person are you anyway?" Oh no, now he was answering the voice back again. He washed her whole body well with a disinfectant, even inside of all of her orifices. Her vagina was very dry, which it probably was, even for the last few years. She had nice, smooth legs. Her toenails were thick, and yellow with fungus in all of them. He checked the body as he washed it and he removed all jewelry, which he bagged up for the family. He removed bandages, and the catheter that was put in by the nursing home. Then he checked for a pacemaker, and she had one. He removed it by slicing over the top of it and taking it out. He then sutured up the incision. It was not her body he was interested in, although he did love cutting her. His favorite part was draining the body. He injected an artery with chemicals that was supposed to break up clots and condition the vessels. When he was finished with that, he injected her abdomen with a solution that would help to liquefy her organs.

He inserted the tube into her carotid artery to pump in the embalming fluid, while he drained her bodily fluids through a trocar inserted into her abdomen. This was going to be a fun night. When he was finished embalming her, he glued her eyes shut. Next, he placed several cotton balls in her cheeks and mouth and glued her lips shut. This first embalming took him about two hours with the cleanup. He had done a decent job with her hair and makeup and put the clothes on her that her family had brought in with them for the funeral. He tagged her right big toe and put her in one of the refrigerated drawers. By the time he finished, he was tired but also felt a sense of excitement. He knew he would not have a problem staying awake for the rest of the night.

Chase thought of some of the things he said he would do to Dr. Clark. This fucking Dr. has ruined his life. He hated her so much. She made him talk about things he didn't want to talk about, especially when he was going through puberty. She would ask him things like how many times a day did he beat off and if he ever thought about killing anyone when he thought about sex. Stupid shit like that. He realized when he got older; another reason that he hated her was because she knew everything about him. She knew things that would make someone else throw up. When he got to be about ten, some of the things he would tell her, he would make up just to see her squirm in her nice leather chair. He liked seeing her reaction to some of his thoughts, even though she tried to hide them, she could not hide them from Chase. After all these years, Chase knew her about as well as she knew him. He had learned early on what each of her facial expressions meant.

Chase remembered a time when he was about thirteen; he brought her a jar candle of her favorite fragrance for Christmas. His Mother made him. He had scooped out all of the wax, except for around the sides and filled it full of spiders. She accepted it even though she said it was not professional for her to do so but since she had been seeing Chase for so long it would be okay. She was as excited as a child would be. When she opened it, she screamed and dropped the jar and it broke. Spiders ran everywhere. He said, "How does that make you feel, you fucking slut". A phrase she had used on him many times except the fucking slut part. She threatened to stop seeing him then. He would use his best smile and charisma to win her back over. He thought she was easy to manipulate. She told his parents a long time ago, he could never be cured. His diagnosis was psychopath with delusional tendencies. She also called him a sexual sadist. Sometimes he thought that she was crazier than he was.

He had her private phone number. It was very easy for him to hack into her e-mails. He covered himself well. He was also glad that Dr. Clark had lived in the same house for years. He had broken into the house several times while she was working. He got as much information as he could. He would always make sure that she knew he had been there. He would get panties out of her drawer and lay them on the bed or move something personal to a different spot. Once, he had even found a vibrator, well actually, several sexual toys of hers and he had taken them. He thought it might be kind of fun to see her face when she recognized them when he used them on her later.

After a few months of working for someone else, Chase decided to check into buying a small funeral home of his own. Chase met the real estate agent outside the front of the funeral home he had seen for sale in the local newspaper. He had been watching for a funeral home to come on the market. When this particular one did, he was ecstatic. It was in his hometown. The funeral home was called Durham's Funeral Home. It had been the Durham family business for generations. When they walked in, Mr. Durham was waiting on them. He seemed excited about getting someone interested in such a short period of time. Mr. Durham showed them everything, from the basement embalming rooms, to the chapel next door. He also said that he was including the two hearses and the limo. Chase wanted to look at all of it and it all looked up-to-date. Finally, Chase and his real estate agent went outside and wrote up an offer, 10,000 less than the asking price. Mr. Durham had accepted right then and there and signed the papers. Chase said, "How long until you are ready for a closing?" Mr. Durham said, thirty days, and Chase said, that was 'reasonable. Chase said, "Would it be possible to still keep your family name on the funeral home? I would pay to keep it since everyone knows it as Durham and it is well established." Mr. Durham said, "Of course, I would be proud my name is still on the funeral home. It has been a family business since 1950". Chase was more than excited. He could hardly contain his good luck. Even though he had made the Durham's an offer and he had saved up a sizable amount of money in the last few years; he would still need a loan from his parents. He hated the thought of owing his father anything but he would have to swallow his pride in order to own his own funeral home. He would call his parents when he left here and ask if he could come over tonight and talk to them. He called and they told him to come on out for dinner.

Molly was excited to see her only son and so she got busy fixing his favorite meal, still spaghetti and cheesecake. His father knew that Chase wanted something or he would not be coming over just for a visit because he missed them. He knew that Chase did not care about anyone, a fact that Molly seemed to like to forget. Caleb asked Molly, "I wonder what he wants. He never just visits." Molly replied, "I don't know, maybe nothing." Caleb said, "fat chance".

When Chase got to the farm for dinner, Caleb let him in. He asked, "How have you been doing son?" Chase replied, "I'm doing really well Dad". Chase walked on down the hall to the kitchen, where he knew his mother would be. They gave each other a light hug and a "Hello".

After dinner, Chase said, "That was the best dinner ever Mother. Better than I, even remember it." She replied, "Thanks Chase". Chase and his father got up and helped Molly take the dishes to the sink and clean up the kitchen. They made small talk. When they were finished cleaning up, Caleb asked, "Why don't we all go in and sit down on the couch?" Chase and Molly both replied, "Okay". When they were all seated, Caleb said, "Well son, what brings you out here tonight on a weekday? You must have some good news for us." Molly asked, "Chase, do you have a new girlfriend?"

Chase thought, "It's now or never." He fidgeted a little and then said, "I did come out here tonight to talk to the both of you about something." Caleb looked at Molly like, "I told you so." Chase started by saying, "You both know how much I love my mortician job." Caleb and Molly both shook their heads, "yes". Chase replied, "Well, I have been working for someone else now for a few months and gaining experience. There is not anything else I can really learn about this business so I decided to buy my own funeral home." Caleb and Molly both said, "That's a great idea!" Chase said, "I found the perfect place. You know, Durham's Funeral Home in Greendale?" They both shook their heads, "yes". He said, "I bought that place. Well, I have not exactly bought it just yet. I made Mr. Durham an offer on it today and he accepted it. It is a very nice funeral home. It has plenty of storage, two embalming rooms, its own chapel, two hearses, and a limo." Caleb said, "That's sounds awfully expensive." Chase said, "I got it for a very reasonable price, 300,000. The only thing is, I need to borrow some money from you. I'm sure that I could pay it back to you within the year." Caleb and Molly looked at each other, then at Chase. Caleb asked "How much money do you need son?" Chase replied, "I need 250,000. I have 100,000, and I would normally only borrow 200,000, but I need the extra 50,000 for start up fees. I need to get some new things in there and hire new employees." Caleb said, "Why would you hire new employees when the old ones know how the place is run?" Chase replied, "I do not want anyone working for me that have already been employed there because it is too hard for longtime employees to change their ways. I am keeping the maintenance man." They both said, "I see. Well, we will have to discuss this and we will let you know tomorrow." Chase said, "That's great, that's all I ask." They all knew that this was just perfunctory, that Chase would get the money he needed. Chase lightly hugged the both of them and then said, "Thanks again for dinner, I have to be going." Molly said, "Drive safe Chase!"

That evening when Chase left, Molly and Caleb sat down and talked about loaning Chase 250,000. They both agreed that it was a lot of money but they both also knew that Chase was a hard worker and that he would pay it back. About 10:00 the next morning, Chase got a call from his father. Caleb said, "Son, your mother and I will loan you the money to start up your business, you can pay us back anytime, no strings attached." Chase said, "Thanks, Dad, I knew you and Mom would come through for me. You do not know how much I appreciate that. Would you mind coming to closing with me since I have never bought property before?" Caleb replied, "Of course I will son, I'd be happy to."

Chase had many delusions over the years, but right now, he thought he was God's disciple, helping rid the earth of females who were not worthy of man's presence. Dr. Clark was the one assigned to him to get rid of because she did not respect men and she did not believe in God. She had told him so at one time. They barely touched on the subject of religion on their many talks. There was one time when she asked him if he believed in God. Chase said, "My family didn't go to church very much. I do not know if I believe in God but I do believe in a higher power." What he did not tell Dr.

Clark was that he hears God's voice all the time. He is not sure how he knows that it is God talking to him, but he knows it is. No one else can hear him, only he was chosen to do God's work, which was to rid the earth of as many female prostitutes and other bad women as he possibly could without getting caught. God also wanted Chase to visit Charlie in prison. God said that Charlie could be his servant and he would advise him, just as he always did.

Chase decided that first; he needed to move from Clifton in Ohio, to Lawrenceburg, Indiana, to be near where his funeral home was located. On the following Friday, he found a small house to rent in the little town of Greendale, five minutes away from his funeral home. The house was empty. The owner had just put in all new carpet and had the whole house updated including paint. Chase signed a one-year lease with the option to buy the house when his lease was up.

It was very nice and would be perfect for him. Greendale was an old neighborhood with a mixture of large and small houses. It is a beautiful, clean little town. The house was move in ready and he could move in immediately. Chase paid the owner a deposit and first month's rent. The owner handed him the key. Since Chase really did not have any friends to help him move, he would leave all of the furniture in his apartment and he would buy new, his old college stuff was cheap anyway. He bagged up his clothes and any little things that he wanted to take and put them in his car and left everything else. That night, he slept in his new place on a blow-up mattress. He had trouble going to sleep. He could not believe how lucky he was to be getting his own funeral home at such a young age.

The next day he called Megan to tell her his good news and to see if she would go furniture shopping with him tomorrow. He had great taste but she was more of a decorator. Then he would take her out to dinner somewhere for her trouble. It would be a win win situation for him because when they finished dinner, he would take her back to her place, and he would fuck her. She told him that she would be more than happy to go out with him furniture shopping, that she loved to spend his money. He told her that he would pick her up around 9:00am the next day.

The next day, he was right on time picking up Megan. Megan was always ready on time, not like some women. Megan hated to be late for anything. When she had to be somewhere, she was constantly checking her watch. They shopped all day and stopped for a brief lunch, then shopped until dinnertime. Chase said, "How about I take you back home so you can shower and change and I will pick you up for dinner around seven?" Megan replied, "That's okay, you don't have to take me out to dinner Chase just because I helped you shop. I would do that for any of my friends, besides, what girl doesn't like to shop?" He responded, "I know you would have done it anyway, I'd just like to take you out to dinner that's all." She said, "In that case, I accept." He dropped her off at her place and went back to his new place to shower and change. After that, he left to go back to pick up Megan. He took her to a fancy restaurant and they had a very nice meal. The conversation was great. Chase knew Megan was very smart and could talk about anything. After dinner, she ordered them both cheesecake. While they were waiting on dessert, Chase said, "Megan, I have something to ask you." She asked, "What is it Chase, you can ask me anything." He talked about the new funeral home he was buying and then he said, "I would really love it if you would come to work for me. You know I do not handle families well and I know how well you handle them." She replied, "I already have a job." He said, "I'll double your salary." She replied, "done". She asked, "Would you like to come back to my place for a drink?" They both knew what that meant.

As soon as they stepped inside her apartment and closed the door, Chase grabbed her and kissed her roughly. She said, "I've been a really, really bad girl lately. I think I need a spanking." He was glad to accommodate her. He ripped her panties off and threw her over his knee and gave her a good spanking, until she had tears in her eyes. He picked her up and took her to the bedroom. He tied her hands and feet to her four-poster bed with belts she had hanging in the closet. He knew she kept her toys on her top closet shelf. He got the bag of toys down. He put nipple clamps on her and made sure they were snug. She moaned loudly and started writhing on the bed. Next, he put her panties in her mouth and told her to shut up. They were both so turned on; they fucked and played games for the next couple of hours. When Chase left, it was 3:00am.

Twenty more days until he could close on the funeral home and then It would be all his. The owner would let him come in a week before closing and go over everything with him. Chase could, also at that time, offer to let any of the employees stay. Previous employees usually stay on. Chase decided he would let the former employees go. He did not want anyone working there that knew the place better than him because they usually were not good with change. He knew that Megan would be great with the families. She was not only a mortician but also a kind and caring woman. She would escort the families in to pick out a coffin, services, or anything else that they needed. Megan loved talking to the families and she was great at it. Chase would do all of the embalming and purchasing himself. He was going to keep the same maintenance man, who could also help drive the limo or hearse. He would also be responsible for picking up any bodies in the daytime. He would have Megan train him on what to do when picking someone up. Chase would also hire a cleaning and laundry person to come in twice a week.

The early closing and the use of the Durham name was negotiated and everything was set in place with ease, thanks to his parents. Now all he had to do was wait until the closing date.

Chase had completely moved into his new house but he was still waiting for the furniture to arrive. Megan was great in helping him pick out the right furniture for his house. If he really liked it here, he would buy the house. It was still seven days until closing; therefore, he thought this would be the only time he would get to go up and visit Charlie.

Charlie was in the Lebanon Maximum security prison in Lebanon, Ohio. He had his own psychiatrist there. Chase figured it was about a ninety-minute drive. He had received many letters from Charlie delivered to his parent's house. Charlie told him about his life there and said it wasn't too bad for him. He had met others like himself and drug trafficking was a lucrative business in prison. He hoped that he did not get caught, if he does, he is screwed. He sees the prison shrink on a regular basis. He has free Doctors, Dentist, Nurses, Psych's, Optometrist, and medications, anything he needs. He was a model prisoner; he could get paroled in five years. Chase wanted to make sure he was taking care of God's Business. He may even give Charlie a job if he ever gets out. Hillary had told him In the beginning, when Charlie first went to prison, that his name was on Charlie's List of people who could visit him. Chase drove up to the prison; it was a beautiful day for a drive. When he got close to the prison, just all of the electrical and barbed wire surrounding the place was intimidating. When he parked and got to the visitor's door, he was escorted inside. An officer looked at his ID and checked to see if his name was on the visitor list for Charlie. Chase did not like his name on the list where someone could put the two of them together. He would ask Charlie to take him off the list. Next time Chase visited, he would just okay it then. Chase was taken to another room where he had to walk through a metal detector and a wand passed over him. You were not permitted to bring anything in for the prisoner. They were leading him to the prisoner's holding area, where he had to go through the sally port doors, where one door was opened, and he stepped in a small area, then the door was closed before the next door opened into the prisoner visiting holding area, which looked like a school lunchroom. A little nicer than talking through glass like you had to at the jail. They told Chase to sit on the opposite side of the table from Charlie, there would be no contact and there would be an officer present at all times. Charlie looked surprised that he had a visitor. He knew it was not his parents. They did not want anything to do with him and moved to another state. Chase was the only person it could be. He was excited to see his longtime friend. When he was brought in and he saw Chase, he smiled from ear to ear. They were permitted to hug briefly. Charlie did not have to wear cuffs in here. Charlie said, Good to see you man." Chase said, "How they treating you?" Charlie answered, "Just like home". Charlie talked a while, and then Chase told him about college and his new funeral home. He told Charlie about God's work and that he needed his help. Charlie, gave him ideas and said when he got out, he would help him, but now it was a different life. Actually, what Charlie was thinking was that Chase had really finally lost his mind. Chase told him about the voices he had been hearing. Charlie was the only person he could ever tell that to. Maybe since Charlie had the same diagnosis as he did, maybe he heard voices also. Charlie looked at Chase funny and then said, "No, man, I don't hear any voices." Chase was then sorry that he had said anything to Charlie about it. Charlie asked Chase, "When did you get so righteous and wanting to do God's work? That does not sound like you. Man, you are really changing." Chase said, "I think that one of the voices I hear is God's voice. I started hearing him about a year ago. I don't know why, it just happens and then somehow I know that I have to do what the voice of God tells me to do or something really bad will happen to me. Does that make sense?" Charlie looked at Chase funny and said, "Man, you are crazy, crazier than I ever was." They both laughed together. It was fun for Chase to have a good laugh with Charlie again. Charlie finally asked him, "Chase, have you killed anyone yet?" Chase answered, "No, but I plan to kill a few prostitutes before I even think about taking Dr. Clark. I want to be a skilled murderer when I finally take Dr. Clark." Charlie said, "That's what I thought, you are always in the planning stage Chase, you will never take the Dr. or anyone else. I knew you would never really do it. I always thought that you would chicken out at the last minute. Chase was not offended by this. He already knew how Charlie felt. They both knew each other so well. Charlie asked, "Will you tell me your plans for Dr. Clark?" Chase was glad to. He wanted someone besides himself to be excited over what he was going to do. Chase spent the next hour talking about the details of Dr. Cl ark's murder, in a whisper of course. Charlie listened intently. Charlie missed being with a woman more than ever now. Chase missed his best friend. Chase could not wait for Charlie to help him take Dr. Clark, but that was okay, because Chase wanted her all to himself. He promised Charlie that when he got out, they would take other women. There was a homeless shelter not too far from the funeral home and it was like a buffet of people. Charlie said, "It's not that bad in here really. I have met other people who think just like us, and I get to do some stabbings and killings in here. It's usually drug related. Man, I did not know, you can get any drug you want in prison, as long as you can pay or negotiate for it. It is much easier to get those in here than it is off the street, plus a lot of the officers are involved. When someone had to learn a lesson, especially about learning to pay for their drugs; they let me be the one to teach them the error of their ways. The officers are paid by the inmates to look the other way, and they do." After a while of visiting, Chase said, "I have to be going now, keep your nose clean so that you can help me when you get out of this place. I need your help in cleaning up the neighborhood for God." Charlie said, "Sure, Chase, whatever you say". Charlie thought, "Man, Chase has really lost his mind now."

Finally, it was the day of closing on the funeral home. His Father went to the Bank with him. His father paid what Chase did not have, which was $250,000. Chase had paid $50,000, and his parents loaned him the rest. He and his father went out for lunch and Chase was so excited. The deal with his Father was that his father would receive 20% of the profit of the funeral home every month, until the loan was paid in full. Chase and his Father went to a gourmet hamburger place in town and most of their conversation was about the funeral home. They talked about how to run a successful funeral business. His father suggested he hire an accountant to do all of the books. Chase thought that was an excellent idea. After they had finished eating, Chase said, "Dad, you and Molly don't know how much I appreciate your financial help and all of your suggestions. Thanks for being here for me. I know, you and I have never been very close and, I have put you and Molly through a lot growing up. I want you to know that I do appreciate all of the help. I know you don't like the business I'm in, but it is what I love doing." Caleb said, "Your welcome Chase, I know that we never got along well. I know I compared you to my brother Henry all the time and I know that was not right, and I am sorry for that." "It's okay Dad, forget about it."

We can all be a happy family doing our own thing. I think your Mother and I are going to do some traveling." Chase said, "That's great Dad, you and Molly deserve to have some fun in your life for a change. Besides, you know you are getting up there in age and you know that farming is too much for you". Caleb said, "You sound just like your mother." They both smiled and Caleb said, "I guess I best be going." His father replied, "If you have any questions or anything I can help with, let me know." Chase picked up the check and said, "Thanks Dad, I will." They both hugged lightly and went their own way.

Chase thought that was a good idea to hire an accountant to keep the books and do the payroll. He would also hire a cleaning and laundry service to come in once a week.

Chase called Megan and told her she could start a week from Monday. She was excited about that and Chase was going to pay her very well, not to mention the extra great sex on the side. What more could a girl ask for? Well, she could think of just a few more things she could ask for. What she wanted most was to ask Chase how he felt about her. He did not have any girlfriends and she had never seen him with another woman. She was in love with Chase. She fell in love with him when they were in their last year of mortuary college. They both had wondered why they had not noticed each other before then. Megan knew that she satisfied Chase in the bedroom, he had told her this often enough, but she did not know how he felt about her. Was she like a sister to him? A friend? She just did not know. She thought that soon, she would just come right on out and ask him. She would be afraid of the answer, but she knew herself well enough to know that she would ask him soon. Chase decided after a few days, to fire the maintenance man because he caught him several times, sitting down in the basement and sleeping. He hired the maintenance man from his old apartment building he lived in. He seemed very good. He called a painter to paint the inside. He had new carpet installed throughout. He also added new light fixtures and pictures. He would reopen a week from today, next Monday.

"PART IV"

Six months later, business for Chase was going great. There were several nursing homes around, in addition, a hospital. He had a steady stream of dead people to embalm. He loved it here. He was ready to take his first living woman. One more prostitute he would get rid of for God, or at least that is what he told himself. He would bide his time and get a girl buying drugs in the parking lot of one of the bars.

For a small town, they had more than their share of bars and liquor stores. There were two bars that featured female dancers. The girls did not get nude. They wore G-strings and pasties. He would get one of those girls who danced in the nearby strip bar. They had regular apartments that they paid a very small amount of rent. Most of them were drug addicts or recovering drug addicts. A few of them had children. Chase sat in his car, in a nearby parking lot away from the bar to watch the people who were coming and going at all hours of the night. He knew each of the girls schedules and also the one bouncer they employed. He also made sure that there were no security cameras outside the bar. He liked several of the girls, the way they looked, but he narrowed it down to three of them that he really liked a lot. He would never take a woman who had a child.

Chase had seen the girls buying drugs many times in the parking lot of the bar after work, at 2:00am. One night he saw a girl standing just outside the bar, in the back, where employees had to go for a smoke break. She was one of the girls that Chase had chosen. They had just passed a law that you could not smoke, even in bars here in Indiana. The girl was smoking a joint outside and she was alone. Chase thought, "Now's my chance". He got his rag and chloroform out of the glove box where he kept it in a small, zip lock plastic baggie. He held his breath while he put a small amount on the rag and stuck the rag inside the plastic bag. He put the baggie under his car seat. He hurriedly got out of his car and walked up to the woman and said, "I have got a lot better stuff in my car", which was parked on a side street. He gave her his best charismatic smile. She said, "What do you have?" He replied, "Oxy's, ecstasy and the best pot you have ever had. She said, "I don't have any money; will you take it out in trade?" He said, "Sure, Baby. Let's go to my car and you can give me a blow job." She followed him and got in his car. When she got in, he locked the doors quickly without her realizing it. He looked at her and said, "Let me scoot my seat back". He reached under his seat and moved his seat back. He grabbed the baggie and pulled it up in his lap. He said, "Oh, I wonder what this is under my seat?" He opened the bag and quickly got the rag out. He reached around and held her head while holding the rag to her nose before she even knew what was happening. It helped that she had been smoking weed, she was like putty in his hands. She passed out quickly and fell over on his lap. He gently moved her aside, readjusted his seat, and headed for the funeral home. He did not see anyone watching them and no one else came out of the bar.

He had told his employees to take the weekend off, he had a family emergency, and he would call them back in to work if he needed them. He told Megan he was going on a weekend long fishing trip with some buddies.

He made sure he was alone and the funeral home was locked up tight. He had driven the girl to his funeral home, right up to the back door and carried her Inside, all without any lights. He took the woman down to the embalming room and put her on a large, stainless steel table with stirrups, just like the ones you would find in a gynecologist office. He felt his heart pounding and the adrenaline rush. He cut off all of her clothes except her underwear, with one of his favorite, large, sharp knives. He pulled her down on the table until her butt was right on the edge of the table. The same position she would be in when visiting her gynecologist. He bent her knees, spread her legs, and placed her heels in the stirrups, then buckled leather restraints on her wrists and ankles, also one across her mid-section. She would not be able to move very much, if at all. She was one of the most beautiful women that worked at the bar and he felt so lucky that he got her. He put a piece duct of tape over her mouth. He was going to cut her. His heart started beating fast and he was breathing too hard. He tried to calm his breathing down. He didn't want to hyperventilate and pass out. He became hard with the thoughts of what he could do to her. He even had little tiny beads of sweat break out on his forehead. He felt like God, he could do with her whatever his heart desired. He did not put that much chloroform on the rag he had held to her nose and he couldn't wait for her to wake up and see her fate. She was starting to come around. He had turned the lights down low when he came in.

Now he stood behind her, watching in the mirror over her head for her to be fully awake. He turned the lights up now. He wanted to watch her face, especially her eyes, as realization dawned on her that she had been taken and was about to be raped and/or killed. She started to move her head around and she was trying to open her eyes against the bright lights. She fought against the restraints. When she got her beautiful, contact blue eyes fully open, she looked around the room. It was slowly dawning on her that she had been taken but she did not know by whom. Her eyes got huge and Chase was thrilled with the terror that he saw there. She looked up at the ceiling and into the mirror and she saw him behind her. She tried to scream but her scream was muffled by the tape over her mouth. She shook her head back and forth "NO!" She was crying now and her tears spilled down the sides of her face. She struggled violently, as he knew she would. Even with the tape, her muffled screams were loud. He walked around the table so that she could see him. "Now calm down baby, I'm not going to hurt you. If you stop screaming and are quiet; I will take the tape off of your mouth. Can you do that?" She shook her head vigorously that she could. He got his finger under the corner of the tape and ripped it from her mouth, along with a little bit of skin from her lips. She was practically screaming when she said, "Who the hell are you and what in the hell do you think you are doing?" He said, "I'm your worst nightmare baby". She screamed, "You sick fuck, let me out of here!" As she struggled against the leather restraints. "Okay, I warned you." He tore off another piece of duct tape and put it over her mouth. "Now, that's better. I am going to cut your underwear off now." He got out one of his biggest, sharpest knives, just for the dramatic effect. He wanted to watch her eyes get bigger and bigger and he was not disappointed. First, he cut off her bra. She had about a DD bra on. Her breasts were obviously not real, her breasts did not even move. They looked like rocks and he would see if they were soft later. Next, he cut off her thong panties. He may have nicked her once or twice while cutting these because they were so tight. Next, he cut off her black g-string. These girls always had a couple of layers on so they could prolong their striptease and get more money thrown at them. Now she was completely naked. She smelled clean and her pussy was shaved bald. Her face was red and he thought that she might pass out. He broke open an ammonia packet and waved it under her nose. He needed her awake and aware of what he was doing. He told her he was doing God's work and she should be happy about that. She looked around and slowly observed her situation. The room was small and all of the white walls except one were lined with white cabinets with glass fronts. The cabinets all held bottles of some kind and instruments that were shrink wrapped. She could smell the formaldehyde. Any kid who ever had to take Biology in high school, knew that smell, from dissecting frogs along with other things. The smell of formaldehyde was one smell that you never forgot. Guys loved that part of biology. The floor had a dark brown ugly tile on it. She thought she was in some kind of Doctors or Dentist office at first, until she started reading some of the writing on the wrappers of some of the instruments. They said "Durham's Funeral Home." She started screaming under the tape again. Chase hated screaming but liked to see her crying. He told her to shut up or he would cut her. He told her if she cooperated, he would eventually let her go, which he knew he would not. If he asked her a question, she should nod "yes" or "no". He poured some kind of oil on her pussy and dropped his pants. He had a raging hard on and he fucked her long and hard. He said, "Do you love this rough?" She was smart enough to shake her head "yes". After he came, he looked at her and asked, "Is this the best you ever had baby?" She shook her head "yes" again. He left her alone in the room for a few minutes to calm down and slow her breathing.

When Chase left the room, she did stop crying. She did not know how she ever let herself get into this kind of a situation. She had always been so careful. She knew she hadn't smoked that much weed but when this handsome man came and offered her oxy's, that's all she could think about at the time. She would give him anything for a few oxy's and was not thinking about anything like this happening. Most of the men at the bar were too shy to talk to her or they were married and just out for an evening of fun. She had let her guard slip and now she had to find a way out of this situation. She decided that the best thing to do was to go along with whatever he wanted. When he got tired of fucking her, maybe he would let her get up. Maybe when he took the tape off of her mouth again, she could talk her way out of this situation. If she couldn't talk her way out, she would have to wait for the right time to take a chance on escape. She would be patient and wait for the first opportunity to get away. She knew that the main thing that she needed to do was try and keep calm, keep her mind sharp. For just a second, she let herself think about what if he killed her? She didn't have any family and knew that no one would miss her. She made herself stop thinking along those lines and tried to slow her breathing and try to think of a way out of this situation. She decided to ask him if she could go to the bathroom and also have a drink of water. Maybe then she would find an opportunity to escape. She knew that this man was a lot stronger than her but she was small and she knew she was fast. She was used to being quick to fend off men in the club and she knew she could hold her own against any woman. If he let her get up, she would look for anything that she could grab for a weapon.

When he came back into the room, he had something in his hand. When he stepped in front of her, she could see what it was. It was a very large, shiny knife. He held it in a way that it glinted off of the ceiling light into her eyes. He asked her, “Isn’t this a pretty knife?” Again, she shook her head, “yes”. He asked, “Would you like for me to cut you with it?” She shook her head “No” and started struggling. She was screaming under the tape again. He wrote his name on her flat stomach, using his knife and barely grazing the skin. Her stomach was barely bleeding but it made Chase get excited all over again. He made shallow cuts on her breasts. He told her she should be still or he might accidentally cut something he should not. She became still and he lightly cut around her neck. He was really hard now but there was one more thing he wanted to try on her before he fucked her again. He attached two clamps to her breasts. She tried to move and she was still trying to scream. Her face was very red from the struggle and he could see the veins popping out on her neck. She could see that the clamps he had placed on her breasts had wires attached to them and ran down the side of the table. She was truly terrified and peed on herself. This made Chase really angry. He yelled, “You bitch, now you have gone and made a big mess!” He quickly wiped off the table and the floor. She shook her head “no!” and her breasts shook the wires running to a box beside the table. He said, "Now, you will pay for doing that." He turned the switch to full power. He shocked her nipples which elicited a cry from her sore throat. She could smell the sensitive tissue of her breasts burning. Chase noticed a small amount of smoke coming from the clamps and hurriedly turn the voltage down to half way. He didn't want to ruin her body. She was a his first gift to God. He wanted her to be perfect.

He rammed a cold, large, metal rod in her as far as he could ram it. She had managed to scoot up on the table and he pulled her down until her ass was almost hanging off the table again. Next, he put on a condom to stay clean, lubed it and crammed it up her ass. He pounded her until he came. He was not surprised at how turned on he was by causing her pain. He asked her, "did that hurt?" She shook her head "yes". He briefly thought about Charlie. Charlie would be surprised that he had gone through with taking this woman. He would also be angry that he was not here to share her with him. Chase was learning that the more pain he caused the woman, the better orgasm that he would have. When he had finished, he put clamps on her pussy lips and shocked her there but had learned not to turn the voltage up all the way. This woman was practice for him for when he abducted his greatest prize, Dr. Clark. He liked watching this woman's tits bounce while she struggled against the restraints. He found that her tits were not as hard as they looked. He would turn the voltage down and then back up again suddenly and she would almost jump off of the table. Her face was so red and she struggled so much, Chase thought that she might pass out. He decided to remove the tape from her mouth so that she could breath better. He asked her if she could be quiet if he removed the tape over her mouth and she nodded, she could. He removed the tape and asked her if she would like a drink of water. She whispered, "yes" He told her not to try any funny business or she would pay for it in the end. She knew that he meant it. "If its sex you wanted mister, you know I would have given you that, you didn't have to kidnap me." He said, "Yes, I did. It is not just the sex I want baby. I want to torture you and see how much pain you can take." She yelled, "Let me go, you sick, fucking, bastard!" He said, "No, I'm afraid it's too late for that. Now be a good little girl." He then re-taped her mouth after realizing that she would not be quiet. He fucked and tortured her for the rest of the night in any position he could think of. On Sunday, she struggled as he hog-tied her, put her in one of the morgue drawers. She didn't like it in here but at least when she was in here, he would leave her alone. He went to church. He had started going to church when God started talking to him so much. After being in the drawer for a while, she listened intently but did not hear any sounds outside of the drawer she was in. She wondered if he had gone and how long he would be gone. She kept trying to untie herself but the task was impossible the way the ropes were tied and then he had put cuffs on her as an extra security. She banged on the sides of the drawer with her hands and feet as best she could, hoping that someone would hear her. She was soon exhausted and lay there in the dark. She still couldn't believe how stupid she had been, letting a man lead her to his car. She had made it so easy for him to take her. All she had on her mind at the time was getting more drugs. That was her life, as pitiful as it was. Sleeping all day, stripping and doing drugs at night. She didn't have a boyfriend. She didn't even have any close female friends except the girls at the club. She hadn't prayed since she was a little girl but now she did. She bargained with God. She prayed that the man would let her go and in return, she promised God that she would change her life for the better. She prayed as hard as she could but she really couldn't see how God would answer a prayer from someone like her. It was all she had.

When Chase returned, he rolled out the drawer he had her in. He gave her a bath because God would not accept her if she were dirty. He would periodically remove the tape from her mouth, give her more water, and let her use the restroom. He went into the restroom with her of course. When he did this, she would beg him to let her go. She would not tell anyone. He said, "That's what they all say isn't it?" He told her he would let her go soon because she had been such a good girl. She said, "Oh, thank you! He said, "I'll let you go after one more session." When she started to protest, he re-taped her mouth and transferred her to an embalming table. "This is my embalming table. After our session, I am letting you go, letting you go to meet your maker." Her red eyes got big and she screamed and cried again. "You should feel honored; God will forgive all your sins because I've chosen you, to please him". She didn't want to die but she hoped that what the man said was true, that God would forgive her. He slowly got out his instruments and made sure she saw each one. He saw the terror in her eyes that turned him on and that he loved so much. He saw beads of sweat break out on her forehead and heard her breathing fast as she struggled against the restraints until her body was red and bruised. He took it all in. This is what he lived for. He put a piece of duct tape across her forehead and around the table so that she could not move her head. He taped her eyelashes to her skin so she could not shut her eyes. He gave her two shots in her neck. She thought it was some kind of drug to put her to sleep, but she was not that lucky. She did not feel sleepy at all. She needed to stay awake and look for a way out of her situation. He walked to the head of the table and stood behind her head. He bent down and got close to her ear. He said, "First, we have to drain your abdomen of fluids". While she tried to understand what he was about to do, she struggled against the restraints as hard as she could. She barely had any strength left in her body. She did not know what he was up to but she knew it was not good. She felt like she had to pee again, so she did it right on the table again. She knew that would make him angry but she was trying to stall for time to think. He did not seem to be as angry this time and he just wiped it up quickly. He got some cleanser and water and washed her private parts. He put a condom on. He wanted her to be clean for God when he sent her on her way. He fucked her again while her insides were dissolving like butter. He knew he had to be quick, because he wanted her alert enough to see and feel the sharp trocar he would insert into her abdomen. He wanted her to feel her life slipping away into the ink black tubing. She violently shook her head no, as she struggled harder to get free.

She could feel pain in her abdomen like nothing she had ever felt in her life. The pain was too much and she knew she was about to pass out. He came quickly, then went and sat on the black stool beside her. He waved another ammonia packet under her nose to keep her from passing out and she hated him even more for that. She was praying that he would kill her soon. She did not know how much more of this pain she could take. As if he knew what she was thinking, he told her, "It's almost over now baby. You should feel privileged, you were my first one". He stuck a trocar, a large, sharp instrument into the side of her abdomen. She almost passed out from the pain and he had to wave another ammonia packet under her nose. He told her of all of the things he was going to do for her, like glue her lips and eyelids shut. He told her he would send her off looking beautiful and she should be grateful to him. He turned on the suction machine and lifted the large tubing so that she could see her life draining away from her. He saw resignation in her face and he did not like that at all. He stuck his dick in her and watched her eyes in the mirror on the ceiling. He watched her eyes until the last bit of life left them. They looked dull and glassed over. He came then, the best orgasm he had ever had. It was one of those moments that seem to stand still in time. He stole the light from her eyes, which he thought was, like the fountain of youth. If he never stopped killing, he thought he would live forever. As he stood in front of her body with his pants down, he listened to the quiet. She was gone. He had given her the gift of releasing her from her pain and torture, from drug addiction, prostitution and hopelessness. It was so quiet he thought he could hear his own heart pounding in his chest. He could hear the ticking of the clock on the wall, he could hear cars passing by out on the main road. He thought, "Was this all there was?" He felt empty inside. Kind of like Christmas morning after you have opened all your presents and you got something that was kind of like the real thing, but not really what you wanted. He felt disappointment and not a lot of satisfaction. This was the best experience of his life so far but he thought he should feel high, on top of the world. Mostly what he thought about through this whole experience was how much better it would be when he finally took Dr. Nancy Clark. He would be an experienced killer by the time he took her. He would practice on a few more women. He would learn how much pain, and torture with electrical shock they could endure. How much and how deep he could cut her without her dying. He wanted and dreamed about taking Dr. Clark to the edge of death many times before he would finally let her escape into the hereafter. He would show her no mercy, as she had shown him none when asking all of those stupid questions about his life. All of the questions that were so personal that she had no business asking. Like, "how many times a day do you masturbate? Did you ever lick a woman's privates? He would also repay her for telling his parents that he should be locked up somewhere. "Yes", he thought, "She would deserve everything he was going to do to her. This one was not for God this one would be for him and him only." He wondered now, how he would feel when Dr. Clark was no longer here for him to obsess about. Would he feel empty and disappointed then also? He knew there would never be another Dr. Clark once she was gone so he had to make her death the most memorable. He knew he would continue to help rid the earth of prostitutes and other undesirables. He knew that God would understand and would want him to have this one woman. He also knew himself well enough to know that after Dr. Clark, there would be someone else that he would obsess about just as much. He was glad that Charlie was not going to be around to share her with him. He had often wondered, especially lately, if he had gone completely mad. Since Charlie didn't hear voices as he did, maybe there was something really wrong with him.

He finished embalming the prostitute. He put small pieces of a cotton balls under her eyelids and glued her eyes shut. He put cotton balls in her cheeks and glued her mouth shut. He removed the restraints and he washed her body again. He wanted his gift to God to be as clean as possible. He wrapped her up and loaded her in one of the hearses. Cops rarely ever stopped hearses. He had recently purchased a metal detector and that would be his excuse for being at the farm should he need one. He threw the detector in the back of the hearse. He headed for the farm.

He knew his parents went to New England this weekend. He gave them a call on their cell phone just to be sure. His Mother answered. He said, "Just wanted to see if you guys were having a good time". She said, "We are having a great time, thanks". They talked a few more minutes and Molly said, "I'll talk to you when we get home Monday night". "Okay, see ya. While driving to the farm, he called Dr. Nancy Clark. She answered and he said, "Real soon baby, you'll be all mine". When he got to the farm, he pulled up to the garage. He looked around to make sure no one was watching him, like the neighbor that was taking care of the few animals that his parents had left on the farm. He took a shovel and drove one of the four-wheelers out of the garage/barn, up to the back of the hearse. He could hear a truck and when he looked, saw the neighbor coming down the road towards the farm. Chase quickly grabbed his metal detector out of the back of the hearse and slammed the door. He got on the four-wheeler and sat there until the neighbor arrived. He was not happy about having a visitor. He was finished with this girl and he wanted to get back home and shower. The neighbor pulled the truck up behind the hearse and got out. Chase said, "Hey, how ya doin. Do you need something?" The neighbor answered, "No, I just thought I saw someone come down the road and thought your parents might be home from their trip and I wanted to tell them that all of their animals were fine". Chase said, "Thanks so much for looking after the animals while my parents are gone. They will not be back until Monday. I just came out to try out my new metal detector for a while." The neighbor said, "Okay, well, nice to see you again Chase". The neighbor got back in his truck. Chase said, "Thanks again, see ya later." The neighbor drove off and Chase waited until he was out of sight before he loaded the girl onto the four-wheeler. He drove out past the fields to the wooded area. He found the perfect spot and buried the girl deep, at least six feet down. He covered the area with brush. He moved a large boulder over on top of the grave to mark it, just in case he ever wanted to remember where she was. He drove back to the barn and put the four-wheeler away, leaving the shovel on the seat. He drove back to the funeral home. He cleaned everywhere and everything she could have come in contact with, with harsh chemicals. Chase had been planning the kidnapping of Dr. Clark for so long now, he wondered, if he was disappointed afterward, if maybe he would find a way to preserve her permanently. Maybe he would film the whole thing. The only bad thing about filming the whole thing is someone always finds the films sooner or later and then there is no denying your guilt. He was tired. He went to his new home, took a shower, and got something to eat. He sat down In front of the television set and fell asleep. He had horrible nightmares, a side effect of one of his medications. He always had dreams that someone was trying to kill him with a knife. In his dreams, he felt the terror that the girl that he killed must have felt and it was terrifying. Maybe that is what the girl felt like when he let her see his knife for the first time. He forgot to take his medication most of the time, but now, since the medications had not kept him from killing anyone, he threw them all in the trash.

"PART V"

Caleb was getting up there in age. He was in his early sixties. He and Molly did want to do some traveling and take some trips, now that they were empty nesters. Caleb had worked hard all of his life and he knew it was time to stop and smell the roses; spend more quality time with Molly while they still had their health. Hillary still visited regularly. She still came to dinner at least once a week. Hillary told Chase and Molly that she would help them find a home for all of their animals. She said, "Are you going to sell the farm also?" She knew her father and other relatives were buried here so if Chase and Molly decided to sell their farm; she told them she would buy it. Chase said he would sell the animals but would never leave the farm. This is where he grew up. Caleb and Molly did not tell Hillary, however, if Katie or Chase did not want the farm, they would leave it to her. By the next week, all of Caleb and Molly's farm animals had new homes. They decided to take a week and drive to New Orleans. They would be gone Tuesday through Monday. Timing could not have been better for Chase. He would take another woman.

Caleb and Molly got back home around six on Monday evening. They had a great time in New Orleans. They ate delicious food, had great tours, saw historical sites, and had great sex. They both admitted that they should have retired a long time ago. They were already planning their next trip to the Rockies. When they pulled in their driveway, they both said they were glad to be home. The farm was their only home and they knew they would never sell. Caleb helped Molly in the house with the bags. There was a message on the answering machine from Katie. Katie had finished college a year ago and had a great job in the emergency room at Christ Hospital in Cincinnati. Molly had told her that they would be gone this weekend but she guessed Katie forgot. She had left a message. She had a new boyfriend and would they like to go out to dinner with them. Katie wanted her parents to meet him. Molly thought that they must be serious. Katie never offered to let them meet any guy she had ever dated and she had dated a lot. Katie turned out to be a beautiful woman, with her green eyes and long red hair. Caleb had a hard time with her dating anyone but he knew she was a grown woman and he had to let her go on and lead her life. He said, "Yeah sure, I want to meet any guy dating my daughter." Molly just smiled and said, "Okay, I'll call her. She probably forgot that we were meeting next weekend, Caleb said, "I'm going to put the car in the barn. This was also their garage. When Chase had started pulling the car into the barn, he could not pull it all the way in because the four-wheelers back tire was in the way. He thought, "That's weird, obviously, when I took the car out before vacation, it was not there, but a few feet over to the left. He got out of his car to Inspect it. The tires were full of mud and grass and there was a shovel propped up against the seat. Caleb had just washed it before they left for the weekend. His first thought was, "What did Chase do?" He would not tell Molly about the dirty four-wheeler, but he called Chase from his cell phone. Chase answered on the fourth ring. He said, "Hi, did you and Mom have a good time?" Caleb said, "Yes, we did. Were you over here the weekend?" He answered, "Yes, I told Mom, I dropped off a bunch of dishes, also linens from my old apartment. Mom said she would like to go through them before I pitched them. If she did not want any of them; she was going to donate them. Caleb said, "Oh, I didn't know about that. I was just wondering who took the four-wheeler out and used the shovel because everything is muddy and I just washed it before we left on vacation. I would not even have noticed, except I could not get the car in." Chase said, "I came out yesterday and it was so nice out, I took my metal detector and took a ride out by the edge of the fields. I shoveled up two whole bottle caps and lost interest. Sorry if I got them muddy, I was not thinking, but it will not happen again. There was a short, awkward silence and Chase yelled, "Oh my God! You think I killed someone? That is ridiculous." Chase laughed and said, "Yeah, sure Dad, I killed someone and buried them on the farm, real fuckin funny." Caleb said, "Don't use that kind of language wi . . ." and then he realized that Chase had hung up the phone. Caleb felt bad about practically accusing Chase of committing such a horrible crime.

Chase would kill now whenever he got the chance, even if his parents were only out of town for one night. Chase berated himself for being so careless. Being careless was more like Charlie, not him. What was wrong with him? He promised himself he would be more careful. He would bury all of the women he killed on the farm. He did not want to get too cocky because when he did, he was careless.

Caleb looked around the barn and saw the box of dishes, so he believed him then. When he got back in the house, Molly was still on the house phone, talking To Katie. She covered the phone with her hand and said, "Is everything okay?" Caleb shook his head up and down that he was okay.

Chase was all ready to take another victim, but he knew he would have to wait until everything was right and his parents were out of town again. He thought that he would go back up to the prison to see Charlie. He wanted to tell him all about the two women he had killed. Charlie would love hearing it. Charlie would not believe that he had finally killed someone. Charlie would love to hear about all of gory details. Chase promised that he would tell him. Chase wondered if he thought he would ever take a man or a child. He knew he would never take a child that would be boring, also predictable. He may take a man someday, he did not know, but right now all he was Interested in was a weak, screaming, and crying woman. That is what turned him on the most, listening to the girl scream behind the tape and see the tears flowing down her cheeks. He liked to torture, to see how much pain a girl could take before she passed out. Not that he ever let them pass out. He always waved an ammonia stick under their nose and it has not failed yet. He planned on taking Dr. Clark, seven months from now, when his parents had a trip to the Rockies planned.

Chase could not believe that his life-long dream was finally coming true. He had gone over and over his plans for Dr. Clark many times, checking for any little mistake that might get him caught by the police. He kept thinking in the back of his mind that he was forgetting something. He did not know what it was he could be missing, it was just a feeling he had in the pit of his stomach. Maybe it was just anxiousness over finally claiming the prize he had coveted for so long. He still wasn't sure where he would take her from but he still had time to work out the fine details. It did not matter because he would go over and over it in his head a hundred more times before it was time to take her, just like Charlie said he would. He really did miss Charlie sometimes. Charlie kept him on his toes. The sloppier Charlie became, the more meticulous Chase became. Chase would put himself in Charlie's shoes and look at his plans from Charlie's point of view and see if he could tell if he was missing anything. Caleb and Molly would be gone for two weeks when they went to the Rockies. Chase thought he may even bring Dr. Clark here to the farmhouse for a few days and tie her to Katie's bed. Katie was nothing but a little bitch and Chase never could stand to be around her. She was afraid of him, so that would be fun to put the Dr. there because Katie still slept in that bed, when she would visit and spend the night. Chase had broken into Dr. Cl ark's house a few times, as well as her car and even her office. He would always do something so that Dr. Clark would know that he had been in her house, in her bedroom. He would take a pair of her panties or some other frilly thing and lay it neatly on the bed, kitchen counter, washing machine, coffee table, somewhere where it could not be missed or mistaken that she had not left them there. After being in Dr. Cl ark's house the first time, he was sure, that Dr. Clark was suffering from OCD. There was not a thing out of place in her whole house. Her clothes were arranged in her closet by color and season. The towels and toilet paper neatly stacked and all going in the same direction. In the kitchen, all of the canned goods were lined up and separated, labels facing front. Same with the dishes. Every picture on every wall was straight, as were the pillows on the couches and her bed, even her throw rugs were perfectly straight. He could imagine her going around with a measure and a leveler to make sure everything was straight. She knew that he knew about her disorder and how fucked up she herself was. Chase would move things just slightly, and by doing this, she knew that he had been inside her house.

One night she and her fiance decided to play with the sex toys and she could not find them. She looked at her fiance and screamed, "Oh My God! It is my stalker, he has been here, and he took them! I am going to kill that bastard when I find out who he is!" Her fiance said, "You probably just put them somewhere else". She screamed at him, "No, I always put them back In the same spot in my closet! Shit, he has been in my panties and everything else I have. I wonder what else is missing." She started searching the drawers. Her fiance just rolled his eyes and got up to go and watch television in the living room. He knew he would not get any tonight. He thought, "She's losing her own mind, and I'm not getting any sex, thanks evil stalker, whoever you are. You really know how to bring a guy down". The police didn't have any leads on her complaints, so they pretty much looked the other way when she called. They chalked her up to being crazy. They said, "That was that crazy woman calling again. No big deal."

Molly called Chase back and told him about their trip. She invited him to go to dinner with them to meet Katie's new boyfriend. "He said, I'll pass, you know Katie and I were never close, but I appreciate the invitation.

Molly and Caleb met Katie and her boyfriend Daniel at La Petite, their favorite nice restaurant in Cincinnati, about an hour's drive away. Katie introduced all of them and Caleb shook Daniel's hand, that was slightly damp. Caleb thought, "Good, the kid is nervous, always a good sign. "The men pulled out the chairs for their ladies, and then also sat down. They were very polite to Daniel without actually grilling him, but managed to fit in a few questions into the actual conversation. Caleb did ask Daniel what he did for a living and he said, "I'm a retail pharmacist." Molly asked him if his parents were still living and how old he was. Conversation flowed well. Caleb and Molly both seemed to like Daniel. He was smart, polite and handsome, but most importantly, and not unnoticed by Molly and Caleb was how Daniel looked at Katie. Daniel was obviously very much in love with her. They all ate way too much but ordered a dessert to split. They had coffee after dinner and more great conversation. Caleb and Daniel talked a lot about hunting and fishing, they each loved both. They also talked about the farm and Caleb could go on forever about the farm. Katie nudged Molly with her foot and said, C'mom, Mom, let's go to the restroom and freshen up. It is just a nice way of saying, 'let's talk in private." Molly looked at the men and said, "We will be back in a few minutes". The guys just kept on talking. Daniel was asking Caleb if there was anywhere to fish on the farm and Caleb told him about their big creek that ran along the back of the property and that he would have to come and fish with him sometime. Daniel said, "I'd really love to do that." When Molly and Katie got in the restroom, Katie asked Molly excitedly, "Well, what do you think?" Molly said, "He's very good looking, smart and I can tell he loves you very much by the way he looks at you. He hardly took his eyes off of you the whole night." Katie was smiling from ear to ear. Katie said, "I love him Mom, he's the one I have been waiting for, he is perfect for me. We both even have the same sense of humor. I know we have only been together for two months, but it feels like I have known him all of my life. I want to spend the rest of my life with him. Of course, it also helps that he makes a good living." Molly said, "I wouldn't be surprised if he asks you to marry him very soon."

Katie smiled appropriately and turned red. Katie knew that she really wasn't in love with Daniel but they were compatible and she thought it would be good for her career to be married. Besides, it would keep other men at the hospital from hitting on her. When the women left to go to the restroom, Daniel nervously said, "Mr. Jones, the real reason I wanted to meet you is" . . . there was a long pause . . . Caleb was not going to make it easy on the man who wanted to marry his little girl. Daniel said, "I'd like to have your permission to marry your daughter." Caleb smiled and said, "You have our blessing son. When are you going to ask her?"

Daniel was so happy he was beaming. He did not say anything else because the women were coming back to the table, they were all smiles, and giggling like two schoolgirls. The men stood as they took their seats. Molly said, "Well, Caleb, are you ready to head on back?" Daniel piped up. "Hold on just a minute okay?" Daniel got up, went over to where Katie was sitting, and pulled her chair around to face him. He got down on one knee. Katie covered her mouth with her hand, totally surprised. Daniel gently took her hand and said, "Katie, I know we haven't been together long, but I know in my heart that you were meant for me the first time I laid eyes on you. I love you more than words could ever express. I cannot imagine my life without you in it. Would you please do me the greatest honor in the world and be my wife?" Katie jumped up out of her seat and yelled "Yes! Yes, I will, I mean I do. I love you so much." Daniel slipped a beautiful silver and diamond engagement ring on her finger. Everyone in the restaurant clapped for them. Caleb said "Congrats to the both of you." Molly said, "We'd be proud to have you as our son-in-law". Caleb didn't want to hang around to watch them hugging and kissing more, so he said, "Now, I'm ready Molly, if you are." She said she was ready and gave Daniel and Katie a big hug and said, "Welcome to our family! Now we have a wedding to plan." She hugged Katie again and told her to call her in a couple of days.

Molly and Caleb were kind of quiet on the way home. Both lost in their own thoughts. Finally, Caleb said, Chase should have been here." Molly said, "Do you think that Chase will ever find someone he could love?" Caleb just looked at her and then she said, "I know, I forgot. He does not have those kinds of feelings like the rest of us do and that is so sad. Is it possible that he might find someone to share his life with." Caleb said, "It's possible, but I doubt it". When they got home, Molly called Chase to tell him that his sister was engaged. He said, "That's great! I only wish her the best." After that conversation, Chase started thinking about getting married. Maybe he would ask Megan to marry him. He could tell that she loved him. He did not care about all of that but he thought it would be better for his new business if he had a wife. He, at least, did not think he would ever find anyone else who shared his same Passions of dealing with dead people." He decided to go ring shopping and ask her soon, maybe this weekend but he did not want to get married until after he had completed his life's plans with Dr. Clark. Chase decided he would ask Megan out to dinner for Saturday night. He did not usually go to the funeral home in the daytime when Megan was working, doing her magic with grieving families while thinking in the back of her mind, what she would sell them. Everyone loved Megan, loved her sweet personality. Yes, he decided that marrying Megan would benefit him and his business. He thought, "What if she says no?" He did not think about that long, because who wouldn't want to marry him?" He was handsome, and charismatic along with owning a great business. Everyone loved him, or the person everyone thought he was. He might even think about having a couple of kids of his own someday. He did not tolerate children well, but he would like to have at least a son, to leave his assets to and to carry on the family name and maybe even occupation. Who would suspect a well-respected family man of murder? When he walked into the funeral home, he went back to Megan's office. He thought she would be surprised to see him. She gave him a big smile and said, "What is so important that brings the vampire out in the daytime?" Chase sat on the side of her desk. He asked, "I came in to ask you if you'd like to go to dinner with me tomorrow night?" She said, "What's the occasion? You mean like a real date?" She had never known Chase to go out on a date with anyone. She always thought that he was just too busy building his career. She had been in love with him for a long time now, but she could never gauge his feelings for her and so she never told him how she felt. There never seemed to be a good time. The way they had sex, rough and loud, wasn't exactly a romantic time to talk about love or feelings. In addition, she thought that Chase would be the type of man to scare off easily by a girl who had real feelings for him. He said, "Yes, a real date." She thought for a minute. She said, "What's the catch, what do you want? You already get free sex." He said, "I just wanted to take you out okay?" She looked skeptical but said, "Okay, what time?" He answered, "I'll pick you up at seven, wear something nice." She said, "Okay, seven it is. Pick me up here. I can shower and get ready after work. I'm usually here until 6:00." He kissed her on the forehead and said, "See you then".

Chase wanted to tell Megan about his mental illness for a long time now but timing was everything. He was afraid if he didn't tell her, that someone else would bring it up in front of her and then she would know he kept it from her. Someone would let it slip, Like his Mother or Katie. Finally, he decided that he would just tell her the truth and then If the subject of his mental health ever came up, Megan would be okay. In the meantime, he knew all of the right things to do and say to a woman, even if he did not feel any of it. He could say "I love you" and all that other gushy stuff so convincingly that she would believe every word.

She had waited for this day for forever. She had loved Chase since they went to mortician school together and the sex was great also. They just seemed to "get" each other. Two people who liked dead people and liked to fuck on top of coffins, "Yep, they were made for each other". She thought, "He's loving and giving during sex but has never said anything to her about how he feels about her". She started to get worried, what if he was going to fire her?" No, he would not ask her out to dinner to do that. She would just go with it. Earlier in the day on Saturday, he had purchased a gorgeous three carat engagement ring. It was in his pocket. He picked her up from the funeral home exactly at seven, the next day. He thought she looked beautiful. Their conversation was easy. They talked about everything except their odd relationship. They had a wonderful dinner. Chase was surprised at how much fun he was having. They could talk about anything. She would make a good wife. He was glad that he went out with her. Even after dinner was over, there were never any awkward silences. After dinner, Chase asked Megan if she would like to go back to his place and have a little wine. She said, "Sure" but she was thinking about what else he wanted. They had known each other for six years now and had been intimate for five of those years, but they had never talked about taking this relationship any further. On the way back to his place, Chase was trying to think of a way to bring up their relationship. He didn't know, he would just blurt it out after a glass of wine. They sat next to each other on the couch, with the gas fireplace glowing. There was a very romantic feel to the room that made Megan wonder what was on Chase's mind. After a glass of wine, Chase turned to Megan and said, "Megan, I wanted to talk to you about our relationship." This made her nervous. He asked, "How do you feel about me? I know I'm your boss, but be honest, please." She thought, "Well, it's been six years, why not tell him" She looked him in the eyes and said, "Chase, I love you. I have been in love with you for the last six years. You just never seemed all that interested in having a relationship with me, so I kept my feelings to myself." Chase said, "Wow, I had no idea." She said, "Well, we never talked about our feelings before, we just did booty calls. How do you feel about me?" He said, "Before I tell you how I feel about you, I have to tell you something else." That kind of scared her but she said, "Okay, what is it? You know you can tell me anything." He said, "Okay, here goes, and this will be your chance to run if you want to and I wouldn't hold it against you." She said, "Okay, tell me already". He said, "I have a mental illness. I have been on medication practically my whole life and have never had any problems with it." She said, "What is the illness?" Chase knew how smart she was and she would know exactly what kind of person he was after he told her, but he went all in. He said, "My diagnosis is psychopath." She stared at him and she did not say anything while she was processing this important amount of information. After what seemed like an eternity, she said, "Have you ever acted out or been in any kind of trouble for your behavior, any trouble with the law?" He said, "No, like I said, it is under control with my medication. I know this is a lot to throw at you. She was quiet for a while longer, and then she said, "Now it all makes sense. Now I know why you never expressed your feelings about anything or anyone, including me. Now I know there was a good reason and not just because you thought I wasn't good enough for you or something." She got tears in her eyes and she said, "You don't know how much this means to me that you would tell me this. Why haven't you ever told me this before?" He said, "Because I never had a reason to, but now I do. First, I want you to know that I do care for you as much as I can care for anyone. I think you are intelligent, funny and I think you are beautiful and we have similar personalities and like the same things. We are also sexually compatible. These are things that even a lot of couples don't have." She mentally noted the word "couples" She said, "Go on." He kissed her gently. She said, "Why are you saying these things, where do we go from here?" He said, "Megan, will you marry me?" She was stunned.

She did not know what to say. He had already caught her off guard, but before she could even answer, he said, "Don't give me your answer right now. I need you to think about this, at least for a week and then give me your answer. You know what my mental diagnosis is. You know that I will never love you like someone else could, but I can show you affection and I can appreciate your beauty and intelligence. I will also, take very good care of you. You would never have to worry about me cheating on you with another woman. You are all the woman I need, and I think we could have a great marriage. If you do say "yes", I would like a long engagement, at least a year, to make sure my business is settled and I know it takes you ladies probably more than a year to plan a wedding." She had tears in her eyes when she said, "Okay, I will give you my answer next week. I will carefully take into consideration all that you have told me and when you do get my answer, it will be sincere and truthful." She did not want to think about his diagnosis right now. They snuggled against each other, while holding hands. Chase was thinking, "This went better than I thought. At least she did not run away and it felt good to tell her, now he would not have to try to hide it. They kissed again and Chase said, "Let's go to bed, okay?" She smiled and started pulling off clothes on her way. At least they were sexually compatible. They made, slow, sweet love, not the wham, bam, thank you that they did most of the time. Chase was unable to have an orgasm this way, however, Megan understood, and she loved him all the more for doing this mostly for her sake. Not that Chase did not enjoy it; he just could not get the same satisfaction that he did when they made it rough. This just showed Megan that he could be giving towards her. At least she knew that she did not have to worry about him having feelings towards anyone else. Megan was a very smart woman and she had touched on Chase's diagnosis a few times in her different courses in college. She knew that most, if not all serial killers were psychopaths. Chase claims to have his mental illness under control, with medication. Megan decided that the person who would know Chase best would be his Mother, Molly. She wanted to talk to Molly about Chase's mental illness, and then she would be able to make a permanent decision.

Megan had called Chase's mother Molly and asked her if she could meet her for lunch but that she did not want anyone else to know about it, especially Chase.

She did not want him to know that she went behind his back and talked to his mother but this was a major life changing decision and she needed to know what Chase was like growing up. Molly thought it strange that Megan would want to go to lunch with her, but as Megan requested, Molly did not tell anyone that she had agreed to meet her. They met at a small restaurant on the outside of town. They both ordered a drink and a salad and Molly looked at Megan and asked, "What's up Megan, what's on your mind?" Megan did not want to tell Molly that Chase had asked her to marry him. She did not want to take that surprise away from Chase. Megan said Chase have been friends for a long time, went through school together and she thought they knew each other quite well. Molly let Megan take her time in getting to the point. Megan said, "You know that I am working for Chase now at his funeral home?" Molly said, "Yes, Chase told me that he was excited that you would be working for him. He said you are a wonderful people person." Megan said, "Molly, I know what Chase's mental illness diagnosis is." She let this sink in a minute and then said, "I wanted to talk to you and ask you if you thought that Chase was under control on his medications, if you had ever had any problems with him growing up." Molly said, "I am not surprised that you know about his mental illness, only a very few people know. So, what you're really asking is if I think it is safe to be around Chase?" Megan said, "Yes, that's what I want to know I guess. I want to know if you think he would ever hurt me." Molly said, "I won't lie to you, when he was little, he did have issues with small animals and he did have problems with authority figures, especially his father. No one really knows what goes on inside his head sometimes, I can only tell you what my opinion is. I think that Chase is a good person. He is smarter than your average person. When he sets his mind to something, there is no changing it. Do I really believe that he would actually harm you or someone else? My answer is "No" I don't believe that Chase would harm a hair on your head. He doesn't have the same feelings as the rest of us do as far as love and concern but he does seem to stay within the perimeters of what we believe as normal behavior. He is a little socially awkward and doesn't make friends easily but I know that he is very fond of you Megan."

"Thank you so much for sharing your thoughts with me about Chase. I am glad that I took the job he offered. I also think that Chase is a good person and I do not think he would harm anyone, especially me. These are things that I just needed to know from his Mother, the person who knows him best. Please, please do not mention this meeting to anyone, especially Chase. I do not want him to think I do not trust being around him. Thank you so much Molly, it was so nice to see you again."

They said their good-byes. Molly was not suspicious at all of Megan's motives in asking these questions. She thought that Megan was really smart to want to know about her boss and good friend. Molly could also see how much Megan cared for Chase. When Megan talked about Chase, her whole face lit up. Molly thought that Megan was in love with Chase. Megan was also smart enough to know that Chase could not really love her back. Molly was happy that Chase had such a good friend as Megan in his life.

Megan thought about Chase and his diagnosis for the past week, just as he had asked her to do. She had talked to Molly, she had read up on his mental illness and she thought that she had all of the tools to make her decision about whether she would marry Chase. She knew that she loved him and had for a long time. She called Chase on the following Tuesday night, when she knew he would be up, she asked him if she could come over to his place Thursday night. He said, "Sure, do you have an answer for me?" She said, "Yes, but I won't tell you what the answer is now, you will have to wait until then." He was thinking, "Uh oh, this must mean bad news." She knocked on Chase's door about 4:00 in the afternoon. He let her in and gave her a kiss on the cheek, which he had always done. He fixed her some tea and then they sat down on the couch. She said, "I have thought about all that you have told me. I have thought through it meticulously, one piece at a time." He said, "As I knew you would. Please, Megan, give me your answer." She said, "My answer is YES!" He took the ring out of his pocket and got down on one knee. Megan started crying, but they were tears of joy." He said, "If you accept this ring, I promise to take care of you, treat you with respect, and be there for you in all ways. Megan, will you please do me the honor of marrying me?" She said, "Yes" again. He slipped the beautiful, three-carat engagement ring on her finger. She said, Oh My God Chase, it is so beautiful!" She hugged and kissed him, He said, "As I've said, I'd like to wait a year before we get married so that I can properly pursue you." She giggled and said, "Yes, that would be nice Chase." He said, "I'd like for us to ride out to my parents' house this weekend and tell them." she answered, "That would be great Chase. Then we could go and tell my Mother". He said, What about you're Father?" She said, "He died when I was eight years old." Chase said, "I'm sorry you don't have your Dad, I didn't know." "That's okay, no big deal about him, I barely even remember him. We are engaged; let's talk about our wedding and how happy we are!" He asked, "Do you like your ring?" She said, "I absolutely love it. It is the most beautiful ring that I have ever seen and it is the perfect fit. How did you know what size to buy me?" He said, "Remember a few months ago when I told you that the family of a deceased woman wanted her wedding ring cut off and given to them?" She Said, "I remember." He replied, "Remember when I had you go to the jewelry store and try on rings so that we could replace her wedding band with something else?" She said, "Oh, you are so smart. I wasn't even thinking about that, at least I wasn't suspicious at the time." He looked at her and he said, "Seriously, Megan, did you really think about my mental condition and are you sure you can handle It if someone should bring it up? Are you sure, you can live with the fact that I adore you but that I do not love you?" She said, "Chase, I'm a very smart woman and I don't do things lightly. I know your diagnosis. I know you have it under control and are on medications. If you're asking me if I will be afraid of you, that you might kill me in the middle of the night; the answer is "NO!" He said, "Your right, that would never happen. I have never thought about killing someone. I adore you and love being with you and that will have to be enough because that is all I can give, no matter how much you love me." She said, "I know, and that's okay, just as long as you always tell me the truth about everything." She had tears in her eyes. Chase said, "I thought you were so happy, are those tears of joy?" She said, "I cry easily". Chase replied, "That's okay as long as there tears of joy." Megan said, "They are, I couldn't be happier. But we do need to talk about some things." He answered, "Like what?" She said, "Well, how do you feel about children? Would you ever like to have one?" He got up and jumped up and down. He said, "I can't wait to have a child!" He had thought about that from time to time and decided he would like to have a child to pass along his family business to. I can't wait to be a father!" Megan was pleased. She had always thought about having a child and she wanted at least one. She jumped up and down she was so excited she could not wait to tell her Mother and friends. "I can't believe we are engaged! She sat back down next to him and said, "Chase, are you sure you are ready for this?" He said, "I'm sure, I couldn't be more ready or any happier". They kissed a nice, long kiss. Let us get some sleep since we are riding out to my parents tomorrow." She said, while looking at her ring, "I'm so excited, I don't know if I can go to sleep."

When they got in bed he said, "Turn over on your side so I can spoon you". When she did, he started gently rubbing her butt. She said, "What are you doing?" He said, "This is called "Booty Duty. I just made that up, it is supposed to relax you so you can go to sleep." She did roll over and he massaged her gently and she loved it. She said, "You know, once we are married, that I will expect this every night." He said, "I will love to accommodate you." Before she drifted off to sleep, she said, "I'd like us to ride out to the farm tomorrow and then go and tell my Mother. I've got a husband and wife coming in tomorrow at ten to purchase their coffins and make plans for their funerals if anything should happen to them. They are in their eighties and don't want to put a burden on their children. We will have to wait to leave until they are finished."

They arrived at Chase's family's farm at 2:00pm the next day. She had met his family before but had never been to their farm. She had always wanted to see where Chase had grown up. She loved the farm and its isolation. She did not like close neighbors and she relished her own alone time.

Molly and Chase were so surprised. Molly said, "Wow, both of my children engaged within the same week!" They all sat, talked, and drank tea and Molly got out some of her homemade cookies. Megan seemed interested in the farm so Caleb asked her if she would like to take a walk with him on the farm, it was such a beautiful day. She said, "Sure, that would be nice". Once Chase and his Mother were sitting alone at the kitchen table, she looked at him and said in a gentle voice. "Chase, did you and Megan talk about your mental illness?" He said, "Yes, I told her all about it, I didn't want there to be any surprises". Molly already knew that Megan knew about his mental illness but she also knew that Chase expected her to ask if he had told her. How did she take that news? Does she know what that means as far as your feelings go?" "Yes, she is a smart girl and we did talk about it at length. She knows what my diagnosis means. I told her I would never love her like someone else could but that I adore her and I would take good care of her." Molly said, "That's good. She must love you a lot." "She said she has loved me for years. I think it would be great for my business and the functions I have to go to, to have a wife by my side. Who knows? I may even run for city council or something one day." Molly said, "Oh Chase, that would be wonderful! You know that we would help you as much as we possibly could." "When do you two plan on marrying?" "I don't know, however, I told her I would like to be engaged at least a year and she said it would probably take longer than that to plan a wedding anyway. If I have my way, we will just go to the courthouse and tie the knot". "Well, we woman are different. We look forward to our special day all of our lives. I really like Megan and I think the two of you will make a great couple." He said, "Thanks Mom, I appreciate that". The fact that he called her Mom didn't go unnoticed by her and she liked the sound of it again."

On Caleb's and Megan's walk, Caleb pretty much asked her the same questions about If she knew Chase's medical condition. She said, "Yes, I do and we talked about It at length. I am prepared to live with Chase and love him without him loving me in return because he says he adores me, and we are good together." Caleb said, "Yes, I do think that the two of you will be good together. You both have the same interest and your personalities gel." They had easy conversation and returned to the house. When they got back, Chase said, "We better go, we have a long drive, we are going to tell Megan's Mother about our engagement." They all kissed and hugged goodbye.

When Chase and Megan got in the car, she said, "Chase, your parents are really nice, I'll bet your sister is to." He said, "Yeah, she's okay I guess. We never seemed to get along very well and with the differences in our ages, we didn't do a whole lot together growing up." Megan said, "I always wished I had a brother or sister, but I was an only child." Chase said, "My sister just got engaged last week however, I have not met the man yet. Mother says he is a pharmacist and a really nice person. We will all have to get together soon. Usually, I just see Katie on Christmas." Megan thought that was very sad but she didn't say so.

An hour and a half later, they arrived at Megan's Mother's house. She lived in a neighborhood in Cincinnati, called Northside. Megan said, "This is the house where I grew up". My mother has lived here almost all of her life. When I was little, this used to be a beautiful neighborhood. The houses and yards were kept up. Everyone knew and talked to each other. Now, everything was run down and broken. There is a lot of crime down here now and some people have bars over their windows. There are drug deals going on, at every corner. I have been trying for so long to get my Mother to move out of here, but she just will not. It has been her home for way too long. I did talk her into getting a dog for protection. He is a rotty and he is a great watchdog. His name is Dyson. Dyson barks at every little noise and sometimes if he sees a stranger near the door, he just sits in front of it until the person sees him. The strangers usually end up running away. Everyone around here knows Mother has a dog, because she has to take him out for walks. She loves him so much.

She said when she walks down the street, and there is someone coming towards her, they go to the other side of the street. Everyone around here is afraid of Dyson. Mother takes great care of him and he is all muscle. He said, "Well, maybe I don't need to meet your mother today." Megan said, "Don't worry, as long as I'm with you, he will only eat one leg". They both laughed.

When they got to Megan's mother's door, Dyson was sitting there and when he saw that it was Megan, he started barking and wagging his tail. They walked in, with Chase walking behind. He held his hand down for Dyson to sniff him and then Dyson snapped at him as if he was going to bite his hand off. Dyson would not quit barking at him the whole time they were there, no matter how much Megan's mother yelled at him. Megan's mother said, "I don't know what's gotten into him, he has never been like that with anyone else." Megan's mother resembled an old, well not too old, hippy, the way she was dressed, beads and all. They all had a seat in the living room and told Megan's mother the good news and showed her the engagement ring. She was so happy for them. She said, "I have some news also. I have a man friend. I have been dating him for a little while now. We will all have to get together so that you can meet him." Megan had a really surprised look on her face. Since her father had passed away, Megan had never seen her show even the slightest bit of interest in another man. Megan asked, "Where did you meet this man?" "I met him at church". Megan said, "If you like him, then I'm sure that he is a very good person." "Thank you Megan. Well, when is your big day?" They told her the same thing as Chase's parents and she said, "Let me know when you are going to shop for your wedding dress and all of the other wedding things and I would like to come with you." Megan said, "Oh mom, of course I will." Megan noticed that her mother kept looking at Chase a little funny. When Chase got up to go to the restroom, Megan asked her. "Mother, what is wrong, why do you keep looking at Chase so funny?" She answered, "I don't know, there is just something different about him." Megan said, "Like what?" Her Mother answered, "I don't know, I can't put my finger on it, but like he has some kind of hidden agenda or something." They had hot tea and homemade cookies.

Chase commented several times how much he loved her mother's homemade cookies. They visited for about an hour and then Megan said, "We better get back to Indiana, it's getting late". They hugged and kissed goodbye and Megan said they would visit again soon. They got in the car. They started to pull away; Megan's mother came running out of the house with something in her hands. She yelled, "Chase, you forgot your cookies!" Megan's mother had wrapped up extra cookies for Chase to take home. Chase got out of the car as she was running towards him with the cookies.

She handed Chase the cookies. She smiled at her daughter, while she quietly whispered, "Stay away from Megan, find yourself someone else." Chase smiled and thanked her for the cookies and got back in the car. Chase said, "Your mother seems really nice. Does she work or is she retired or something?" Megan said that she was on disability due to autoimmune diseases but that she still kept very active. She told him that her mother was an artist, and kept busy with her creations. She also belonged to a couple of woman's groups and had quite a few friends. She felt that her life was very full.

They were both quiet on the long ride home. Chase asked Megan, "Do you want me to drop you off at your place or are you coming back to mine?" She said, "I guess I'll go back to your place and . . ." just then, Chase's cell rang. He said, "Hello? Uh huh, okay, put him in the cooler and I will be in after I catch a couple of hours of sleep. Okay, see ya." Megan said, "You have to go to the funeral home tonight?" He said, "Yes, we just got a new customer, so I'll go in tonight. You will have the family there to talk to you in the morning about their plans for the funeral." She said, "In that case, I guess you better drop me off at my place so we can both get some sleep. Besides, I don't have any extra clothes or anything at your house." Chase had a weird look on his face and she said, "Oh, don't worry; I'm not moving in or anything". He said, "That's good. I do not want us to live together. That would defeat the purpose of me dating you. I cannot very well pick you up for a date if you live with me can I?" She said, "No, you're right. Besides, I'm just getting used to us being a couple." They both admitted that they were tired and Megan asked, "Are you going to try to get some sleep tonight before you go in?" He said, "Yes, I'm beat. I will probably get a couple of hours sleep and then go on in."

When they got to her apartment, Chase walked her up to her door. He kissed her goodnight and said, "I'll see you tomorrow babe." She liked the sound of the pet name on his lips. She smiled and said, "Okay, tomorrow."

While driving home Chase wondered why Megan's mother had warned him away from Megan. He had been very polite, the perfect man. Her mother probably was some kind of sensitive that could tell what the real Chase was like. Oh well, he didn't care what Megan's mother thought of him as long as she did not dissuade Megan from marrying him.

When Chase got home, there was a message on his answering machine. It was from his aunt Hillary, asking him to call her as soon as he got in. It was 10:00, he knew that Aunt Hillary stayed up late, and he also knew that she never called him unless it was something important. He called her up and she said, "Hey, Chase how are you?" He said, "Fine, what's up?" She said that she wanted to let him know, before he heard it from some other source, that Charlie had killed a man in prison, in front of witnesses, mainly officers, and that he would probably never get out of prison, if he didn't die first of some kind of retaliation." He said, "That's too bad, I was hoping and I know that he was also, that he would get out early for good behavior. She said, "I know when you are in some kind of gangs, you don't really have a choice sometimes. You have to do what they want you to do or they will kill you. I think that Charlie must have gotten mixed up with some people like that. Almost everyone in there is in some kind of gang." Chase said, "Thanks, Aunt Hillary for letting me know. I'll talk to you later." They both hung up at the same time.

He wanted to tell her about his and Megan's engagement but not along with that kind of conversation. He did not feel too many emotions but he felt angry. Angry that Charlie did this and he knew that he was waiting for him to get out of there so he could help him carry on God's work of getting rid of prostitutes and other sinful people in this world. He felt like punching the wall or something. He did not have feelings like normal people do but one emotion he did have was anger and when that anger escalated, he went into a rage. He had not felt like this in a long, long time. Was Charlie trying to destroy his plan? Charlie had a lot of nerve doing this to him after they had been friends all their lives. Now he was too worked up and angry to go to sleep. He decided that he would go on in to work now. It was 1:00 in the morning.

When Chase got to the funeral home, he was still feeling angry with Charlie. He could feel himself starting to go into a rage right now. He was so angry with Charlie that he thought by coming to the funeral home he could do an embalming; he would feel better and not get into that full-blown rage where he could not even think straight. That was a dangerous place for his mind to be. It made him feel out of control, the one thing that made Chase afraid. He needed to feel in control of himself at all times.

The main lights in the funeral home were off, just the security lights were on, so he knew there was none of the workers here. He let himself in the back door and went straight on down to the bottom floor where the cooler and embalming rooms were. He put on his protective clothing and set up the embalming room with the tools and the chemicals, he would need. Everything else he needed was prepackaged in neat little trays. Right when he was getting ready to go to the drawer to get the deceased out, he heard the front door bell, which was connected to a bell down here so he would know when the doorbell rang. He wondered who could possibly be here this time of night. He thought that maybe it was the FBI. He quickly pulled off his protective clothing on the way upstairs and to the front door. He could see through the side glass that it was a woman. He opened the door, and to his surprise, it was Megan's mother. She asked, "May I come in?" He answered, "Yes, of course you can. Did you drive here by yourself?" She said, "Yes, I did, I didn't want anyone else to know that I was here." She came in and he said, "Why don't we go and have a seat in my office?" She followed him to his office and he helped her remove her coat. He said, "Here, why don't you sit on the couch? Can I get you something to drink, some tea or something?" She responded, "No thank you, I won't be here long. I came this time of night because I knew by what Megan said, you would be alone. She doesn't know I'm here, and I'd like to keep it that way". He said, "Yes, of course, if that is what you want. What can I do for you?" She said, "I warned you away from my daughter." He said, "That's correct, but I have no intention of giving up Megan. We are still getting married. Have I done something to offend you or something?" She said, "I know you, I know your kind, you are an evil man. I can see it in your eyes, even the way that you move". He answered, "I assure you, I am not evil. Is it because I own a funeral home?" She said, "Of course not. Megan is a mortician herself. I am very sensitive to people and I can tell that you are an evil man, with hidden agendas and I'd like it very much if you would break it off with Megan". He said, "I'm sorry, Megan and I are both adults and we want to get married and that is what we will do. I am sorry that you feel that way about me, but I am not an evil, sinister man and I am sorry if you got that impression". She said, "I can see it in your eyes. If you decide to go ahead and marry my daughter, I want you to know that I will be watching you closely. If you ever do anything to hurt her, you will answer to me, and I promise you, it won't be pleasant". Chase actually thought it was kind of funny that she thought that he would be afraid of her". He said, "I'm sorry, you have it all wrong. Megan and I will get married, and I hope that you can get use to that fact for Megan's sake. I hope that you don't ruin her happiness". She answered, "Don't be so snide and try to lay her happiness off on me when you clearly are the one who will eventually make her unhappy". That made Chase angry. He pulled her up off of the couch by her arms and squeezed them tight. He got close to her face as he said, "Megan is mine and there is nothing you or anyone else can do about that fact. I'd advise you to leave now before my "evil side" really shows". She replied, "Turn me loose. I knew it; I knew what you were when you first walked into the room. That is why Dyson did not like you. Yes, I am leaving now, but remember, I am watching you and if you are not afraid of a little, old woman like me, then you surely are miscalculating my intent". He replied, "And what would that miscalculation be?" She said, "The fact that if you hurt my daughter in the least little bit, I will kill you, and you can take that to the bank. At that she grabbed her coat and rushed to the front door to leave. Chase beat her to the front door and put his hand on it so she could not get out. He said, "Okay, I'll admit you are right. I have even killed people myself, a lot of women like you. Would you like to be my next victim?" She said, "Don't be redundant". She yanked the door open and headed for her car. Chase started laughing and could not stop. He thought that she was hilarious. She was annoyed by his laughing. No, he would not bother to tell Megan of her mother's visit and he knew that her mother would not tell her either. He would not even give her a second thought. If she weren't Megan's mother, he may of even have thought about killing her tonight. She was one lucky bitch.

He went to the cooler and pulled out the drawer, expecting an old man from one of the nursing homes but the man was not that old at all. Probably, younger even, then his own father. His paperwork from the nursing home said, he was fifty-four and he was being taken care of in the nursing home because he had brain cancer. Chase transferred him to the metal gurney and rolled him into the embalming room. He cut his clothes off and went through the routine of trying to loosen up his muscles from rigor. He was not a very big man, probably 120lbs. His body looked wasted. Chase knew that was what cancer had robbed him of. While

Chase was draining his bodily fluids, he started thinking about the man's brain cancer and wondering how big his tumor was and what it looked like. He decided he wanted to see it. He knew it was against the law and his training to open up the man's scull but he also knew that he would be able to hide it from the family or anyone else looking at him at the funeral. Besides, he was tired, bored, and pissed. Maybe this would put him in a better mood. He took a body saw and cut a large portion of the man's scull off on the back of his head. He really enjoyed cutting into the bone, it made him feel better. He decided when he kidnapped the good Dr., he would cut on her a lot without killing her. He would enjoy that. He did not know why he did not think of that with the girls he had already killed, which at his last count was six. He cut some of them very shallow but got more of a kick out of just showing them the shiny knife. He lifted the scull flap and there was the man's gray brain matter. Chase cut into the brain until he saw something that looked like a tumor. He excised the tumor and lifted it out of the man's head. He felt like a surgeon. He had thought about being a surgeon at one time, he was certainly intelligent enough but when you were a surgeon you were supposed to make people well and he rather kill someone. He placed the corpse scull bone back on his head and then he sutured it back on tightly. There was no way that you could see the sutures in his hair and the family would never know. He cut the tumor open and inspected it closely. It did look different from the rest of his brain tissue, but not that much. He put a piece of the tumor under his microscope. Of course, he did not know what he was looking at but it was still interesting to look at it. When he was finished looking at the tissue, he was trying to decide what to do with it. He had heard of people eating parts of someone that they had killed, but he quickly threw out that thought. He might try it if it were regular tissue but not cancer. He could not put cancer in his body. He found that he was not even thinking about Charlie anymore and he did feel much better than when he first got here tonight. Maybe he would taste a little piece of Dr. Clark, and maybe he would do it while she watched him. He thought about what piece of her he would not mind eating and all of the gory thoughts were starting to turn him on. He decided that he needed to think more about exactly what he did intend to do to Dr. Clark after he kidnapped her. He liked to have things planned. If he planned things carefully, it was less likely he would get caught. He never really thought much about getting caught. He thought the police were really stupid. After all, did they find out who was calling Dr. Clark? No, they gave up after a while, as he knew they would. If they could not solve a case in a timely manner, they just put it away on a shelf and called it a cold case. That is what he was counting on anyway if he ever made a mistake. He knew that making a mistake was highly unlikely but always a possibility. That was one reason that he needed Charlie and was so angry with him because if he ever did get caught, Charlie was his scapegoat. Okay, enough about that idiot Charlie and back to planning Dr. Cl ark's gruesome death.

He had not quite decided yet where and when he would take her but now he had to make a plan. He thought the best place to take her would be in her garage at her office building, but then he decided "no" there may be cameras there. He finally decided that the best place would be to take her from her own home. He would park his white "work van" which would really be a rental in her driveway when he knew she would be leaving for work. When she came out to investigate or to go to work, he would snatch her and quickly knock her out with a chloroform soaked rag and put her in the van. He would torture and rape her of course, but he had to have something a little bit more special for her. After all, she was his lifetime goal. It was July and he only had to wait four more months until his parents would be leaving on their vacation to the Rockies. He could not wait for the day that Dr. Clark would be his, all his, to do with what he wanted. He was getting more turned on thinking about what he would do to the doctor. He decided that he would wait for Megan to get here in the morning. He would ask Megan to come into his office and then the both of them would cum in his office. He took his time finishing up the embalming of the man since he decided to stay all night and wait for Megan.

His father and Molly would be leaving on their two-week vacation to the Rockies. He would give all of his employees a head's up that that was when they were all to go on vacation. He would give them all a full two weeks paid vacation, unless there was an emergency and he would have to call someone in. They would be happy about getting two weeks, instead of one week that most employers would give them.

Back to the task at hand. He put the tumor in a small jar of formaldehyde and placed it in the embalming room refrigerator that held the chemicals that needed to be kept cold. He did not really know why he wanted to keep it, he just did, at least for a little while. He finished up the old man and he had done a great job, as usual. He had gotten so good with makeup that the dead people really did look like they were just sleeping, as a lot of old women like to say. He tagged the body and put it in the refrigerated drawer. The bodies were marked with a tag on their left big toe and on their right wrist so there is not a chance that someone would come to the funeral home for a visitation for "Uncle Ed" and ended up at a visitation for "Aunt Dolly". He returned to the embalming room and did his usual cleaning until everything was spotless. By the time he finally finished, showered, and changed his clothes, it was 4:00am. He had a full bathroom with a large shower installed next to the embalming room. He liked to shower before he even put his regular clothes back on, because if he did not, he could smell formaldehyde on his clothes and in his car for weeks.

He was finished early and feeling a little bit tired. He decided to lie down on the small couch in his office and take a rest until Megan came in at 8:00. As he lay there, he thought about what other cool stuff he was missing out on in the bodies that he embalmed by not even thinking about what they died from.

He was feeling the itch again. He was ready to take another prostitute. He would have to wait until next weekend, when Megan would be shopping with her Mother and looking at wedding reception halls. Apparently, the best reception halls were rented more than a year in advance, so Megan had to get out there. He gave Megan his credit card and told her to pick whatever she wanted for the wedding, but within reason. He told her that men did not really care about such things, well maybe some men, but not many. He wondered if he was doing the right thing by getting married because with Megan living with him, she would know when he was gone and she might even check at the funeral home. He would just have to be extra careful. He thought that God and lust were pulling at him to take another prostitute. Once in a while, he would think about taking a man but that really did not excite him like taking a woman.

Sometimes his head felt so mixed up. What if the Devil disguised himself as God, telling him to kill these women? He really could not answer that, all he knew is that he had an overwhelming urge to take them that he could not control. He was planning on taking Dr. Clark and she wasn't a prostitute, she was just a mean, stupid woman, and he thought that she sucked as a therapist. He thought he would make a much better therapist than she was. Dr. Clark basically told his parents that he was not curable, but that medication should help keep his thoughts in control. The medication did not seem to help that much, even when he did take it. On the medication, he still wanted to kill a woman.

He was a psychopath and nothing she could say would ever change that. His therapist knew it and so did his parents. Katie knew it better than anyone. He must have fallen asleep because that was the last thing he was thinking about before Megan was there and shaking him, trying to wake him up. He sat up on the side of the couch. He gave her a quick kiss on the cheek and he said, “Megan, meet me back here in fifteen minutes”. She answered, “Why?” He did not say anything, just gave her that devilish grin. He went downstairs to his own bathroom and brushed his teeth, then went back upstairs and grabbed a cup of coffee before returning to his office. When he got back to his office, he sprayed on a little cologne that he kept in his desk drawer and sat down at his desk and closed his eyes. He started thinking about some of the women that he had killed so he would be ready to go when Megan came back. There was a couple of light knocks on his office door and he said, “Come in”. Megan stepped into his office and he said, “Is there anything going on out there this morning?” Megan replied, “There is a family coming in at 9:00 to make arrangements for their grandmother.” He said, “That’s okay, this won’t take long”. He came around the desk in a flash. He grabbed her in his arms. He gave her a long, passionate kiss and she melted in his arms. He said, “Does my baby need a spanking this morning?” She, of course said, “No!” He pulled her over to the couch and pulled her down over his lap. He reached up under her skirt, found her thong panties and ripped them from her body. He pulled up her skirt to expose her cheeks and he gave her a good spanking. Not enough to really hurt her or make her cry, just enough to make her beautiful ass red. She did yell at him to stop and he did. She stood up and both of them quickly undressed. He sat her on his desk and spread her legs then he licked at her clit until she came, which did not take long. He always let her have hers first. When she stood up, he leaned her over the desk and fucked her from behind while he was pulling her hair. He also had a quick orgasm. When he was finished, they both quickly dressed. Both with satisfied looks on their faces. When Megan got to the door, Chase grabbed her again but this time he kissed her very sweetly. He said, "See you tonight babe, maybe we will have a repeat performance". She smiled at him and answered, "Okay, but I'm almost out of thong underwear because you keep ripping them off. I will have to go buy new ones." He answered, "Or you could just not wear any at all". She said, "Later baby".

Megan went back to her office to wait for the arrival of the family that was making plans for their grandmother. She sat down in her office chair. Her face was flush and warm. She tried to concentrate on her work for the day. She kept thinking about her relationship with Chase. Even though their relationship was new, she had loved him for years and so their relationship did not really feel new to her. She was having second thoughts about marrying Chase, she was thinking about how her life would be married to him. She wondered if later on, she would need that emotional connection that she could not have with Chase. If she had the need for comfort, would she feel that in his arms? When they had the baby, would she be all alone in feeling the joy of a child? She knew the answers to these questions already. She would never have any emotional connections with Chase. She thought about their relationship before agreeing to marry him but there was so much to think about, she knew that she had not covered all the bases in her own mind. They were both sexually compatible as far as they both liked rough sex, but sometimes, she wanted to have slow, easy, loving sex. Chase was good at pretending to do this, as he had done the night they got engaged, but she knew what he said to her during these times was a lie. Was their whole relationship a lie? She loved him and couldn't imagine living her life without him but now, she was starting to imagine her life with him and she was not sure if she could live without what Chase could not give her.

There was one of the paramedics that brought in the deceased from the local hospital that flirted with her every time he came in and she flirted back. He was very good-looking. He was tall, at least 6'2" a tan complexion, high cheekbones, straight nose, and very kissable, full lips. He had gorgeous hair of black ringlets that fell naturally around his face. She thought that he looked like he was part American Indian. she looked forward to him coming in all the time. Every time she got a call from the hospital that they were bringing someone over; she always hoped that it would be he that brought the person. Just then, her phone rang, they were bringing a deceased person over from the hospital. God how she hoped it was the paramedic she thought was attractive. Her thoughts were interrupted by Chase sticking his head in her office door and saying that he was going home and would be back tonight. When he left, she started thinking about the paramedic again. Shortly after, the bell had rang on the back door and she knew it was the delivery from the hospital and that Dan, their maintenance man would let him in. After he checked in with Dan, he would come up to her office with the paperwork.

About ten minutes went by and there was a light knock on her office door. She said, "Come in". It was her favorite paramedic and her heart skipped a beat. He said, "Hey sweetie, here is the paperwork for the deceased." She had never let a man call her by anything other than her name and she didn't really know why she allowed it now. She guessed it sounded sweet coming from his lips. She had to sign the papers stating that she had accepted the deceased. As he handed her the paperwork, his hand touched hers and it was like an electric shock. She noted that he was not wearing a wedding ring. She stood up and went around her desk to face him. She said, "I've known you for a while now and I don't even know your name, would you tell me what your name is?" He answered, "My name is Ben. I know your name from your signature on the papers. Do you mind if I call you Megan?" She answered in a daze, "No, you can call me Megan". She was thinking that he could call her anything that he wanted to. She walked closer to him, while starring at his beautiful lips. His look was smoldering. He grabbed her and kissed her deeply. When he had finished kissing her he said, "Megan, I'm so sorry, I do not know what came over me. It won't ever happen again." She said, "That's okay, don't worry about it, it just happened that is all. You do not have to worry about your job, I will not tell anyone. I should not have allowed it, I am engaged you know." He was embarrassed and his face was red. He said, "I'm sorry, if you'll just sign the papers, I'll be gone." Megan took her time signing the papers. She looked up at him and said, "Please don't be embarrassed and please don't hand off any deliveries to here. I hope that you make the next delivery Ben. I'd like to see you again". He looked a little confused, especially since she told him that she was engaged, but he said, "I'll come back again. I'd like to see you also". They left it at that. She finished signing the papers and handed them back to Ben and he left.

When he left, Megan was thinking about what happened. Why did she allow him to kiss her and even worse, she returned the kiss and asked him to come back. What was going on with her? Maybe it was the fact that she was thinking about Chase not having any feelings and she wanted to be held by someone who did. She had to admit to herself that she really loved being held and kissed by Ben.

When Chase got home and climbed in bed, he felt exhausted. He thought about his business and it was doing better than he had ever dreamed it would. It only took a couple of minutes and he was sound asleep. Late that evening, he went to the funeral home and Megan said that the man's family were here earlier and paid for his arrangements. Chase told her she was doing a fantastic job. She told Chase, "You know, I'd like to do the next embalming, I have to stay in practice." Chase said that would be fine and asked her if she needed him to help her and she said, "No, I'm fine. He told Megan, "I guess I get a night off tonight and that he would see her tomorrow.

The next dead body came in that night and Megan called Chase from her cell. She said, "You left in such hurry this evening. The work is never-ending. I have a body here now, a woman that died in the hospital. I'm going to do the embalming on her." Chase said, "Would you like some help?"

She answered impatiently, "No, it's just like riding a bicycle, you just jump right back on. Do not worry I have done quite a few bodies you know, before I came to work for you." He said, "I'm not saying you're not capable, not at all, I just thought you might be tired and like some help, that's all." She said, "No, its fine". Chase told her to have the maintenance man sit upstairs, in case anyone calls or comes in while you're downstairs." She said, "Don't worry, it's all covered. Get some sleep, I know you need it." He said, "I will." She said, "Love You" and he replied, "Bye" which is all she expected.

The deceased woman was brought in by Ben. He had come back again as promised. When he came upstairs to her office for her to sign the papers, she said, "I was just going downstairs. I am going to do the embalming on this woman." Ben said, "I thought you were just the secretary". She laughed and said, "Well, you might think that but I am also a mortician". He said, "Wow, I didn't know that. That is great. I'd never kissed a mortician before and it was a great kiss by the way". She said, "I don't know, maybe we should kiss again, just to see if it was that good". They came together in the middle of her office. They kissed passionately for a while and then they started pulling each others clothes off. He whispered in her ear, "Is this okay with you?"

She said, "Yes, just do it". They made passionate love on her couch in her office. The whole time, Ben was whispering in her ear how beautiful and sexy she was and how he had been waiting for this moment, even dreamed about it. Megan was not use to this. She was not use to making love to someone who actually cared about her, who thought she was passionate. When they were finished, they kissed goodbye at the door and Ben asked, "Can I see you again? can we go out on a date?" She said, "I will think about it Ben. Since I am engaged, I have to think about what all of this means". They kissed again and he left. When he was gone, Megan sat down in the chair behind her desk thinking, "What in the hell did I just do?" She was very attracted to Ben and she threw caution to the wind. What kind of woman was she to cheat on her fiance? She would really have to do a lot of thinking to sort this all out.

Chase knew he was going to take another woman next weekend; the urge was just too strong to deny himself. This time, instead of a prostitute, he would take a young woman who did not wear a ring. He would take her from the UC campus. He wanted to try to get a virgin. Of course, there was no way to tell if the woman he takes is a virgin, just by looking at her, but he would try. He would try for God. He thought that God would be more pleased with a virgin than with a prostitute. God would appreciate the pureness. The next Saturday, everything fell into place. Megan was gone for the weekend with her Mother and he gave his few employees the weekend off, barring any emergencies, that is. His parents had driven up to New England to do some sightseeing and would be there for four or five days. They were leaving early Saturday morning.

He had been watching the campus for the last couple of days and he saw a woman who was rather mousey looking and she was not wearing a ring. She would go to the nearby coffee shop for a latte before heading to an on-campus apartment. He knew that she probably had roommates, most college kids did. If he took her, he would have to take her while she was between the coffee shop and her apartment. If she reached her apartment, it would be too late. Too much of a chance of him getting caught. He had gotten to the coffee shop before he predicted she would get there. He got his coffee. He sat at a little round table by the door so she was sure to notice him. He positioned his chair, so that when she came in she would hit it and he would pretend to spill his hot coffee all over himself. Here she came, just as he had predicted. Everything went like clockwork. After he spilled his hot coffee, she grabbed his arm and repeatedly asked him if he was all right. He struck up the conversation. Chase was not only good-looking but very charming; Molly always said, "Chase, you could charm the feathers off a chicken." He invited her to sit and have coffee with him. She did, mainly because she had never been asked out on a date before. She was the one who accidentally ran into him. After an hour of talking, he asked if she would like for him to give her a lift home. She thought about it for a few minutes. She knew she shouldn't since she didn't even know him but it wasn't every day that a handsome, charismatic man even noticed she was alive. He looked and acted as if he was someone she could trust. He didn't bring it on heavy like he had any ulterior motives and it was getting a little dark out and it had started to rain. At a lull in their conversation, she said, "I guess I should be going, and I will take you up on that ride if the offer is still open." He smiled his perfect smile at her and said, "Sure, no problem at all, let's go." They left the coffee shop. The coffee shop had been so crowded, hardly any place to stand, that no one would remember either him or her being there.

He had her now. She was strapped to his favorite table with the stirrups and her mouth was taped. She was not exactly beautiful but she did have a model's body. She was long and lean with small breasts. He said, "Shake your head "yes" or "no" if you are a virgin. She shook her head "yes". He was so happy because he knew that God would be pleased with his present. He had never had a virgin and he did not really know how to tell for sure if she was one. He took one of his small dildos, one that he thought any woman would consider small and slowly inserted it into her vagina.

He felt a resistance at a certain point. He kept taking the dildo out and pushing it back in again, Just a little farther each time. Finally, he pushed it past the resistance that he felt and It went in all the way and she was bleeding. He mopped the blood up with a cotton ball. That was it. That must be what guys mean when they say they "popped a cherry." Of course, she was crying and trying to scream and wiggle just like the rest of them. He said, "Thank you for the present, God will be pleased with you and me. He pulled her down on the table and fucked her ass until he came. He told her he could not defile her vagina. If he did, she would not be a pure gift. It was at this moment that she realized that, he was going to kill her. The look of terror on her face would satisfy him for a while. Her eyes were wide and bright with tears. She pleaded with him with her eyes for him to let her go. Then he did just what she knew he would. He killed her.

Just as he had kept the piece of brain tumor that he took out of the man, he thought he would like to keep a piece of this girl to remember this very special night. He was trying to think of what it would be that he would keep, that would last. He decided to keep the cotton ball. This is what he would keep. He would put it in a bag and label it with "God's pure gift." that way; it was still unidentifiable to anyone who just happened to find it. He would have to think of a safe place to put it. He would take it to the farm with him and find a special place for it.

He dressed the girl in white and took her to the farm and buried her not too far from the Six others he had already killed. He thought he might dig all of the others up, just to get some kind of trophy from them, but then decided it would be way too much work and too much of a chance of getting caught.

"PART VI"

A couple of days after Molly and Caleb had come home from their trip up to New England, Molly had gone out to the barn for something and she noticed that one of the four-wheelers had been moved again. When they had made their trip to New Orleans and came home a few months ago, Caleb had brought the bags in and had gone back outside to put the car in the barn, Molly remembered asking him what took him so long and he told her he had to move the four-wheeler out of the way and that Chase had left the dishes that she had wanted. She did not think about it at the time, but she started to notice that every time they went away for a few days, one of the two four-wheelers would have been moved. She did not say anything to Chase; she did not know what was going on with that, only that she thought that Chase was up to something, but she did not know what, and she did not want to alarm Caleb. He would think the worst about Chase he always did. She hated it when Caleb thought that way, especially about his own children but she knew it was because of how he grew up with his stepbrother Henry. She liked to think that Chase just liked to come over and ride by himself for a little alone time. He always did enjoy riding a four-wheeler. Maybe he brought Megan along with him, but no, the other four wheelers had not been moved. She had made an unnoticeable mark on the barn floor where the tires were on both machines so she could tell if they had been moved or not.

After their second trip, she started seeing fliers and articles in the local newspapers about women who were missing. She had counted four in the last five months. She prayed that Chase did not have anything to do with their deaths. She did not want to think that way. because he had a great career and was newly engaged. She did not think that he would take a chance on messing all of that up. Besides, he had not done anything violent since he had killed the kittens at five years old. The worst thing he had done since then was set one of their small outbuildings full of hay on fire, playing with matches. The whole thing was old wood and went up in a flash. Although Chase said he was sorry and did not mean to do it, he was smiling when the building was burning. Since then she had seen the perfect son. He had not been the perfect brother to Katie though. She knew that. He had never done anything sexually to his sister. Molly and Katie had talked about that once but he did abuse his sister physically, every chance he got. They hated each other. They never had a kind word for each other, all they ever did was fight and argue. Molly would catch Chase hitting, strangling, and doing other physically abusive things to his sister. After a while, Molly never left Katie alone in the house with Chase. She did not think that Chase would really go too far in hurting his sister on purpose, however, he may accidentally. To this day, they still did not like each other and could hardly stand to be in the same room together. Molly thought that things would be different between them once, they were grown, but it was not, they still hated each other. Molly never really knew why they hated each other so much. Neither one of them gave her an inkling as to why they did.

When Katie was about twelve, she had begged Molly and Caleb for a pet. They finally decided that she was responsible enough for a small pet. They let her have a parakeet. She named her bird Ruby. Ruby had her own, very nice cage in Katie's room. Katie talked to her every day. She thought that Ruby was smart enough to talk. She really loved all animals, but especially her bird Ruby. One day, her parents went into town to go grocery shopping and left Katie and Chase alone. They had been getting along pretty well lately so they felt that they would be okay together until they got back from shopping.

Katie went in her room, Rubies' cage door was open, and Ruby was nowhere to be found in her room. Katie's door was shut so she knew that Ruby could not have gotten out of her room. She looked everywhere and she started crying. She went looking for her brother, thinking he might help her find Ruby. He was not in his room. She opened the bathroom door and Chase was sitting on the toilet, with the lid down. He was beating off with his right hand and squeezing Ruby in his left hand. Katie screamed at Chase, but it was too late. Ruby was dead. Chase had squeezed the life out of her.

Chase grabbed Katie around the throat and told her if she ever told anyone, especially their parents, he would kill her. When Katie saw the look in his eyes, she believed what he said. When their parents came home and saw that Katie was visibly upset; Katie told them that she had opened her window in her room and got Ruby out to hold her and she flew out the window. They were very sympathetic. They told her they would buy her another bird. She said she did not ever want another bird. Their parents never did know about that day and what really happened to Katie's pet. That is why she hated her brother Chase and she would hate him until the day she died. She could not believe her dear, sweet, parents had such an evil child. When she got to be an adult, she understood his mental illness but she still refused to forgive all of the things he had done to her. When they were all together at Christmas or any other time, she barely nodded a "Hello" to him and nothing more. If either she or her brother found out anything about the other, it was only because their Mother would tell them. Katie knew that it broke her Mother's heart that they did not get along and her Mother had asked her many times "Why?" but Katie would say, "I don't know, we just don't get along." and she would leave it at that.

A couple of days after returning from New England, it was August and very warm out, Molly decided that she wanted to learn how to ride one of the four-wheelers. She asked Caleb if he would teach her. He was shocked, "He said, "I will, but why? We have been married almost thirty-five years and you have never wanted to learn before." She said, "I just thought that now you are retired and we are trying to take better care of our health, that we should do something outside together. Don't you think that would be fun? I would like for us to be able to ride back to the creek for a picnic or swim if it is hot out. Besides, Hillary rides and I'd like to ride with her." Caleb still looked at her as if she had lost her mind. He Said, "Sure, I'll teach you, it's not hard and we can ride together. That is why I never ride anymore, because it's not much fun to ride by yourself." She said, "How about now? We are not doing anything else." He smiled at her and said, "Okay, c'mon". They went out to the barn where the four-wheelers were kept.

Caleb always kept an extra woman's helmet here for Hillary. He said, "If you really like riding, we will go into town tomorrow and buy you your own helmet so that you can ride with Hillary when she comes." They put helmets on and Chase showed her how to fasten it. He told her, "You ride the little smaller four-wheeler and I'll ride the big one. He showed her how to start it, how to stop, about the throttle, and everything else while they were just sitting there. She said, "Okay, okay I get it. Can we ride now?" He said, "Safety first. I do not want you to get over confident your first ride and get hurt." She said, "Caleb, it's not like I'm going to fly around curves, pop wheelies or take it in the creek. I just want a nice, not too fast, ride." He laughed and said, "Okay, here we go, ready?" "Yes!" They started up the four-wheelers and rode to the back of the property, stopping at the creek. They got off and he said, "Molly, you are a natural four-wheeler driver." Her cheeks were pink and she was breathing a little harder and she said, "Chase, I should have done this years ago. I love it! No wonder Hillary rides every time she comes over." He was beaming. He was proud of her for trying something new. He said, "How about a swim, I'm so hot." She said, "We didn't bring our swim suit." He said, with a devilish grin, "We don't need one." They were still so much in love and Caleb said, "We should do this every day." Molly said laughing, "down boy". Molly had never swam in a creek before. She didn't know if she would like it because there were fish, turtles and who knows what else was lurking in the water. She wanted to please Caleb and if everyone else did it, she thought that she could do it also. She surprised Caleb by stripping off her clothes and jumping in the creek before he even knew what was happening. He did the same. He said, "How do you like swimming in the creek?" She said, "It's wonderful! The water feels so nice. I don't know why I had not done this sooner. They swam for about an hour and then got out to dry off in the sun. They talked about the places that they wanted to travel to, grandchildren that they hoped for and how much they loved each other.

Even though Molly had sore muscles where she did not even know she had muscles, she went out riding on the four-wheeler, every day that the sun was bright. Sometimes Caleb went with her and sometimes when he was out working the farm, she went alone, but Caleb was always listening for the four-wheeler when she went out alone. By the end of the week, she felt very comfortable riding.

The next Thursday when Hillary came over for dinner and after dessert, Molly said, "Hill, how about we take the four-wheelers out for a while?" Hillary looked at Molly and then at Caleb, to see if she had heard right. Caleb nodded his head. Hillary said, "Oh My God Molly! Really?" She responded, "Yes, Caleb taught me how to ride last week. I have been riding almost every day this week and I love it! I even got in the creek and swam with Caleb. I do not go very fast, but I love it. He even bought me my own helmet, a pink one. She winked at him. Hillary said, "Molly, you got in the creek? Wow, you are turning into a regular country girl. I would love to take a ride with you." They rode back to the creek, got off the four-wheelers, and sat on a big rock next to the creek. Molly said, "Hill, are you ever going to get married?" Hillary said, "Can I be honest?" Molly said, "Don't give me the "I'd rather be single speech again". Hillary said, "Have you ever noticed me dating or going out with any men?" Molly said, "No, just the one guy you were fond of in college." Hillary said, "Right and he was not even a love interest but more of a good friend. Well, I will tell you why I have never found anyone yet, it's because I prefer women." Molly did not look too surprised. Hillary turned and searched her face, expecting to see disgust there. Instead, Molly was smiling. Hillary said, "Molly, you knew I was gay?" Molly said, "Caleb and I both figured you were when we hadn't seen you with any men. We figured it out after a couple of years." Hillary said, "Oh, I thought I was going to give you this big revelation and wondering how I was going to tell you." Molly said, "Hill, its okay with me and Caleb. We do not care what your sexual preference is, we still love you just the same, and we do not think of you any differently. I am just wondering why you are telling me even now. This must be someone special. Maybe you are not in a "Normal" relationship but Caleb and I would just love it if you found someone you could spend your life with and be happy." Hillary said, "Molly, I am so happy. I have found the love of my life, the woman of my dreams and we are both so thrilled to have found each other. I came here to tell you both tonight that I was gay and that I would love it if I could bring my girlfriend over here to meet the two most important people in my life". Molly said, "Well, when you put it like that . . ." They both started gigging like two little girls. Hillary said, "Her middle name Is Marion, that is what she goes by. She is a wonderful person. She is the same age as I am, fifty-four. We have a lot in common. We actually met across the street from my office, at the sandwich shop. Marion is a Dr." Molly replied, "That's funny, I didn't know that shop was still open. That is the sandwich shop that Caleb's brother Henry worked for when he was younger. Molly came right out and asked, "How long have the two of you, been dating? Do you love her?" Hillary said, "We have been dating for a year now, and yes, we love each other very much. You know I am not getting any younger and I thought I would never find someone but Marion and I are perfect for each other. Molly said, "That's so wonderful Hill, we have to tell Caleb. He will be so happy for the both of you." They hugged and then rode back to the house.

When they walked in the house, Caleb said, "By the looks of you two, it must have been one hell of a ride." The women laughed. Molly said, "We were talking about Hillary's new love, well, old love." Caleb said, "Oh Yeah? Who is it?" Hillary said, 'Her name is Marion." She saw the shock on his face for a moment and then a big smile. He said, "Hill, Molly, and I are so happy for you." Molly said, "They are coming over next week for dinner so we can meet her, It's getting serious". Caleb and Molly both said, "We can't wait to meet her." Molly told Hillary about Chase's engagement and she was shocked by that news. Molly said, "Would you mind if Chase and his fiance, Megan join us for dinner, then we could all meet together." Hillary said, "sure". However, Molly saw a little bit of doubt on Hillary's face. Molly asked, "Hill, would it be okay if I gave Chase a heads up that you are dating a woman? That way he will be prepared and it will not be so awkward for you and Marion. Hillary visibly relaxed and said, "Yes, that would be great Molly, if you would do that". Molly said, "Okay, next Thursday it is. How about if I make my homemade pasta, you bring dessert and I will have Chase bring some wine." Hillary said, "Okay, that sounds wonderful!"

When Hillary left, Molly called Chase and asked him and Megan to dinner on Thursday night to meet Hillary's girlfriend. Chase said, "That'd be great". He did not seem too surprised that his aunt Hillary was gay. Molly guessed that sometimes the gay person was the last to know that everyone else already knew they were gay. Chase said, "I'll talk to Megan, but I don't see why not. We don't have other plans." That night, while he and Megan were having dinner together at his house, he asked her about Thursday. He said, "Megan, my parents would like for us to come to dinner on Thursday to me my aunt Hillary's new love interest. Do you mind going with me?" Megan hesitated for a minute. She was thinking that this might me a good opportunity to see Ben again if Chase was at his parents for the evening. Chase looked at her strangely. He said, "Megan, what is going on? You have been acting very strange lately. Have you changed your mind about marrying me?" She answered, "No Chase, of course not. I just have some things on my mind that is all. I've just been worried about my mother and her new boyfriend and what his intentions are." She really was not worried about that but it was the best she could come up with at the moment. She said, "Of course I'd like to go with you to your parents' house on Thursday for dinner." Chase said, "Would you like to take the day off on

Wednesday to go and see your mother?" She thought for a moment. She said, "Thank you Chase, that would be very nice". He said, "Your welcome, now finish that beautiful steak that I just made for you." Chase did not feel jealousy and so he never had a clue as to what was going on with Megan. He never once thought that she would cheat on him.

"PART VII"

Ben had given Megan his phone number and on Monday, she got up the nerve to call him. She asked him if he was doing anything on Wednesday? Could she see him? He sounded excited and he said, "Sure, you can come over to my place and he gave her the address and told her to come about 1:00 in the afternoon." She said she would see him then.

Wednesday came and she was at her own place and she had fixed herself up and she had to admit that she looked really nice. She wanted to look nice for Ben. She drove to his house and was there at exactly 1:00. She sat in her car for a few minutes thinking about what she was about to do and wondering if she should just turn around and go home. After a few minutes, she decided she would go in. After all, this is what she had planned on all week. She went up the walk, noticing all of the landscaping and the flowers that had been planted, and she rang the bell. Ben answered right away. rushing her into the house. He did not want any of his neighbors to see her but she thought that he was just happy to see her. They walked to the back of the house to the kitchen and he told her to have a seat. He asked her, "Would you like a drink?" She responded, "No thanks, I don't drink but I would like some bottled water if you have any." He got her the water from the refrigerator and was fixing himself a drink and while he was doing that, she took her time looking around the kitchen. It looked like a woman's kitchen. There were matching, flowery potholders, and dishtowels, kick-knacks along with plants in the windowsill. Obviously, a woman lived here. She was hoping it was his sister or something. He said, "Let's go into the living room and sit". She replied, "okay". They went into the living room and sat down on the couch. Again, she looked around the room and she saw flowery throw pillows on the couch, doilies on the furniture, and a couple of vases with silk flowers. Ben looked at her and said, "Megan, what's wrong"? Megan asked, "Does your sister or another woman live here?" Ben replied, "Yes, my wife, I am married. She is at work now, that is why I told you to come over so early, before she gets off work at 3:00." Megan's face turned red and she practically screamed, "You're what? married? Don't you think that is something that you should have told me about before you asked me out?" He said, "I thought since you were engaged, you just wanted sex and me being married was no big deal". She yelled, "You are an idiot and don't let me see you at my funeral home, or anywhere else again and do not call me. You are just one of those "pieces of shit men" and you made me feel like some whore just because I was attracted to you. At least I let you know that I was engaged right up front so you at least had time to think about it. You never told me you were married, you do not even wear a wedding ring. You did not give me the same courtesy of being able to think about it! I really feel sorry for your poor wife because you probably do this all the time." He lost all color in his face. "Maybe I should let her know what goes on here in the daytime when she is working. Of course she knew that she would never do that but he did not know it. He needed to suffer a little bit. She slammed the door and left.

She decided to go on to her mother's after all. The drive gave her time to think. She loved Chase and she would marry him. Even if Chase does not have any feelings, she at least knows that because of that, he would never cheat on her. She knows that he adores her and respects her and now she knew that he would be man enough for her. Chase was so much more of a man than Ben was. At least Chase has integrity. She felt so guilty about what she had done. She thought about coming clean with Chase and finally she decided that she would tell him, just not the whole story. It would be hard, however, she would do it.

Megan called Chase on the way to her mother's house. She asked him if she could see him tonight at his place, she wanted to talk to him about something. Chase said, "Is it something serious?" She said, "Yes, but I don't want to talk about it over the phone, I'll come by about 7:00." They both hung up at the same time.

Megan needed to see her mother. It was times like these when a girl needed her mother the most. Thank goodness, her mother was home when she got there and not out with her new boyfriend. She told her mother all about her situation and she ask her what she should do about it. Megan's mother said, "I think you are doing the right thing by telling him. Otherwise, there would always be that one thing between the both of you." Megan said, "Mother, you don't like Chase very much do you?" Her mother answered, "There is something cold and calculating about him. I do not know exactly what it is, I just know it's there". Megan said, "Mother, I wasn't going to tell you this because it's not just something you advertise. Chase is a psychopath". She watched her mother's face for any reaction but only saw a blank stare. Megan said, "Mother?" Finally after a few moments, Megan's mother said, "I guess that is it then. That is what I felt so different about him. We both know what this means. Do you still want to marry him?" Megan replied, "Yes, I love him and at least I know he would never cheat on me. Megan's mother knew there was no chance of talking her daughter out of marrying Chase. Once Megan had made up her mind, nothing she could say would change it. All her mother said was, "Megan please be careful of him." Megan reassured her mother by telling her about her lunch date with Chase's mother Molly. Molly was certain that he would never hurt her and has never done anything illegal. Megan's mother felt a little better, just a little. Megan thanked her mother for the advice and told her she had to be going and promised to visit again soon.

Chase was waiting for Megan when she arrived at his house at 7:00. He had been frustrated all day. He could not figure out what Megan was going to tell him. Maybe she wanted to break off the engagement. Maybe she decided that she could not live with a psychopath. maybe, maybe, maybe.

Megan arrived at his house at 7:00; He offered her a glass of wine, trying not to act as if he had been dying to know what she would tell him. He offered her a seat on the couch next to him. She smiled at him, he thought that was a good sign. Finally he said, "Well, what is it Megan? You know you can tell me anything." She did not know how to start this conversation, so she just jumped right in. She looked at him with rather sad eyes and she said, "Chase, I have a confession to make. Please do not talk, just listen." He nodded for her to go on. She told him that there was a paramedic that came to the funeral home often. Chase's facial expression did not change. She said, "I think he really started to care for me as he told me so many times. Last week, I let him kiss me and he did so passionately. I wanted to kiss someone who had real feelings, the feelings that you don't have, to see if it made any difference in how I felt about you and marrying you." Megan had already decided not to tell Chase they had sex because that would not make any difference to him and it would only alleviate her conscience. Chase asked her, "How do you feel? Does it make that much difference to you? Do you not want to marry me, because if you don't, I told you from the beginning I would understand." Chase was holding his breath and looked at her expectantly, certain that she would break their engagement. She said, "Yes, the guy had feelings for me and I felt that in his kiss, but I have decided again, that you are the only man for me, the only one I want." Chase looked her in the eyes and said, "Megan, you know I don't get jealous, I don't even know what that feels like. I am not angry with you but I also cannot say I love you or any of the rest of the things that go along with telling someone how much you care for him or her. If kissing that guy helped you figure something out about yourself, that you really could be happy with me and you still want to marry me, then I forgive you." Megan said, "Well, I had to tell you anyway. I would never keep something like that from you. I am glad you are not jealous or angry; I just wanted you to know that nothing like this would ever happen again, I love you and only you Chase. You are all the man I need." Chase said, "Does this mean you will still marry me?" She answered, "Of course I will". She thought to herself, that was way too easy and he probably wouldn't have cared if she had sex with someone else, but she did not want to push her luck.

Thursday evening came and Chase and Megan were the first to arrive to Molly's dinner party. They were right on time at 7:00. Molly had to have dinner so late because Megan didn't close the funeral home until 6:00 and it was an hour's drive out here. Chase brought a nice wine. They went into the living room and visited and they enjoyed easy conversation. It was 7:30 and Hillary and her girlfriend were not here yet. Something must have come up because Hill was never late to anything. Molly guessed that Marion was the one that was making them late. A minute later, they heard a knock on the front door and Hillary just came on in like she always does. They walked quickly back to the living room. Hillary started apologizing over and over for her tardiness when she realized that everyone was staring at Marion and she at them, with their mouths open and shocked looks on their faces. Hillary stumbled through the introductions and still no one said anything. Hillary said, "Okay, what's going on here? Would someone please let me in on it?" Hillary looked at Marion with the question. Marion said, "I already know all of the family except Megan. I was Chase's therapist for thirteen years, from the age of five through eighteen." Chase said, "Hello, Dr. Nancy Clark". Now Hillary was the one with the shocked look on her face. Molly said, "Hillary told us your name was Marion, so there was no connection I guess." Marion said, "Marion is my middle name. It's what I use in my personal life." Hillary looked at Marion and said, "Mare, we can go if you'd like, if your uncomfortable." Marion said, "No, I'm fine with it as long as they are. That was a long, long, time ago when I was Chase's therapist." She looked at Chase and the rest of them and said, of course, if that's okay with everyone else." Everyone else politely said that everything was okay. Chase was even smiling a lot at Marion and Hillary thought she had not seen him smile that much in his whole life. Megan thought that his behavior was a little strange also. He starred at the Dr. all night, which did not go unnoticed by any of them, especially Megan. Well Chase may not have one but the little green monster was coming out in her. Megan and Chase had talked about where they had met and how long they had known each other before they had gotten engaged. Hillary and Marion properly goo-good over Megan's engagement ring. Chase ask Marion, "Are you and aunt Hill serious?" They both said in unison, "Yes, we are very serious. We have been dating for almost a year now." Chase wondered to himself why, since he was stalking her, had he not known about Hillary's and Dr. Clark's relationship. He only knew of the man that left Dr. Clark because he thought she had lost her mind because of her stalker. Chase really liked that he left, liked the fact that he thought Dr. Clark was as crazy as some of her patients. After dinner, the women helped Molly clean up the kitchen. Shortly after everything was cleaned up, they all had to get going it was getting late.

Chase was kind of quiet on the way home. His plans for the good Dr. would now have to include getting rid of aunt Hillary for at least a week. He could not have aunt Hillary looking for the Dr. while Chase was having his fun with her. He had waited too long for anything or anyone to come between what he had planned for Dr. Clark and him. He would think of something. He did not really have many feelings except rage but if he had to say that he cared for anyone, even just a little bit, it would be his mother and his aunt Hillary. He would not feel bad about killing Dr. Clark because she was Hillary's girlfriend and he would not feel remorse afterward. He just did not feel those kinds of things but he did not like the fact that he was taking away someone that Hillary loved. "Oh well", he thought, "She would find someone else. Megan said, "What's going on in that mind of yours Chase, you have been so quiet on the ride home?" He said, "You know, it's just weird that my therapist was having dinner their at my parents' house." Megan said, "You sure were all smiles and Google eyes at her all night." "Jealous?" he said. "You don't have to be. By the time my therapy ended with Dr. Clark, I think she hated me and I was ready to be turned loose from her. She knew everything about me. My life up until the age of eighteen. Things that no one else knew or would ever know. It was just strange, that is all. I'm sure that Dr. Clark is the man of the house in that relationship. Believe me when I say, you don't have anything to worry about." Megan knew he was sincere and said, "I'm sorry if tonight was so uncomfortable for you Chase. I believe she is a good fit for your aunt Hillary. Chase I believe you when you say I do not have anything to worry about, I wasn't worried, just curious as to what your relationship was with her now?" Chase said, "The last time I went for therapy at eighteen, that was the end of our relationship. I had not seen her since. "Let's talk about something else. How the wedding are plans coming? Have you found your perfect wedding dress yet?" Megan answered, "No, not yet, but I hope I do soon."

The next day, while Megan was at work at the funeral home, Chase was watching television and channel surfing. He saw the answer to his problem of getting rid of aunt Hillary for almost a week and a half. It just popped right on up on the screen. It was a reality program about brides-to-be finding their perfect wedding dress in New York at a The New York fashion show week and they were showcasing wedding dresses. New York fashion week just happened to be one of the weeks that Molly and his Father would be taking a vacation in the Rocky Mountains. He would be able to kill two birds with one stone, so to speak, getting rid of Hillary and Megan at the same time. He was a genius. He even amazed himself. He got on the phone right away and ordered plane, hotel, and fashion show tickets for Megan and aunt Hillary. They would be there for a week and a half. He could check ahead on the doctors schedule by going into her office computer. Yep, she was booked up that week. He called Hillary, the Dr., and Megan and ask them out to lunch for the following Wednesday. It would take him that long to get the paper work for their trips. He wanted to make sure he had them in hand. He stressed that there was something important that he had to talk to them about. They were all thinking the worst. Maybe Molly or Caleb were dying or something. Chase had never asked any of them out to lunch before. Just like Chase thought, they all agreed to meet him. They met him at a fancy French cafe in Cincinnati located on the levy, by the Ohio river. They all thought it was a long way to go for lunch, and expensive.

Chase was waiting at a table for them when they got there. He stood up and kissed Megan on the cheek. He pulled her chair out for her. Megan said, "Well, you are smiling from ear to ear so it can't be that bad, can it?" They were all seated and had ordered drinks, Chase said, "Why do all of you look so sad? This is really a big surprise for you, not a death sentence." They all murmured that he had made it sound like such an emergency when he had called them. Their drinks arrived and they all ordered salads. When the waiter left. They all said, in unison, "What is the big surprise Chase?" He said, "Megan has told me that she has been having such a hard time trying to find the perfect wedding dress." She shook her head yes for the benefit of the other women. He said, "I have a surprise for you Megan and Aunt Hillary." He reached inside his suit pocket and pulled out the paperwork and handed one stack to Megan and one stack to Aunt Hillary. They all looked at the paperwork and Megan said, "Oh My God Chase! You really know how to surprise a girl! This is so awesome; I can't wait to go to New York!" These tickets are so hard to get and so expensive. How did you ever manage to get them?" Chase said with a little grin, "Well, it pays to know people." Actually, he didn't know anybody and had paid three times the price for the tickets. Aunt Hillary and Marion we are not smiling. Aunt Hillary said, "Did you get the same thing for Marion?" Marion touched Hillary's arm and said, "Oh no, it's perfectly fine with me honey, you will be the one in the wedding dress, not me. Besides, you will have fun with Megan. Hillary answered doubtfully, "But don't you want to see me in my wedding dress?" Hillary replied, "I'm not supposed to see you in it until the day of the wedding, remember?" Chase said, "That's what I thought you would say. I thought it would be a good bonding time for Megan and our family, but, yes, I did bring Marion a gift also. They all smiled and said, "What is it?" He handed a packet to Marion. It was a gift of one week at a well-known spa in California, where she could go and be pampered and relax. Marion said, "Oh My Goodness Chase, you didn't have to do that! But this is incredible!" I have never been to this spa, but I do know they are usually booked three years out. How in the world were you able to get this? He said, "Like I said, I have connections." Chase thought to himself, "My connections aren't that good, that's why your trip is not real!" Marion said, "I would much rather be getting a message and drinking champagne then looking at wedding dresses in busy New York! A couple of my friends go to New York once a year to shop and they always invite me to go although I never do. Shopping is just not my thing." Marion was so secretly happy that she did not have to go to New York to look at wedding dresses. That sounded like one of the most boring trips she could think of. The trip to the California spa was incredible. She knew that Chase was doing well in his business, but she did not know that he was doing that well. It was really strange for one of her previous patients to give her a gift. She wasn't even sure she should accept it, but for now, with all of the happiness going around at this table, she would.

They all looked wide-eyed at Chase. None of them ever thought of him as a generous person. Chase said, "You are all very welcome. Consider this as my wedding gift to you. Things could not have worked out better and maybe my fiance will find the dress of her dreams in New York." Megan said, "If I can't find one there, then it doesn't even exist and I will wear my sweats to my wedding." They all laughed easily, then aunt Hillary had a worried look on her face. Chase asked, "What's wrong?" I was just thinking about Katie. She is getting married also. Maybe we should invite her along to go to New York with us." Chase looked a little uncomfortable. He said, "I feel terrible about that. I know Katie and I have never gotten along but I honestly did forget that she was getting married also. I will extend the olive branch myself and call and ask her if she would like to go." All of the women said that would be a very nice gesture on his part. This made him look really good to all of the women. They could not believe that he had organized all of this, much less paid for the whole thing himself. He thought, "Sometimes, I'm just too smart for my own good." He was beaming until lunch was over. All three women were looking at him as if he were some kind of God. They all thanked Chase over and over and over again. They could not be happier. He would finally have the good Dr. Nancy Clark, a.k.a. Marion, all to himself for at least a week. The women would be in New York, his parents would be in the Rockies, and he would be alone with Dr. Clark. His parents would be leaving on Sunday on their trip, and Megan and aunt Hillary would be leaving on Monday for New York. Dr. Clark was scheduled to leave on Tuesday. Little did Dr. Clark know, she would never be leaving to go to a spa in California; she would never make it there. She would be leaving for Chase, for a sex and torture fest. Since aunt Hillary would be leaving the day before Marion, Chase offered to pick her up and take her to the airport. Dr. Clark thought for a minute and said, "Yes, that would be very nice of you Chase but I could take a cab". He said, "No, it's no problem; I will drop you off at the airport." She said, "Okay, that would be great.

The next day, Chase called his sister Katie. He told her congratulations on her engagement and she told him the same. He told her of his plans to send Megan and Aunt Hillary to the New York fashion show and he wanted to know if she would like to join them, expenses paid by him of course. Katie kindly refused, saying that she already had her wedding dress and that she probably couldn't get off work from the emergency room for that long of a time but thanked him for thinking of her. When they had hung up the phone, Katie thought, "I wouldn't take any kind of gift from that monster, even if I were desperate." She wondered what the motive was behind Chase being so generous to everyone. She knew Chase better than anyone else did. She knew he did not do anything that did not benefit him in some way. She knew he was up to something; he was just not that generous. She also knew that to be so nice to her had cost him a lot; she just did not know what he was buying yet.

Later that night Katie brought up that conversation to her fiance She said, "I talked to my brother today." Her fiance looked surprised. Katie proceeded to tell him about the gift Chase offered her. Her fiance looked surprised as he said. "That's really nice, did you accept?" She responded, "Of course not. Chase always has ulterior motives, he was not just being nice, he does not know how to be nice." Her fiance said "Oh, don't be so hard on your brother, maybe he is just trying to mend fences." That was the end of their conversation. Katie never brought up her brother again. How could she possibly explain to her fiance or anyone else for that matter, what kind of monster her brother really is.

"PART VIII"

Chase was getting so excited planning what he wanted to do to Dr. Clark. He couldn't stop himself from going out to find another woman to kill. He was practicing his torturing techniques on them.

There was starting to be a lot of talk around town about all of the missing women. Most of them were prostitutes without families and no one missed them or even reported them missing but Chase had started taking virgins and rich women from well off families and the small town was starting to take notice of the missing women, even though a lot of them were missing from the tri-state area of Kentucky, Ohio and Indiana, the news about the girls still ran in their local papers. Chase started taking some of the more affluent women to see how they reacted to his torture because he knew that Dr. Clark had been raised with a silver spoon in her mouth. He thought they would react differently than the prostitutes he killed and he was right. The prostitutes seem to be able to take a lot more. He thought it was because some of the prostitutes had already gone through hell in their lives. A lot of them had already been through a lot of pain growing up. The women who had led a charmed life seemed to be able to take a lot less pain. He thought that this was very interesting but didn't like the fact that Dr. Clark probably couldn't take much pain, at least not as much as he had planned to give her.

Molly was still checking the four wheelers all the time. She could not help herself from worrying. She started noticing the dates of when the girls were missing and when one of the four wheelers would be moved. Her heart did not want to think about her son being involved but her brain started telling a different story. She had been riding the four-wheeler every day almost. She did not want Caleb to get suspicious of her, which he would if she hardly rode the four-wheeler. She rode around the property in addition, through some of the woods that the four-wheeler would fit through. She had seen a couple places where the dirt had looked freshly dug. She told herself that it was just animals digging there. Today, she had seen another spot in the woods. She thought that if it was Chase, he was going to great lengths to hide the spots with brush and boulders. It was time, she needed to talk to her husband, and she needed to talk to her son before she left for her vacation. Their vacation was only six weeks away now. If she did not clear her head of these suspicions before she left, she would not be able to enjoy herself on her vacation. She would be fixated on what Chase was up to. She wasn't sure what to do about it. She would just worry constantly. She did not know how she was going to approach her husband about it yet. She thought that he would understand her concerns. God, how she prayed that it was not her son, her only son killing all those women. She had decided it was time, she would talk to Chase tonight right after she and Caleb were finished with dinner. She would make some excuse to Caleb that she needed to go out.

That night after dinner, Molly told Caleb that she wanted to talk to him about something. He said, "Go ahead, Molly what is it?" She said, "Well, you know when I asked you to teach me how to ride the four-wheeler? There was a reason for that." Caleb replied, "I knew there had to be, since you never wanted to learn in the last twenty years. Why the sudden interest now Molly?" She asked, "Have you been reading in the local paper about all of the women who have been missing over the last year?" He knew where Molly was going with this and said, "Molly, do you think Chase killed them and buried them on the farm?" She said, "I do keep seeing freshly turned earth in spots when I ride out to the wooded area." Caleb said, "Molly, don't worry, Chase wouldn't do something like that in a million years, what with his funeral home business and new fiance at stake." She said, "I guess you are right, it was just in the back of my mind is all but if you think that it's unlikely, then I won't worry about it." Caleb said, "No, honey, don't worry about that. It's probably just where some animal has been digging." She answered, "Okay, if you think there is nothing to worry about then, I will not". Caleb hadn't told Molly, but he had also noticed the number of missing women, the muddy four-wheeler, and the freshly turned earth in the woods. He did not want to think it could be Chase killing those women. He had tried to put it out of his mind, but now that Molly had the same concerns, he was not so sure. He was sure that he did not want Molly to worry. He said, "Don't worry honey, everything is okay. Give me that big, pretty smile of yours now, and he pulled her on his lap." She forgot all about Chase, for the moment anyway.

After she cleaned up the kitchen, she told Caleb I am going shopping for girlie things and I will be back later". He said, "Do you want me to go with you?" She said, "No, I don't want you hanging over my shoulder." Caleb smiled, "Okay honey, I'll just sit home by myself and do nothing". Molly thought, "He is such a baby, and he tries to make me feel guilty when I don't ask him to go out somewhere with me. He just doesn't like to be alone too much." Molly told Caleb that she might also be shopping for his upcoming birthday and that was another reason he couldn't tag along. She thought that she might get him another dog. Caleb loved dogs and had Satan for almost twelve years. Maybe she would buy him a new dog, a smaller dog that he could keep in the house. As soon as Molly was safely gone, Caleb was thinking about the missing women. He had also noticed the four-wheeler being dirty at the same times they went on vacation. He had never really thought to go out and look for a fresh grave like Molly had done. Now, he really was suspicious. He decided to take a four-wheeler ride himself and take a look around. He rode around the property for quite a while and only saw one spot that looked freshly dug up but did not think it was big enough to be for a human. He had brought the shovel and so he decided to dig anyway and see what was buried, if anything, down there. He dug down about five feet and he found a human skeleton. The bones looked very old, not the body of someone who had recently been killed. He knew that there were probably people buried all over this property because of people burying their loved ones themselves a hundred years ago. The skeleton did look very old and could have been at least a hundred years old. He reverently replaced the dirt and said a prayer for the person he had dug up. After all this, he still had his suspicions about Chase but he did not think that Chase was stupid enough to bury a body in their own back yard. He dismissed this idea with the same reasoning he gave Molly. It was probably animals digging and burying something.

Molly was actually going to see Chase, and she did not want Caleb to know. It was almost seven.

Molly was almost to Chase's house. She had gone over and over in her head about how she was going to bring up the subject of the missing women. Finally, she decided, I will just come right out and ask him. She knew even if he did have something to do with the girls, that he surely would not admit it to her. She always knew when he was telling a lie. She just wanted to see the reaction on his face when she asked him about the missing women. Sometimes, when someone is lying, you can just look at them and know they are lying.

She knocked on Chase's door and he opened it right away. He said, "Hello Molly, come in and have a seat. Would you like something to drink?" She said, "Yes, I'd like some hot tea if you have any." He said, "Sure, I will be right back with your tea." This gave her a few minutes to look around. She saw a few woman's things but knew they must be Megan's personal items. When Chase came back into the living room, she said, "Chase, your place really looks great. I didn't know you were such a decorator." He said, "Oh, that was all Megan; she decorated the whole place for me." She said, "Has Megan moved in with you?" He said, "No, she stays here sometimes because it's easier than driving all the way back to her apartment." She laughed and said, "I just wondered because you have some pretty pillows on the couch and it looks like a lady has taken over." She laughed to break the tension. Chase knew she wanted something because she never just "stopped over". He said, "Molly, I know you didn't stop over here to see my pretty pillows." She said, "No, I have something serious to talk to you about." He thought, "ooh, no". She turned on the couch to face him and looked him in the eye. She always did this when she wanted to talk about something serious. She said, "Chase, don't get all riled up, I just have to ask you something". He said, "Okay, what is it?" She said, "There have been a lot of missing women around here in the last year. I want to know if you had anything, anything at all to do with their disappearance?" He looked her in the eye, making sure; he had a hurt look on his face and said, "No, Molly, I certainly did not have anything to do with that. You know I am not a violent person. I do not go around kidnapping young women." She said, "Okay, I just had to ask and now I'm satisfied that you didn't have anything to do with it."

They talked a little more about the upcoming weddings, her, and Caleb's trip. Chase knew that they still had a few animals left on the farm and when they took their trips, they had a neighbor down the road from them, Jim Taylor, take care of the animals. Chase had run into him once at the farm when he had his first victim in the back of his hearse. Chase asked Molly, "Is Mr. Taylor going to take care of the animals while you are gone on your trip? If he cannot, then I could probably get over there and look after them. Molly said, "Oh no, I know how busy you are with your new business, Jim doesn't mind, he's happy to do it for us." Chase said, "Okay, just let me know if you need me for anything." Molly replied, "Thanks Chase, you are a good son. I am thinking about getting your father a new dog for his birthday. A dog that is small and can stay in the house. What kind do you think I should buy him?" Chase replied, "I cannot believe you would let a dog in the house. You always said there was no way you would ever let an animal in the house. Maybe a mini poodle or something?" She smiled at him, "I was thinking maybe a beagle hound. I know they do not get really big. I think your father misses having a pet and I think he gets lonely when I am not around. It is not like when he was younger and worked on the farm all day. I was also thinking maybe a basset hound would be more his style." She stood up and she said she had to go because it was getting late and the pet store closed at 9:00. He kissed her on the cheek and walked her to her car. He said, "Be careful on your way home. I know you do not see as well as you use to, driving in the dark." She answered, "Don't worry, I'll be just fine". She thought to herself, "Chase is a good son.

She went on to the pet store to pick up the beagle hound puppy for Caleb. She had already called the pet store a couple of days before. She knew that they had what she wanted. She was the cutest little puppy. She was only eight weeks old. She purchased the puppy, along with dog food, dog bowls, collar and leash.

On her way home she thought that she felt better after having talked to Chase and she didn't think he could ever kill someone. Now I can feel good about going on vacation." until she was about half way home. As Molly was driving home, she got more and more upset. She was replaying their conversation over and over in her head. She was upset because, first of all, she never said a word about kidnapping and she never said they were young women. She was hoping that he was just making assumptions. By the look in his eyes though, she could usually tell when he was pretty satisfied that he had convinced her of something. She really was not sure what to think, but she wanted to believe he was not lying, but she was not sure he was not lying to her this time.

Caleb's birthday was next week so she thought that Caleb would love this present. Caleb already had everything else he wanted, but he did not have a dog. Molly got home about 10:30 that night. She left the puppy and all of his things in the car. When she walked in the house; Caleb walked up to her and hugged her. He said, "It's getting late, I was just starting to worry about you". Molly answered, "I'm fine Caleb. You know how we girls are when we are shopping." He replied, "Well, did you buy some sexy underwear or did you just buy granny panties?" She said, "Actually, I didn't buy any underwear." Caleb said, "But isn't that what you went shopping for?" She said, "No, that was just a set up". Caleb looked at her suspiciously. He said, "Set up for what?" Molly got a big smile on her face and she said, "I wanted to go out and find you the perfect birthday present". Caleb said, "You didn't have to Molly. We stopped buying each other birthday presents a long time ago." Molly said, "I know, but it's something that I think you need and I'm hoping you want it." Caleb replied, "Well, then, let's see, it's not too early to give me a birthday present." She said, "Okay, but I need for you to sit down over there in the recliner and close your eyes tightly". He did as she had told him. She went down to their bedroom and got one of her scarfs to use on Caleb for a blindfold. She wanted to make sure that he did not peek. She told Caleb that she had to go out to the car to get his present but that she would be right back and for him to stay right there in the chair and leave the blindfold on. He said, "Yes Mam!" He had a big smile on his face and Molly loved teasing him. Caleb heard the front door shut and then he heard her come back in a few minutes later. While she was coming down the hall, she yelled, "Caleb, do you still have your blindfold on?" He yelled back "Yes!" He heard her walk into the room. She told him that she was going to stand behind him and place his present in his lap. She told him he had to guess what it was before removing the blindfold. He agreed. Molly had the little beagle hound lying on a towel. She leaned over the chair that Caleb was sitting in and placed the puppy on the towel on Caleb's lap. She said, "Okay, you can touch it now and try to figure out what it is!" As soon as he touched the dog, he knew it was either a dog or cat. He could not wait and jerked the blindfold off. He said, "Oh My God Molly, you bought me a dog? You don't even like dogs." She said, "Well, I do like this one, she's very sweet and won't get too big so we can make her a house dog." Caleb said, "Molly, are you feeling okay? I mean, you never let animals in the house before." She said, "I am fine with the dog in the house as long as she is trainable." Caleb gently picked up the puppy and looked her over well. He loved her already. She was beautiful. Caleb said, "I love her and she has beautiful markings". Molly said, "She was the runt of the litter and she just gravitated towards me. I think she was the sweetest, prettiest of the litter. I thought maybe you could train her for hunting." Caleb replied, "Sure I can, as soon as she is old enough. Daniel and I will take her rabbit hunting!" Molly said, "I have to go back out to the car to get the rest of her things. Caleb offered to do it but Molly said "No, just look at your new puppy and decide what to name her." When Molly came back into the house with the dog things, she put them on the kitchen table. Caleb put the dog on the chair for a minute and walked into the kitchen. He turned Molly around and gave her a big hug and kiss. He said, "Thanks' honey, for the dog. I know you don't like dogs very much, especially in the house." Molly answered, "Well, I'm mellowing out in my old age." Caleb found a box to put the puppy in, along with a blanket and an alarm clock. The sound of the alarm clock would take the place of the puppy's mother's heartbeat. This was supposed to keep the dog from whining and crying all night. Caleb put the dog's box right next to his side of the bed. The alarm clock thing did not work; the puppy whined and cried for a couple of hours. Finally, when Caleb could not take it anymore, he scooped the puppy up and held her next to him. The puppy was quiet for the rest of the night. The next morning when Molly got up, she said, "Caleb, what are you doing. We cannot let the dog sleep with us because then it will start to think that our bed is her bed. Caleb said, "I guess your right." He still had no intention of not sleeping with Minnie. That was the name he had given her. She reminded him of a little, tiny mouse and so he thought Minnie was a good name for her.

When Chase did not have any bodies to embalm at night, he would work on his plan for Dr. Clark. He decided that Dr. Clark deserved something special, something different than the rest of the woman he had killed. He had waited for this for so long, he wanted to stretch out the Dr.'s death for as long as possible. He had modified one of his cheap, wooden coffins for her. He decided he would not kill her but that he would bury her alive. That was most people's fear. He would not be able to feel the life drain from her body, but most importantly, he would be able to see her eyes on the small camera he had mounted inside the coffin.

He was home during the day while Megan was working; this gave him time to make his plans for Dr. Clark. He built a panel in the side of the coffin to put a tank of oxygen and some tubing in with a nasal cannula. On the other side, he affixed the small camera and a microphone so that he could see and hear her. He could also talk to her if he wanted to. This was the perfect set up and he was so proud of himself for coming up with the idea. Well, he had to admit, it was not really his idea, he had seen it in several different horror movies and on a couple of soap operas, while he was home during the day. He doubted that the Doctor had ever seen anything like this. Not very original, he will admit that, but lots of fun none-the-less. First, before he buried her, on his family's farm, of course, he would bring her to his funeral home and put her on his special table and strap her down to sexually torture her for long periods of time. He also planned on doing some cutting on her. He had pretty much cut up his last three victims, he could do that, without untying the leather restraints. Just the thought of cutting her and watching her bleed really had him hard again. He told himself to pay attention to the details. He did not want to get sidetracked with his gruesome thoughts. Before he was ready to bury her alive, he would tell her exactly what he was going to do. He would knock her out with some rohypnol, the date rape drug, when she woke up, she would be in her grave. No, he decided that he did not need to drug her to get her in her coffin. He would simply make her get in it herself when he was finished raping and torturing her. That would be much more satisfying, watching her get in herself. Of course he knew he would have to help her a little bit. He knew she would not be cooperative with anything he had planned for her. Everything about the coffin was tested and retested and everything worked, as he wanted it to. This would be the highlight of his life. He would take every necessary precaution. He enjoyed the planning almost as much as he enjoyed the act itself. He would fuck the Dr. in every position he could think of. He took great steps to make sure that he did not get caught by the police or by Megan. The coffin that he had custom made for the Dr., was hidden behind some others that looked just the same in the warehouse.

Megan wanted to do the embalming on the woman that came in from the nursing home, to keep her skills up and Chase agreed that she should. She had done several autopsies since she had been working here. He told her to go over to his house to get some sleep. It was afternoon and he would look after the office, which he hoped no one came in. He really hated dealing with the deceased family. He told her to go and get some sleep. She said, "Thanks, I think I'll take you up on that."

Megan went to Chase's house. He had already made her a key. She went to the kitchen to get a drink of the wine she had left here the last time she was here. A glass of wine would help her relax and go to sleep. She sat down on the couch and turned on the television. She channel surfed then sipped her wine until it was gone and she was feeling sleepy. She took the glass to the kitchen, then she went to the bathroom to wash up before lying down. On the bathroom vanity, sitting there in plain sight, was a tube of lipstick, which did not belong to her. She wondered what was going on. She knew Chase and she also knew he would have a good explanation for it being there. She went ahead and washed up and got ready for bed. She went into the bedroom and pulled off all of her clothes and she set Chase's alarm clock for 9:00pm. She climbed under the warm, down comforter. As soon as she got warm she was fast asleep.

Megan got back to the funeral home about 10:30, after taking a nice, long, hot shower. When she walked into Chase's office to let him know she was back and that he could leave if he wanted, he grabbed her and kissed her hard. She smelled clean. He could smell his soap on her skin. He picked her up and carried her over to the couch in his office. They continued kissing until both of them were hot and ready. She whispered, "I've been a really bad girl today". He answered, "Oh, what have you done, tell Big Daddy all about it." She said, "I drank your wine and messed up your big bed". He said, "Well, you know you will have to be punished for what you've done?" She answered, "Yes, I know." He turned her over on his lap and spanked her good until he was rock hard. When she got up, she looked at him with a smoldering look and she said, “I think Big Daddy needs a spanking also.” He looked surprised as he asked, “What for?” She said, “I found a tube of woman’s lipstick on your vanity in your bathroom and it is not mine. I think you need a spanking yourself.” He said, “That was my mother’s. She was over the house the other night.” Megan replied, “I don’t believe you, get up”. She pulled him over to the chair behind the desk. She said, “Bend over the chair and hold on to the arms”. He replied, “Okay”. She said, “Okay, What?” He answered, “Okay mistress”. Both of them were completely naked. She took the belt out of his pants. She hit him hard on his buttocks and made a red welt. He did not know what had gotten into her but he loved it. She did not take this role very often.

He played along, “It was my mother’s, I swear it was!” Megan said, “You’re lying”. She hit him about another ten more times. She asked him “Have you learned your lesson yet?” He said, “I didn’t do anything”. He knew this answer would get him some more blows with the belt”. She thought, “Apparently, he wants more”. She gave him ten more hard blows. He had had enough. He stood up straight and turned around. He gently laid her down on his desk, with her butt almost hanging off of the end. He spread her legs and licked her clit until she came. He was still rock hard and she was still very wet. He fucked her hard and long until he came. After they were both spent, he helped her up off of the desk. He held her close and kissed her very gently. She was secretly proud of giving him what he wanted. He said, “I don’t know what got into you but I loved it.

Maybe you need to go and take a nap more often." She said, "Thanks, maybe I will, but I still do want to know whose lipstick was in your bathroom". He repeated, "It really was my mother's. She stopped over the other night before going birthday shopping for my dad." Megan believed him. It did look like his mother's color of lipstick. She said, "Okay then, I better get downstairs and get to work and you better get home and get some rest and maybe even soak your sore butt." She laughed and he smiled at her. He said, "I don't know how lucky I was to find a woman like you". She said, "I know". She was still smiling when she said, "I'm going downstairs, don't forget to lock the front door when you leave." He replied, "Yes, mother". He didn't have work on his mind this morning and had forgotten to ask Megan about the last embalming she had done. A little while later he called Megan to ask how things went with the embalming. She said, "It went like clockwork, just as expected." He said, "You did a great job on the old lady." she said, "Thanks baby". That was the first endearment she had ever used on Chase and Chase did not know if he liked it or not. Before he hung up, she said, "Oh, by the way, I found something really gross in a bottle in the back of the refrigerator. I was going to pitch it but I thought I would ask you because I did not know what it was." He said, "Oh, that is a cancer I removed from someone's face. I wanted them to look good for their funeral. I didn't know what to do with it at the time, so I put it in the jar, sorry." He thought. "It's a good thing I'm a quick thinker." She said, "No problem, I was just wondering".

The next morning Chase got a call from his aunt Hillary. She wanted to let him know that his friend Charlie had escaped from prison two weeks earlier. She was just finding out about it. Chase said, "How? What happened?" Hillary said that he escaped from a transport van but that she did not know the details. She just wanted to let Chase know that if he had not already, he would probably be receiving a visit from the FBI, looking for Charlie. After Chase had hung up the phone from talking to Hillary, he wondered how Charlie had escaped the officers, but more importantly, he wondered where Charlie was now. He knew they were transporting Charlie to a new facility down south for his own protection. Once you kill a gang member in plain sight of everyone, you were considered pretty much dead. He secretly hoped that Charlie got far, far away. Chase was a little worried after the call he had received from his Aunt earlier this morning. He was afraid the FBI would show up here at the funeral home looking for Charlie. He disassembled the coffin he had made ready for the Dr. He put the pieces in several different places where anyone else seeing them would not know what they were, especially the FBI. Sure enough at 5:00am the next morning, the doorbell on the back door rang. Chase thought that this was very strange because no one ever went to the back door. When Chase went to answer it, he could see through the window, that it was two men in black suits. He knew immediately that it was the FBI. He knew what they wanted. He opened the door and the two FBI agents introduced themselves and showed their badges. Chase asked, "Would you like to come in?" He wanted them to know that he was being cooperative.

When they came in, he took them upstairs to the lobby and asked them to have a seat. They said they would stand. One of them asked Chase, "Do you know Charlie Thomas? Chase answered, "Yes, he was my childhood and school friend." The other agent asked, "Did you know that Mr. Thomas was in prison for killing a young girl?" Chase answered, "Yes, I am aware of that." The same agent asked, "Did you know that Mr. Thomas has escaped from a prison van?" Chase truthfully said, "Yes, I knew that he had escaped but I did not know from where." Agent, "Have you see him or has he been here?" Chase said, "No to both questions". Agent, "Do you mind if we take a look around?" Chase, "No, help yourselves, look all you want. I will be downstairs in the embalming room if you need any assistance." One of the agents said, "I will go with you while my partner searches. They did not want him to alert Charlie if he knew where he was. They did not say another word just started looking around. An hour later, one of the FBI men knocked on the embalming room door. When Chase opened it, one of them asked what Chase's address was. When Chase gave it to them, they asked, "Can we go with you to your home and search it?" Chase said, "Of course you can, like I said, I have not seen him. I do not think he is stupid enough to come around here right after an escape. I will be finished here in just a couple of minutes.

When Chase was finished with the body he was working on, he put the body in a drawer and left the funeral home. He locked the back door and told the FBI agents they could follow him home. The agents said, "No, we will drive you and bring you back". Chase knew that they were afraid that he might call Charlie from his home. Chase said, "Sure, whatever you say". The FBI drove to Chase's house and searched it thoroughly and found nothing. They took Chase back to the funeral home. They told him "If you see or hear from Charlie Thomas, we expect you to contact us immediately". Chase answered, "Of course". They left and Chase was glad to be rid of them. When Megan came in the next morning, Chase told her about the visit from the FBI and also told her that she could expect a visit from them at any time because of Charlie's escape.

One morning, Megan asked him, "Chase, when there is no one to embalm, what do you do there at the funeral home all night?" He said, "Oh, a little bit of this and that. I do some cleaning, take inventory, and whatever else needs to be done." She said, "Okay, I was just wondering". The next night while he was at the funeral home, he decided to give the Dr. a call, he hadn't called her in quite a while now. He was also a little upset that he did not know that she was dating his aunt Hillary. He thought that he knew every aspect of her life, then he realized he had not been keeping up with her as well as he did previously. Her phone rang and she picked up, "Hello" He said, "Hey Baby, when I get through with you, you will not be a little gay bitch anymore".

Dr. Clark and Hillary said they met at the sandwich shop where Henry used to work. They also said that they have been in a relationship for a year. How did he miss this important tidbit of information? Chase guessed that since Dr. Clark's fiance left her, she decided she would try something new, or she actually went to see

Aunt Hillary over a legal matter and they got together. Chase also decided the best plan would be to lay low, not break into her home anymore. When he finally took her, he wanted it to be a complete surprise.

Marion met Hillary at the sandwich shop across from Hillary's office. She was running some errands. She stopped in for a little bite to eat and she sat at the counter. Hillary was sitting on the stool beside her. The Sandwich Shop was a throwback to the fifties, decorated with records, a jukebox, and red and white stools and booths. They even had one of the old soda fountains and made shakes and malts. The shop had been here for as long as she could remember, it was the place to go for lunch, located in the middle of their small town. Marion thought that Hillary was one of the most beautiful women she had ever met. Like her, she was tall and slim. Marion loved her long, curly, red hair and beautiful green eyes. She had full lips and a gorgeous smile. She didn't know it at the time but Hillary thought the same of her, so different from herself with long, dark brown. straight hair, light blue eyes, and beautiful olive skin color. Hillary started a conversation with her first, asking her if she were new here in town. Marion said, "I have an office in the next town over". I had some errands to run and everyone always talks about this place so I decided to try it." Their conversation flowed from there. They were both undeniably attracted to each other. Marion had never had a relationship with another woman but often thought about what it would be like. She never thought about whether she was bisexual. She didn't think she was but she wanted Hillary. She wanted to lie next to her and feel her smooth skin. She wanted to feel Hillary's soft lips on hers. When they left the sandwich shop, Hillary held Marion's hand and she loved that.

Marion and Hillary had been dating for over a year and wanted to get married. When their relationship first started to get serious, Marion told Hillary about her stalker she had had for years but that she had not heard from him in a long time. Hillary said, "That kind of goes along with your line of work doesn't it?" Marion said, "Not really, I only treat children." Hillary said, "If you are asking me if I am afraid, I am not, so do not worry. I will be there for you." They wanted the whole world to know that they loved each other but in a small town like this one, where one was raised by prejudice, southern people; it was not the wisest choice for them. They had to lay low. If some of their clients knew they were gay; that may just cause their business to collapse. They were both so excited about the prospect of getting married and becoming a couple. They had decided that once they were married, Marion would move into Hillary's Victorian mansion with her and move her office there also.

"PART IX"

As each week went by, Chase was getting more and more excited. He could not believe it. His life's dream was about to become a reality. Even Megan noticed. She asked, "Chase, you have been so happy lately, what's up with you?" He replied, "I am just excited about being a married man that is all. Of course, being married to the most wonderful woman in the world helps." She did not believe him and said, "Sure, Okay, if you say so". She asked him, "What are you going to be doing around here while I'm in New York?" He said, "Nothing, just the usual, or maybe I'll go out and find me a hot chick to fuck for a week." She knew that he was teasing her. She said, "I think you can make it for a week without me. You will not just disappear or anything. You will still be alive when I get home." He thought, "Yes, but Dr. Clark won't be".

Chase thought that all of his plans were final now. He had gone over and over his plans for Dr. Clark very carefully. He would pick her up and take her from her house in his van to the funeral home and he would bury her at the farm. Of course, she would still be alive when he buried her. She would be so terrified. He was so glad that he had a speaker, a light, and a camera installed into the coffin so that he could hear and see how terrified she would be. Charlie always told him that he just planned way too much and that he did not need to go over and over everything a million times. Charlie was also the one who thought that he would never actually complete the act of killing someone. Charlie knew him and Charlie knew that planning was more satisfying for Chase than the final act. Chase guessed that Charlie was right, he wouldn't kill Dr. Clark, or rather she would die all alone, except for the sound of his voice which was very satisfying for him. Today was the Day, now it begins. His parents left this morning for their trip to the Rockies. All of their farm animals were gone now and all they had left was Caleb's beagle, Minnie. His parents were taking the dog with them. Caleb loved that dog so much; there is no way he would leave her with anyone. They had to stay at hotels that allowed pets and taking the dog on the plane cost them a small fortune. Caleb said if he left the dog, the dog would have separation anxiety but everyone knew it was the other way around. Caleb had already trained Minnie to run rabbits. He had trained Minnie so that he and Katie's husband Daniel could go hunting on the farm. Minnie was a great hunting dog. She slept with Caleb and Molly every night but Molly made her stay at the bottom of the bed when she went to sleep. It never failed, by morning, Minnie would be up at the top of the bed, sleeping in the middle of them both with her head on a pillow. Caleb loved this dog so much and he took excellent care of her. He kept her bathed and nails trimmed. Molly allowed Minnie to sleep with them because she also loved Minnie. She didn't like pets in the house but Minnie was like part of the family. Molly thought the dog acted as if she was human. At least, that is how Caleb treated her.

Megan and Hillary were leaving in the morning, on Monday and Dr. Clark thought that she would be leaving the next day, Tuesday. She was packing and getting ready to go. She was so excited about going to the famous spa and relaxing. She still could not believe that Chase had given her such a nice gift. Professionally, she knew that Chase could not change who he was but he did seem to be a lot nicer and actually pretty normal. She never dreamed that she would never make it to the airport. Chase knew that people were starting to get suspicious of the missing girls. His mental track record told him to stop for a while or take prostitutes or someone who did not have any connections to anyone else." The prostitutes could take a lot of pain so they were more fun to torture than the rich city girls. Dr. Clark was a city girl. Dr. Clark would be the last woman he takes for a really long time or maybe even forever, so he better get all of his needs met. He did not know what he would do once Dr. Clark was gone. He had spent years planning her death. Would it just be a great void after she was gone? Would he be very unhappy? Would he ever be able to do anything else that would top this? Since his excitement came from the planning, not the actual killing, he supposed he would have to plan a death for someone else then. Maybe his sister Katie. He had always hated her. Almost as much as he hated Dr. Clark.

The next morning, he drove Megan and Hillary to the airport. They were giddy with excitement, like two young schoolchildren. When they got to the airport and were waiting in line to check in, Hillary pulled Chase aside and whispered to him, "Chase, I just wanted to let you know that they haven't caught up with Charlie yet. Has he been to see you? He replied, "No, I haven't seen him. He is too smart to come and see me because he knows that my place is where they will look for him. He has not contacted me in any way. Hillary reminded him one more time, "Chase, please don't see or talk to him. If you do you are asking for real trouble." Chase replied, "Don't worry, I won't. How could something like this happen? I thought Charlie was in a maximum security prison". Hillary told him, "Apparently he was with two other in-mates in a prison transport van and they were being transported down south to another prison. They wrecked the van on a country road and all three in-mates escaped. They already have one of them back in custody. Chase told her, "Charlie is very smart, just careless sometimes. I am sure they will not catch up to him very soon. He has already been on the loose for a month now. Chase was quiet. Before the women had to go through airport security, Chase kissed Megan on the cheek and hugged her. "Hope you have a great time baby and find your dream dress." She said, "I have your credit card, so I intend to! Love you baby."

Dr. Clark was supposed to leave the next morning for the spa. He called her and offered to take her to the airport again since they really had not discussed it. She said "Yeah, that would be great Chase." That was one small step for him, otherwise he would have to take her before she reached her car. Marion still did not fully trust him, she realized that he was grown up now and was not that irritating little boy anymore. In fact, she rather liked him now. He had also grown up to be very handsome, which she could tell even back then that he would be. Dr. Clark and her fiance had broken up over a year ago. She could not control her anxiety sometimes, due to her stalker and he could not control his anxiety over her anxiousness. She was glad they broke up. He had not been supportive of her at all. When he should have been there for her, comforting her, instead of complaining about not getting any. From her experience anyway, she thought all men were the same. If you could cook and give them a good blow job, they were as happy as a pig. Maybe that is why some women called them pigs. She really was not a man basher it was just her state of mind back then when she and he broke their engagement. Instead of being devastated, she felt free instead. It was one of the best things to ever happen to her, because if he hadn't broken the engagement, she would have never have been with Hillary now. She loves Hillary so much.

The night before Chase was supposed to pick Marion up and take her to the airport, he could hardly contain himself. He was so excited; he knew that he would never sleep. He tried but could not. All he did was toss and turn and kept looking at the clock. This night was going so slow. He ended up getting up and going to the funeral home. He wanted to make sure that everything that he wanted for Dr. Clark was laid out and right where he needed it to be. He went home then, stopping at a store and purchasing a six-pack of beer. He had never drank because it interfered with his medications but now that he had thrown them away, there was no reason why he couldn't have a few. Besides, it would help relax him so maybe he would go to sleep. When he got home, he drank three beers while going over his plans in his head. He checked and rechecked his plans for Dr. Clark, looking for any loopholes or anything else that would get him caught by the authorities. He finally decided that he had the plan for a perfect murder. He was tired now and went to bed. He set his alarm clock and then he checked it at least twenty times before drifting off to sleep. He had to be at Dr. Clark's house by seven.

Chase was at Marion's house to pick her up a little early the next morning to pretend to take her to the airport. He was trying to figure out how to put the rohypnol in a drink for her, when she asked, "Would you mind pouring me some orange juice?" He thought to himself, "This couldn't get any better." He poured the small vial of liquid into her orange juice without her knowing. She came into the kitchen. She grabbed the glass of orange juice and drank it down. She told Chase, "I don't know why I'm so thirsty this morning." After a few more minutes of her rushing around, she started to become dizzy and she sat down on the couch. She yelled for Chase, "I'm not feeling too we . . ." Before she could get the words out of her mouth, she had passed out on the couch. Chase knew that she would not remember anything about this morning, which was great because he wanted her to be totally surprised when she woke up.

He opened the garage door and then pulled his white van inside. He quickly closed the garage door so no nosy neighbor could see him. He went around to the side of the van and opened the door. He had laid a sheet of plastic inside on the van floor in case he was a suspect afterward, they would not even find one of her hairs for evidence. He gently picked her up, along with grabbing her purse. When investigators came to the house, he wanted it to look like she had left on her own, in addition, of course, taking her purse with her. He gently laid her and her purse inside the van. He gave her enough drugs it would be a couple of hours before she woke up. Chase quickly went back into the house to make sure he had wiped off anything that he had touched like the orange juice glass and doorknobs. He hurriedly got in the van, locking all of the doors. After backing out of the driveway, he had closed the garage door and everything here at the doctors house looked perfectly normal. He also did not see a soul while he was leaving the neighborhood. He was on his way back to the funeral home to complete his life's work. Chase was so excited that he could hardly contain himself. His dream was finally coming true. This was going to be the best week of his whole life. His heart was pounding out of his chest, he was short of breath and beads of sweat were popping out on his forehead. The adrenaline was rushing through his veins and he love it, loved the rush.

When he arrived at his funeral home, he pulled around back, making sure there was no one around to see him. He opened the side van door and the door to the funeral home and drove the van as close to the door as he could get so if anyone around did see him; they would just think he was hauling in supplies or something.

He gently picked up his prize and took her on the elevator straight down to the embalming room that he had prepared for her. He went back upstairs to park the van where he usually parked it, came back in, locking the door behind him. Now, she was his, all his. Chase took her purse and laid it right outside of the embalming room next to a chair. He slowly cut off the summer, denim dress and bra she was wearing. He starred at her beautiful body. Even though she was fifty-five, she took good care of herself, evident in her muscle tone. Next he cut off her thong panties. He would have never guessed a woman of her age wearing thong panties. He rubbed her panties on his face, savoring the smell of her. She was starting to stir a little bit. Chase wasted no time in putting her feet in the stirrups and putting her in the leather restraints as he had all of the women he killed.

While he sat admiring her body, he thought he heard footsteps upstairs. He knew it was just his imagination. All of the doors were secure. As he sat there admiring her under the bright lights, waiting for her to slowly wake up, he heard a voice behind him say, "Hello Chase". He turned around in complete shock and surprise to see his friend Charlie standing there. Chase said, "I'd heard that you had escaped, why on earth would you come back here?" Charlie said, "I knew you had probably heard about the escape. I just wanted to drop by and see you before I go back to prison again. I know they will catch up with me sooner or later." Chase said, "How did you escape?" Charlie answered, "They were transporting me down south to another prison, when the van me and some other in-mates were in, had an accident. I managed to get out of the van in a hurry and I just took off into the woods. The driver and the accompanying guard were both knocked out and never saw what direction me and the other guys went in." Chase said, "How did you know where my funeral home was?" Charlie said, Hillary told me one time." Chase responded, "Don't you think they will look for you here?" Charlie said, "Everyone is looking for me Chase". Charlie asked, "I thought you were going to wait for me to join you?" Chase said, "Well, after your recent murder, I knew they would never let you out, so I decided to go on without you. You have to leave, especially with Dr. Clark here. I can't have the authorities finding both of you here." Charlie said, "Well, what's it worth to you?" Chase said, "How much Charlie?" Charlie said, "five thousand. That will get me on a bus or a plane out of here."

Chase said, "Let me secure the "Little Lady" here and I'll get it for you". Charlie said, "I could also use a quick fuck." Chase said, "Go ahead, while I go upstairs and get you the money. Charlie took one look at her almost comatose state and replied, "No man, I like them to be awake to see the fear in their eyes before I can fuck one."

Chase was thinking fast. He thought about killing Charlie and putting him somewhere easy to find so that the FBI would not come here looking for him again. He changed his mind. For once, he didn't know what he was going to do about Charlie being here now. Chase had planned the doctor's death for so long, he didn't feel like he wanted to share her with Charlie or anyone else. She was his, and only his, to do with as he pleased. Chase decided to just wait and see how things played out. Of course he would be on his guard.

He went back to the embalming room. Charlie said, "I see you finally kidnapped the wonderful Dr. Clark you have been thinking about all of these years. I gotta tell ya buddy, this is one chick that I thought you would never kidnap or really anyone else for that matter. Chase replied, "Yes, you knew I would." Chase never thought for a second that Charlie thought that he would never go through will killing or kidnapping and killing Dr. Clark. Charlie said, "Well, now that I am here, we can both have some fun." Chase said, "Charlie, I told you, she is mine, only for me." This made Charlie angry and he replied, "Do you know how long it's been since I've fucked a woman? I want to fuck her when she wakes up." Chase said, "I know, but the FBI is still looking for you. They have already interviewed me three times since you have escaped." Charlie said, "They won't look here again, they think I'm long gone, to another country by now." Chase said, "If the police come here; it will ruin my plans and spoil my life's work." Chase said, "Okay, if I give you another thousand, will you leave then?" Charlie said he would and Chase told him to wait right there and he would go upstairs and get the money out of the safe. Chase went upstairs. Charlie did not fuck the Doctor. Charlie was just like Chase. He could not fuck a woman unless he was hurting her, and she was still knocked out. He picked up Marion's purse off of the chair, noting how heavy it was and just put it next to the chair and sat down to wait for Chase. A few minutes later, Chase was back with an envelope full of money. Chase said, "Charlie, how did you get in my funeral home anyway? This place is locked up tight". Charlie responded, "Common Chase, you know how good I am at picking locks, or don't you remember me showing you?" Chase asked him what door he broke into so he could fix it right away. Charlie told him. Chase said, "I see, you didn't fuck the Dr. did you?" Charlie said, "No, I'd have to torture her first. Chase, I promise I will leave if you tell me your plans for the Dr. in detail. I might get killed by the police trying to apprehend me and that is one last thing you could do for me, just tell me, that's all, then I'll be gone." Chase looked exasperated because he wanted Charlie out of there so he told him everything as quickly as possible, down to the last detail. Charlie said, "Chase, that's a great plan but why don't you let me have her, I'll be going back to prison, and you will have the rest of your life to kill more women." Chase said, "No, I've waited too long for this and I'm not turning her over to you. You have planned nothing; I've done all the work." Chase could see Charlie getting angrier and so he turned his back on Charlie and started for the elevator and said, "Common, you have your money now you have to get out of here." Charlie got up, grabbed Marion's heavy purse and swung it at Chase's head, knocking him out and he fell to the floor. Charlie was not going to let a crazy nut like Chase stand in his way of having one last torture fest with a real woman. He got some tape from the embalming room and tied Chase's hands and feet and put a gag with tape over it in his mouth. He dragged him to a closet in the hall that had shutters for doors, then Charlie locked the shutter doors. When Chase woke up, he would not be able to make a sound, only see through the slats in the door. He would see all of the fun that Charlie was having because of his careful planning. Charlie thought Chase was crazy and an idiot. Charlie decided to do the same things that Chase had planned, that way it would really piss off Chase. Charlie didn't know what had happened to his friend but he had changed, and changed for the worse. Chase had become too nice, too polite. Chase no longer had that killer instinct. Charlie guessed that maybe Chase's church was starting to rub off on him. Charlie decided that he probably would get caught and sent back to prison, so six thousand was not nearly as attractive as doing what he was going to do to the Dr. He liked Chase's plan a lot.

Marion was slowly waking up and didn't remember Chase being at her house this morning or drinking anything. She was in what seemed like a fog. Her mind was cloudy and she could not think straight. When she tried to move, she could not. She inspected her wrist and ankles and they were all tied with heavy, leather straps. The kind of straps that you saw in movies to hold people down. She slowly looked around the room, making her eyes focus. She was on some kind of medical table, was she in an accident on the way to the airport? She realized then that she was not in a hospital. The walls were painted a light tan and were lined with white cabinets with glass fronts. You could see inside some of the cabinets. There were stacks of dressings and tools and dark brown bottles of liquids. She looked to her right and saw some type of machine with thick hoses attached to it and a black stool with rollers. The kind of stool you would see in a doctors or dentist office. There was a tray next to the stool that held all kinds of stainless steel instruments, not unlike the dentist office. There was a large mirror, angled above her head, near the ceiling. It was quiet; you could not hear anything, Where in the hell was she and why was she naked? She screamed, "Help! Please someone help me!" She listened, wait . . . she did hear something. She heard the sound of her breathing. Was she breathing that hard? She tried to slow her breathing and tried to think about what was going on. After a few short minutes she remembered. She was on her way to the airport to go to the spa in California and Chase was picking her up . . . . Chase! She knew it; she knew she should not trust that bastard. Was he the one haunting all her dreams for the last few years? She listened for any other noise and she also heard the sound of someone else breathing. There was someone else in here with her. She didn't know where she was or who could have done this but she could almost bet this was Chase's doing. Oh My God! She started to remember some of their worst conversations when Chase was still under her care and they were to terrifying to think about. She was in a panic. She was trying to calm her mind and think about what she should do but she was too terrified to even move. It was like a bad nightmare when someone was going to do something bad to you and you could not move. Charlie watched her eyes in the overhead mirror. He could see everything. He could tell by her eyes that she was feverishly thinking about what in the hell was going on. He loved watching her slowly wake up. He watched her eyes as it slowly dawned on her what was happening. When she finally looked above again, she could see herself and a man looking over her head. It felt like her heart skipped a beat and she started sweating. She was terrified, too terrified to move or make a sound, or so she thought. She did not realize she was screaming with her mouth-taped shut. She did not know who the man was for sure; he was wearing some type of surgical mask. She looked into his eyes and Charlie saw terror and surprise in her eyes. She had seen those eyes before, but where? She noted that he was also naked. When he bent over her, and she could see more of him in the mirror, she knew that it was Charlie! her patient from eight years ago. She knew it; she knew that Charlie and Chase had never been truly cured. They could not be cured. She did not know why she did not trust her instincts. She realized where she was now; she was in Chase's funeral home. Marion was sure, Charlie or Chase intended to kill her. You did not need much intelligence to figure that he would kill her. Her heart was pounding inside her chest so hard, she was sure he could hear it. She was so scared. She started to sweat even on the palms of her hands. Her heart was pounding so hard, she was sure Charlie could hear that. She tried to calm herself, to think of a way out of this situation. She knew Charlie as well as she had known Chase and she knew what made them tick. She concentrated on her breathing and tried to remain calm. Now he was here, her stalker and he has her just as he had said he would for the last ten years of calls. She realized that by Chase sending the other women away was all part of Charlie and Chase's plan. She should have guessed by that, that Chase is just not normally that generous. She also knew as his doctor, that he could never be cured. How could she have been so stupid as to fall for something like this? How did Charlie get out of prison? She guessed she was just too wrapped up in Hillary to think about anything else. She had been hyper-aware, for the last ten years, since the calls started and as soon as she relaxed, he had her. She knew he had been planning this for a long time, at least since the calls and break-ins started. She had just been led like a lamb, or should she say like a pig, to slaughter. She was a psychologist and she thought she should be able to talk her way out of this situation but Charlie had tape over her mouth. She wouldn't do what he needed her to do, which was scream, cry beg. She knew his mental illness well and she knew that he needed these things to make this whole plan complete. She would not give it to him. This would be her revenge. He talked to her now. He said, "Do you want me to remove the tape over your mouth?" She shook her head "yes". He said, "Okay, as long and you are quiet. If you aren't, then I will be forced to put it back over your mouth and maybe your nose. He laughed at that comment. He reached over and got one of his fingernails under the tip of the duct tape, and then he yanked it off, along with a little skin. She yelled, "Ouch!" He said, "Dr. Clark, we are going to have a lot of fun together aren't we?" She said in a whisper, "Yes, where is your partner in crime, Chase?" He said, "I have been waiting for you for ten years now and now I have you, it's so exciting for me." She said, "It's exciting for me also Charlie but where is Chase?' He got angry that the Dr. did not think he could have planned this by himself, that she thought Chase was so much smarter than he was. He looked her In the eye and he said, "Chase isn't here, he does not know anything about this, I planned this all for me. I have been the one calling you all these years. He could see in her eyes that she believed him. He said I'll bet you have been waiting for me for a long time." She replied, "Yes, I'm glad you finally took me. The phone calls were getting really boring." He replied, "Well, I guarantee you, I will not be bored in the least." Her voice was starting to rise, "How did you get Chase to let you use his funeral home. Is he in on this with you?" Again, that made Charlie feel like she thought he could not do this without Chase. He answered, "No, he's not in on it. I broke in with my excellent breaking and entering skills. We have so little time together, only a short few days before . . ." She said "Before what? They catch you and take you back to where you belong?" Charlie replied, "Before our time will be up". She said, "God knows people like you. People who commit sins like yours and he will forgive you for your sins if you turn me loose". He said, "Enough talk, God has never cared about me before." "Man," she said, "You are a lot more fucked up then I thought you were. More than Chase even." He rewarded her with a slap across the face for that one. She did not make a sound, cry, or anything else and that really pissed him off." He said, "Don't worry; I will give you something to cry about". She said, "You better, or you won't get your rocks off." He slapped her again. He thought, "This is starting to be not quite as fun as I had thought it would be." He wanted her to scream and yell and curse, do all of the things that he did after one of his visits with her. She said, "Charlie, why are you doing this to me? It was your parent's idea to send you to my office to be treated." He said, "Yes, but it was you who made Chase and I talk about our thoughts about sex and other things that young boys do not want to talk about to a woman. I think you got your own rocks off listening to us. It was you who made us feel like outcast when we were with our peers. It was you who made us feel like crazy people and I surely am not crazy, at least not nearly as crazy as Chase, Just different, that's all." If it were not for you, I would have lived my life the way I wanted to and without having to explain anything to anyone. My parents sure did not care about me. They sent me to you to keep me out of their hair and to pretend that they we're being good parents." She said, "I didn't . . ." Before she could get a sentence out, he said, "Shut up now, it is time to see how far you can go, see how far I can take you before you admit to being the worst therapist in the world, admit that you fucked up all your young patients heads." He quickly put another piece of duct tape over her mouth. He attached electrodes to her pussy lips and he could see terror in her eyes. She was trying to free herself from the restraints. She was wiggling her body back and forth and raising her head to see what he was doing. Now that is what he wanted to see. Now he was getting really turned on and getting hard. It had been so long since he had had a woman. Men in prison just we are not the same. He stuck his dick in her then. He reached over and turned the knob up on the electric machine and she jumped.

By this time, Chase had come around and he was listening intently to their conversation. He was as angry as he had been in his whole life. He would kill Charlie with his bare hands for taking this away from him. That piece of shit, he better not kill her, she was his.

Charlie could also feel the electricity in his penis, but not as much as she was feeling it. He said, "Doesn't this feel good Doc?" She shook her head yes and closed her eyes, trying to remain calm. Since this did not seem to bother her, he reached over and turned the knob all the way up. Her body jumped, she opened her eyes then. He said, "Do you like this better?" She shook her head that she did like it. She countered his thrust. He went soft. "That bitch!" he thought." He pulled out and turned off the machine. Her body relaxed. He looked her in the eye and said, "I wasn't going to go this far this soon, but I think you need a little something now to get you in the mood to be terrified and in pain. I think I will cut off your nipples. What do you think about that?" He knew that Chase was watching, this made this more exciting for him. He thought the nipple thing was a nice touch. She shook her head "no.", she wasn't stupid and didn't want to antagonize him too much because there was no telling what he would do to her. He reached over and picked up a sharp knife and ran his finger over the top of the blade, slightly cutting himself, to show her how sharp it was. She screamed under the tape and she started crying, tears rolling down the sides of her head. He said, "Oh, I see I have your full attention now don't I?" She shook her head "yes". He came toward her with the knife. She tried to move but was strapped down too tightly. He slowly circled her nipple with the tip of the knife taunting her. He proceeded to slowly cut off one of her nipples, he said, "How did that feel? Was that nice?" She shook her head "No." and kept screaming under the tape. He said, "Well, you need a matching pair now don't you?" He reached over and slowly cut off the other nipple. He could tell that she was ready to pass out from the pain. He waved an ammonia packet under her nose to keep her conscious. The packet had been lying on the tray with the instruments. Chase had thought of everything. There was quite a lot of blood running down the sides of her breasts and sides to the white sheet below her. Charlie was mesmerized by the site. She was still screaming under the tape. He yelled at her, "Shut up before I decide that you can do without another body part!" She quieted as much as possible. She knew he meant what he said. He stared at the blood and slowly dipped his fingers in it and brought them to his lips.

He said, "Um-mm, you taste so good." He picked the nipples up and took them over to the refrigerator. He saw the jar with the tissue in it and wondered what it was. He took the tissue out and put Marion's nipples in the jar then put them in the refrigerator. He held the tissue in his hand and said, "I wonder what this is?" He knew it must be a piece of brain. He had seen brains before in prison when guys got their sculls bashed in by other in-mates. He took the piece of brain matter and showed it to her, and then he ripped the tape from her mouth. Before she even had a chance to say anything; he stuffed the brain tissue in her mouth and held her mouth shut until she swallowed it. He knew that Chase had not thought of this because he did not mention it in the details. Charlie thought it was a nice touch. Charlie quickly re-taped her mouth. Charlie told her that piece of brain was the only brains she had and maybe it would make her a little smarter. He laughed loudly at his own joke. Charlie loved the taste and the smell of her blood, but didn't want her to die too soon and thought that he should give her some fluids. He did not know how to give her an iv so he ask her, "Would you like a drink of water?" She shook her head "yes". He said, "Okay, but don't try any funny business." He ripped the tape from her mouth again and gave her a drink of water through a straw. She drank down the whole glass of water, trying to get rid of the taste of the nasty tissue he had made her swallow. When she had finished, he pushed her head back down on the table and she started pleading for her life, but all she got out was "Please, don't kill." before he re-taped her mouth shut again. "So sweet" he said. He got hard again. He went down to the bottom of the table and fucked her again. This time he got the satisfaction he deserved. He told her, "Be a good girl and I might just sew those nipples back on for you. Would you like that?" She shook her head "yes". He said, "I will take the tape off of your mouth so that you can get another drink, if you do not make a sound. Do you think you could do that?" She shook her head "yes" again. She was so thirsty from trying to scream through that tape. Her mouth was so dry; she could hardly swallow her own saliva. The pain of him cutting her nipples off was almost more than she could bear.

She knew if she were ever going to find a way out of this situation, she had to keep a clear head and that meant doing what Charlie wanted and giving him the satisfaction that he craved. She would be constantly aware of a moment when she could possibly escape or get the upper hand. Charlie jerked the tape from her mouth again, which was sore from the last time he jerked the tape off and she yelped, "owww!" He raised her head and let her drink water through a straw. She drank the whole glass straight down again. She said, "Charlie, I have to pee, would you take me to the bathroom?" Charlie did not think about her having to use the restroom. He said, "I will take you to the bathroom, but don't try anything or what I do to you will seem like child's play compared to cutting off your nipples." She believed what he said. She was truly terrified but trying to think of what she should say to him.

She said, "I won't try anything Charlie, I promise." He undid the leather restraints and helped her stand up.

She was feeling dizzy and she swayed a little. Charlie held her tightly by the arm and led her the short distance out of the room to the restroom. He went in with her and held onto her while she did her business. Charlie thought he heard footsteps above his head upstairs. He listened but did not hear any more. He thought, under the circumstances, he was probably just being paranoid or maybe it was just Chase making noise in the closet again. On the other hand, he thought he better get on with business. Dr. Clark said, "What's wrong?" He said, "Nothing, just shut up."

He could tell she was in a lot of pain from her breast when she moved, and he was enjoying her facial grimaces. She said, "Charlie, are you going to kill me?" He said, "No, I have so much more planned for you. Just to kill you would be way too boring and I thought since you were my Dr. all of those years, you deserved something special." When she was standing, he jerked her arm and said, "Come on, let's go." When they turned to leave the bathroom, They heard a noise from somewhere. Charlie knew now that it was Chase making noise in the closet. Charlie said, "It's time for us to get going." Marion said, "Where?" Charlie said, "You don't need to know". Dr. Clark was so scared because she knew if they left here, there was little chance anyone would find her. She was in terrible pain from all of the injuries inflicted upon her, when she stood up after using the restroom, she almost passed out. She was more afraid of Charlie than she was Chase, because Chase at least thought things through and Charlie was just too impulsive. She could not really gauge what Charlie would do next. He said, "We have to move somewhere else." She said, "Charlie, I'm dripping blood all over the place, shouldn't you let me wear my dress?" Her clothes were just outside the embalming room, still folded over the chair. He told her. "Okay, put your dress on while I clean up this mess. We do not want the FBI finding me too soon, now do we?" She retrieved her dress While she was getting dressed; he went back in the other room and was cleaning it up, with her in view the whole time. He said, "Don't try anything funny or you will pay for it later." She said, "I won't." She saw him looking at her every few seconds she would have to be fast. She had to time it just perfect, when he looked away from her. He looked away for about five seconds. That was enough time for her to slip the gun out of her handbag and into her dress pocket. The dress was made of denim and the skirt of the dress was full, so the gun was not noticeable. She always carried a small gun in her purse for protection. She started doing that when she first started getting the phone calls from her stalker, which she now knew to be Charlie. She had been so use to carrying it that she had forgotten about taking it to the airport. She stood there waiting for the right time to use it.

Chase was tied up in the closet with the gag still in his mouth. He tried to make enough noise so that Charlie would let him out or at least remove the gag from his mouth, so he could tell him what to do. Chase had already told him every detail of his plan, but like Charlie, he was not exactly sticking to it as Chase would. He saw Dr. Clark slip the handgun out of her purse and into her pocket. He was so angry with Charlie right now that he was actually starting to root for Dr. Clark. He hoped that she killed Charlie and then sometime down the road, he would get his chance with the Dr. a second time. Chase really started to try to make noise when he realized that they were leaving the funeral home. He would not be able to see her or know what in the fuck Charlie was doing. He better not fucking kill her. If he did, he would plan something really special for Charlie. Charlie grabbed her arm and said, “Common, let’s go”. He put her in the trunk of Chase’s car and tied her hands and feet together. There was no way she could reach her gun with her hands tied. The trunk was very small and she was a tall woman. She was crammed in here pretty tight. She looked for a trunk release but there was none in this old car. She tried to lie on her breasts in the trunk as much as possible so she could keep them from bouncing. The pain she was in when her breasts shook was almost unbearable. Charlie headed out towards the farm. She did not know where Charlie was taking her but she hoped this ride ended soon. It seemed to go on forever and ever.

When Charlie and Hillary arrived at the farm, an hour later, he opened the trunk and untied Dr. Clark’s hands and feet. He realized Dr. Clark was too weak to climb out of the trunk and too crammed in there so he would have to help her. He pulled Dr. Clark out of the trunk by her hair and one arm. She was hoping that he did not feel the gun that was in her pocket. If he did, she would never get out of this alive. Her body was so stiff from the trunk that she could barely walk, so Charlie pulled her along. She was in agony and she tried not to think about what Charlie would do to her next. She thought she might be going into shock. The whole front of her dress was soaked with her blood. Charlie pulled her up to the processing building. She did not have time to retrieve the gun and take a shot at him. She would have to wait for the perfect moment. She was sure she would only get one chance to kill him. She thought about doing it when he opened the trunk but she was so cramped up in there, she could not get to her gun and she was sure she would not be quick enough. "Charlie, what is this place?" He replied, "This is where they dress the hogs." She said, "What is dressing the hog?" He did not answer her. She took a quick look around and saw the house and then she knew that she was at Chase's parents place in the country. She remembered the place from when she and Hillary had come here for dinner to announce their engagement. He took her over to a chair near a big white basin and told her to remove her dress. She did it slowly. She did as she was told because she did not have a chance to get the gun out of her dress yet. He dragged her by her hair over to the basin and she complied. He told her to stand in the middle of the basin. She did, but with the way the basin sloped, it was hard to stand on. He tied her hands together in front of her. He lowered the large hook and hooked it through the rope that was tied around her hands and wrists. He slowly raised her up until her feet were about a foot above the basin. She turned and twisted and struggled but could not break free. She felt so much pain in her shoulders from hanging from her arms. She thought her arms would come out of their sockets. He tied each ankle to a spreader bar. He noticed her feet were bleeding from walking on the sharp rocks outside, and he loved it. He began to touch and pinch her everywhere. She said, "Why are you doing this? I've been nothing but good to you Charlie." He said, "Good? You were good to me because my parents paid you to be and that is the only reason." She said, "I was just doing my job". He said, "Shut the fuck up or I will put the tape back over your mouth. I will allow you to scream but no talking to me anymore." She said, "Why would I scream?" He took a knife out of the bag that he was carrying. She had not noticed him carrying a bag, a very large bag, Her eyes got huge and she had a look of disbelief on her face. She said, "Charlie, what are you going to do? Do not do something that you will be sorry for later, you will be in more trouble. Think about Hillary. We are getting married. She represented you for free. What about her?" He replied, "Doc, I couldn't be in any more trouble, I've maxed out, they will never let me out of prison now". He said, "Did you like my phone calls that you received all those years?" She asked, "Oh My God, was that you? "He replied, "Of course it was me, who else would it have been, Chase? Chase is a piss ant. He does not have the balls to do anything like that. He told her just what he thought Chase would say. "I've been dreaming and planning this day for the last ten years. Although I have killed a couple hookers, they deserved to die. She thought desperately of what she should say and she said, "Charlie, I am not a prostitute. He took one of the knives out and approached her. The look on her face was so much more satisfying then how she looked in her office for his visits. He started at her throat, barely skimming the surface of her skin and cut her all the way down to her pubis bone. She screamed appropriately. There was blood trickling down her body and into the white basin below her. He like the contrast between the white and the red. She screamed, “Charlie stop, I’ll do anything you want!” He replied, “No, I’ll do anything that I want. It’s my turn to play Doctor now.” He started cutting her all over. There was a lot more blood dripping from her body and she was in so much pain that she passed out. This made Charlie angry. He took out the electrical machine out of the box that he had found and used on the doctor at the funeral home. He hooked an electrical clamp up to her lower lip, a finger on each hand, the the top of her labia and on each big toe. He turned the machine on and gave her electrical shocks. He loved the way her tits bounced and her body jerked every time he shocked her. She unfortunately finally came around and her nightmare and pain started all over again.

He wanted to fuck her, he was so hard and excited, and the smell of her blood was intoxicating. He lowered her down until she was standing in the basin, in a pool of her own blood. He started licking the warm, red blood that she had all over her body. He unhooked her hands but left her ankles tied to the spreader bar. He threw her over his shoulder and laid her over one of the stainless steel tables. He dropped his pants and started fucking her. He asked her, “Do you love this? Tell me that you love this.”

She barely squeaked, “I love this Charlie, give me more”. Her answer turned him on even more. While he was fucking her from behind, he took his knife and cut two stars on her ass, one on each side. She kept screaming. Charlie said, “You can scream all you want to, there is no one around to hear you”. She screamed louder and Charlie said, "Yeah, common baby scream for Daddy." When he had finished, he was spent and he needed to take a break. He told her that he was going to take a rest in a nearby chair. He removed the spreader bar from her ankles and she slumped to the floor. When he sat down, again, she asked, "Charlie are you going to kill me?" He said, "Oh no. I have waited too long for you. It is not about killing now but it is about doing things to you that I have always dreamed of since you quit being my Doctor. If I kill you, it will all be over to soon and I do not want that, but yes, you will die but you will be alone. You will eventually die but not from me actually killing you." She said, "What do you mean, kill myself? That is absurd. Why would I kill myself?" He said, "I didn't say you would be by yourself. I said you would be alone and on your own. He wanted to see the fear on her face with what he told her next, it would surely elicit the right response. He said, "With Chase's help, I have dug a grave for you in the woods. It has a coffin in it. I picked out a special coffin just for you. I have equipped it with an oxygen tank, along with a light, camera, speakers, and microphone so that I can stay in contact with you the whole time you are down there, or at least, until you run out of your oxygen. What do you say?" She said, Thank you Charlie." He said, "I plan on burying you alive." She gave him an agonizing look and begged him not to bury her alive but she was secretly grateful because this may give her longer to live and more of a chance to be saved by someone. She did not know who that someone could be. Hillary and Megan were gone away. She knew Charlie was smiling at the look on her face. He said, "You have rested enough, get up and dance on the pole like the girls do in the strip clubs." She was not quite sure how that went but she knew that now was her only chance at escape. She knew she had to dance like a professional pole dancer on the pole that had been put up only a few days before. Charlie said, "You look like you have done this before. She had done this many times for her fiance After about ten minutes of dancing, she said, "Would you like a lap dance Charlie?" He answered, "Sure, why not." Her dress lay in a heap behind his chair. She gave him a lap dance, while getting her blood all over him. He was in such ecstasy that he closed his eyes so that he could concentrate on the slickness and smell of her blood. He licked her blood when she came close enough to him. She strutted around him and when she did, she grabbed her dress. She quickly found her loaded gun. She was behind him, rubbing herself on him when he felt something cold next to his ear. She whispered, "You move and you are a dead man". He jumped, turning around to look at her. She stepped back, while pointing the loaded gun at him. He was surprised and he said, "Where did you get that?" She said, "It doesn't matter but I assure you, it is loaded. He started toward her and she shot him in the left shoulder. As he dropped to the floor, she said, "See, I told you it was loaded. That was for all of the phone calls you gave me and for breaking into my house numerous times. You will go prison. You will not kill me because you are better than that. Better than I am. You know you would go to prison for the rest of your life." She said, "No, not after they have seen and taken pictures of my mutilated body, they would know it was self-defense." Charlie was starting to fidget while holding his shoulder and he broke out in a cold sweat. He was trying to think quickly how to reverse this situation. How could he have been so careless? He knew that Chase would not have been so careless and that really pissed him off. He said, "What are you going to do, turn me in?" She said, "No, I think the plans that you had for me would be just as good for you." If I were you, I would tell me where the grave site is and maybe I will give you a chance to plead your case." She had her dress in her hand and she slipped it over her head, without ever breaking eye contact with Charlie. He said, "We have to get on the four-wheeler to get back there." She said, "Okay, get on and I will sit behind you and don't try anything or I will shoot you right through that thick skull of yours." He said, "I can't steer with one arm." She answered, "You will and you will do a good job of it or else." He didn't want to know what the "or else" meant. She said, "You get on first, then I will get on behind you and hand you the keys. He climbed on the four-wheeler while she stood next to him. She climbed on behind him and held the gun to his head while he drove. She said, "Don't hit any big bumps or this gun is likely to go off on its own". He knew what she meant. He did not think for even one second that she would not kill him if he did not do what she said.

They got to the back of the property and started through the woods and went back in the woods pretty far. It was starting to get dark out. They finally stopped and Dr. Clark said, "Well, where is it?" He said, "He looked around and saw it and said, It's over there", looking over toward his right. She said, "Turn the four-wheeler off and hand me the keys. She got off the four-wheeler and she said, Common, show me". He took her to the spot and he uncovered the grave. It was, in fact, six feet deep with a silver coffin in the bottom of it, with the top open. She said, "Okay, get in". He turned and lunged at her but he was not close enough, and she shot him in the shin, which shattered. He fell into the grave and landed in the coffin. She said, "I guess that's one way of getting in there." He howled in pain. She said, "Shut up before I tape your mouth. On second thought, scream some more, it turns me on." She said, "I know you men are such babies, you can't even take a little pain. "Lay down in the coffin like you are supposed to". It took him a few minutes, but he did as she asked. She asked, "Where are the oxygen tank and the rest of the stuff? He removed a panel on each side of the coffin to show her. She said, "Where is the microphone so I can talk to you and hear you?" He said, "It's up in the barn on the work table." She said, "Okay, put everything back and close the lid". He didn't think she would really bury him because she was not a big, strong woman and she was already weak from loss of blood. He did not think she could cover him up with the dirt all by herself. He was thinking that if he opened the coffin and got up to the top of the grave fast enough, he could over power her and if she did not hit a vital place, then he could take the gun from her. It was better than lying here. He would bleed to death from his wounds. He tried it and he did not get any further than opening the lid of the coffin back up, he was too weak from loss of blood and he could not move fast because of his wounds, especially his leg wound. She said, "Sorry, Charlie, you can't get out that easily". Put the lid back down. He did what she told him to do. He thought that he really did not have a choice at the moment and maybe he could find a way out of here. He had to think fast. "That bitch! I will surely kill her when I get out of here, Chase or no Chase. He never liked being in complete darkness as he was now. He was also feeling a little claustrophobic. He started breathing hard and he thought he would pass out. He got the oxygen tank out of the side panel with the nasal cannula on it and he put it in his nose. At that moment, he was glad that Chase was such a good planner. Damn that woman, it should be her in here, not him!" He started yelling, "Let me out of here you God Damned Bitch!" She yelled back, "No, sorry, and you can scream all you want, remember, but no one will hear you." The next thing he heard was dirt hitting the top of the coffin. He thought that she would tire soon, especially with the amount of blood that she had lost, but then, she was in great shape for her age. He thought even with some dirt, he should be able to get out of here. The dirt kept falling and falling until he could not hear it hit the top of the coffin anymore. He could not hear anything. He started screaming himself for someone to let him out of this damn death trap.

Chase struggled in the closet for a long time before he was somehow able to get his hands loose, then his feet and remove the gag from his mouth. His mouth was so dry, the first thing he did was open a bottle of water. He grabbed the keys to the van and he took off for the farm. He vowed to himself that if Charlie killed Dr. Clark, he would kill that son-of-a-bitch Charlie with his bare hands. Chase drove just fast enough not to get caught by the police until he was out of town, then he went 90 miles an hour on the back country roads. He hoped that he got to the farm before it was too late. He was sweating and his heart was pounding and all he could think about was getting to the farm as quickly as possible. If Charlie had killed the Dr., all of his careful planning and work would be for nothing. He hoped that the Dr. was not dead and that Charlie was still at the farm. It would be like Charlie to take off quickly once he killed the Dr., and he had money to go anywhere, thanks to him.

After a while, Charlie heard through the speaker inside the coffin. "Yeah, common and scream for Momma, you bastard." He knew then that she was back in the barn. He screamed, "Let me the fuck out of here!" She said, "Oh, sorry, you want out of there? You made it so comfortable in there for me, I thought you would enjoy it, especially the peace and quiet. The FBI would never think to look for you in a coffin. In a way, I am protecting you. You better shut up now before you use up all of your oxygen". "Let me out of here you crazy bitch!" "You want out of there? Too fucking bad." He heard a click and he knew that she had shut off the speaker. Now he knew what it was like to know that you are going to die. He would die of no oxygen if he did not bleed to death from his wounds first. That bitch was crazier than him and Chase put together. How could he have been so stupid not to check what was in her purse when he knew it had felt heavy and had even hit Chase in the head with it. Chase, he had almost forgotten, he would get loose and come and get him out so he could put the doctor in here. He hoped that Chase was not too late.

Hillary tried and tried to call Marion, Dr. Clark, her fiance, and did not get an answer. She thought she was probably busy at the spa getting a massage or something from some young, great looking woman. Although, they had agreed that she would call Hillary before she boarded the plane this morning, on her way to the airport, she had not called. Marion's flight should have arrived in California at 8:00am. Hillary would try and call her again in a couple of hours. Hillary tried calling Marion several times that morning and she got Marion's voice mail. Hillary had a bad feeling in the pit of her stomach, and her instincts were usually right. Megan was getting ready to go to the bridal show, which was a three day event. Their rooms at the hotel were right next to each other and had a connecting door. Hillary had been really bothered the night before when she started thinking about Chase. Why would Chase be so generous as to send them all off somewhere. It just was not like him. As a matter of fact, he hardly ever talked to any of them. She wondered what his motive was and then she really started to be afraid for Marion, especially since she could not get a hold of her on her cell. When 10:30am rolled around, Hillary placed a call to the spa in California again, where Marion was supposed to be staying, and they said that she had never checked in. Hillary knew that the spa was close to the airport and that Marion should be there by now. She politely asked the receptionists to have Marion return her call after she checked in. Hillary wanted to call someone back home but realized there was not anyone there, except Katie and Katie and Chase never talked to each other. Hillary thought that it was worth a try to call Katie anyway. Katie had told her that she had not seen Chase in a few weeks. Hillary told Katie that she had not been able to contact Marion. She was worried. Katie did her best to reassure Hillary that Marion was fine, probably just relaxing with a drink somewhere at the spa and just had not had time to call her yet. When Hillary hung up with Katie; she got really scared because no one answered at the funeral home or Chase's house. She called the airline and got a ticket back home at 12:00 noon.

Hillary did not want to alarm or upset Megan with her fears, especially since she was engaged to Chase. Hillary knocked on Megan's door and when Megan let her in, Hillary explained that she had an emergency with one of her clients and had to return home right away. She said it would not take long to take care of it and that, she would be back later that night or at the latest the next afternoon. Megan was disappointed that she would be going to the bridal show alone but she understood. Hillary left right away for the airport. By the time she arrived at the airport, she had no fingernails left.

Katie knew her brother better than anyone else could ever know him. Molly had told her the week before about Chase's generosity and sending all of the women somewhere for a wedding gift. Katie thought it was strange at the time because Chase never gave anybody anything that she knew of. She had a feeling that Chase was up to something. She knew he was a planner he liked to plan things. She also knew about his dark side. How he loved to kill animals. She wondered if her brother could ever kill a human. She decided that he probably could. She was hoping that Chase didn't have Hillary's fiance but she decided that Chase would not have harmed her, especially since he spent ten years in her care.

"PART X"

When Hillary got off of the plane at home, she dialed Chase right away and did not get any answer. Next, she tried calling the funeral home and got a recording, which she thought was strange. She decided that she would take a ride out to Molly and Caleb's farm, to see if Chase was there but just in case Chase was at the funeral home, she would stop there first on the way to the farm.

When Hillary got to the funeral home, it was closed. All of the doors were locked and she did not see any lights on. She went around back and she saw Chase's maintenance man doing some yard work. She asked him, "Where is everybody?" He told her that Chase gave everyone the week off because he wanted to take a vacation. Hillary thanked him and left for the farm. She was even more worried now. Why would Chase take a whole week's vacation at the same time that Megan was gone? Hillary drove fast out to the farm. It took her forty-five minutes to get there instead of an hour. She was going as fast as she thought she could get away with without being stopped by the police. When Hillary turned down the long driveway to the farm, she saw Chase's car parked in front of the barn. Hillary thought, "That's good, he is probably here just doing some work for his parents while they were on their trip." When she pulled behind Chase's car, she saw Marion peek around the door of the barn to see who it was. When she saw that it was Hillary, she ran towards her crying. Hillary was in shock. Was this her beautiful Fiance Marion? She was covered in caked on, dried blood. She was battered, bruised, and crying. She ran to Hillary and Hillary hugged her. Hillary said, "Oh My God, what happened to you Marion?" Marion said in a sobbing voice, "its Charlie, he did this to me. He had been planning on killing me if he ever got out of prison. He is the one who has made all of those phone calls. He is the stalker! He has killed other women as well, in his lifetime. I didn't even know he was out of prison!" Hillary was frozen to the spot as she said, "Oh My God, Charlie did this to you? I cannot believe it. Where is that bastard, I'll kill him myself." Marion said, "Don't worry about him, I have him secured". Hillary said, "What do you mean you have him secured?" Marion told Hillary all of the gory details. She told her that Charlie had kidnapped her and took her to Chases funeral home and then brought her here in Chase's car. Hillary asked, "Where is Chase then?" Marion said, "I don't know". Hillary said to Marion, "Show me where Charlie is buried. Then, I am calling an ambulance to take you to the hospital." Marion could hardly talk she was crying so hard, just grateful to be alive. Marion told Hillary that Charlie cut off her nipples, which Hillary had already guessed by where and the amount of blood that was on Marion's dress. Marion told her where to find her nipples, so that maybe they could be put back on. She asked Hillary to take them to the hospital. Hillary said she would, right after Marion showed her where Charlie was buried alive. Marion was reluctant for two reasons, one, she was terrified of him and two, she was also afraid for Hillary. Hillary had Marion give her the microphone and the gun that she had used to shoot Charlie. Hillary drove the four-wheeler out to where Charlie was buried, trying to go as easy as possible with Marion on the back. After Marion showed Hillary where Charlie was, Hillary took her back up to the house, then called an ambulance. It did not take long for the ambulance to arrive. They must not have been very busy tonight because it usually takes a long time for anyone to come out here to the farm. When the paramedics got there, they tried to strap Marion on a gurney for safety's sake and Marion got hysterical. Hillary gave them a look and said, "No straps". Hillary kissed Marion, which shocked the ambulance drivers in the first place and then Hillary told Marion, I will practically be right behind you, after I retrieve your nipples. The two ambulance drivers stood there with their mouths open. Finally, Hillary looked at them she said, "Hello?" When she got their attention, she told them that Marion had been raped, and tortured for hours. She would need a rape kit done at the hospital. They just nodded their heads. Then she yelled, "Get the fuck out of here and take her to the damn hospital!" The men jumped in the ambulance then took off towards the local hospital.

Hillary had the microphone and she was going to go out to the woods where Charlie was buried, to let him out and talk to him. She turned on the microphone and said,

"How did you get yourself into this situation Charlie?" He yelled, "It was all just a big misunderstanding, that is all Hillary. Please, you have to let me out of here before I suffocate." She answered, "No, I do not have to let you out Charlie. You are getting what you deserve. I guess Marion did this to herself?" "We were just having a little fun, that is all. I didn't kill anybody, I swear". Hillary replied, "You can stay down there. You can rot in hell for all I care. I'm not sorry for you". Charlie started yelling, "Please, please, for the love of God please let me out of here!" Hillary turned off the microphone and turned to leave when she ran right smack dab into Katie. Katie had heard the whole conversation and figured out what was going on. Katie said, "Aunt Hillary, I suggest that you help me dig up Charlie or you will be an accessory to murder and you will lose everything, including Marion. Is he worth all of that?" Hillary thought for a minute and she said, "You are right, he's not worth it. 'll go back to the barn and get some shovels and flashlights". While Hillary was gone, Katie got on the microphone and said, "Charlie, this is Chase's sister Katie. Charlie thought, "Oh God Katie, now I know I will never get out of here". Katie told him, "Hold on, we are going to get you out of there". Charlie said, "Oh, thank God. I am bleeding badly from where Marion shot me. She shot me twice, once in the leg and once in the shoulder. I might need some help in climbing out of here!" It took both Hillary and Katie quite a while to dig down to where Charlie was buried. Hillary was surprised that Marion had the strength to bury him. They opened the lid to the coffin and Charlie sat up, gulping in air. He was looking very pale and weak. Both women struggled with getting him out and back up top on the solid ground. Both women were breathing heavily. Charlie saw the gun sticking out of the back of Hillary's jeans. All three of them were lying on the ground, trying to catch their breath when Charlie quickly reached for the gun and got it. Hillary was surprised at how quick Charlie was. Apparently, he lied about being so weak. Charlie struggled to get up. He had to balance on one leg. He pointed the gun at Hillary and Katie and he said, "Thanks girls but now you need to throw the microphone in the coffin and put the dirt back in the hole and cover it up." They did as he asked, all the while, looking over their shoulders for a chance at escape. They saw none. After they filled in the grave, Charlie told them to put some brush over it. When they did that, it did not look like anyone had ever been there. He told them to turn around and start walking. When the women got a good distance away from where the coffin was buried, he said, "Okay, now dig another grave". They both said, "Charlie you can't kill us, you will never get away with it, besides you know Chase will kill you for this". Charlie said, "I'll see, won't I? It couldn't get much worse than it already is, could it"? Both women started digging and when they had dug about a four-foot deep grave, Charlie said, "Okay, stop and come around here to this side of the hole. They did as they were told.

Charlie said, "You know Katie, I don't mind killing you in the least. Some sister you turned out to be for Chase. You never showed him any sisterly love, your own brother, only your mother loved him. No one ever loved me. I'll shoot you in the stomach so maybe you will die a little slowly." Then Charlie looked at Hillary and said, "Hillary, you have helped me in the past, so I think I will let you go last for showing me kindness and for representing me in court for free". You were also a good aunt to Chase, my best friend. I'll shoot you right in the heart so you won't suffer any at all." He looked at both of them and then he said, "How does that sound girls?" They both dropped to their knees and started begging Charlie not to kill them. He lifted the handgun to take aim and then he felt something in the small of his back and a female voice say, "Charlie, don't do it, or I'll shoot". He backed up a little and looked to his side, it was Chase's Mother standing there, threatening to shoot him. He said, "What are you doing here, is this a fucking party or what?" Hillary looked at her and said, "I thought you and Caleb were taking a vacation to the Rockies this week? She said, "It doesn't matter why I'm here, I just am. Charlie, you know you cannot kill these women; you will never get out of the prison mental institution that they send you to". Charlie answered, "What makes you think I want to go back there for life?" I have escaped, it could take years for them to find me now." Hillary said, "I won't be able to help you if you shoot me." "Molly said, "You know Chase wouldn't like it if something happened to you. You have been his best friend since kindergarten." Charlie answered, "Well, we were best friends until he had gone crazy on me. Talking about hearing voices and shit." Molly said, "That's enough chit-chat. Charlie, drop the gun or I will shoot you." Charlie answered, "Chase said you wouldn't hurt a fly, much less shoot someone. Surely, you wouldn't shoot me now would you?" Charlie still had the gun aimed at the two women. He said, "I know you love Chase, he is one of the luckiest people I know.

My Mother did not give a shit about me as long as I stayed out of trouble and she did not have someone knocking on her door. I know you wouldn't do anything to harm anyone, especially me." Molly said, "Charlie, I was really expecting to see Chase here, not you, so I am happy it is you. I will shoot you. I am giving you one last chance. Put the gun down, put it down now. Please don't make me do this." Charlie really felt like Molly would not shoot him. He aimed his gun at Katie again. Molly pulled the trigger and shot Charlie in his other leg. His gun went flying out of his hands and he fell to the ground, screaming in pain. He yelled, "What the fuck did you do that for?" She answered, "I told you I would shoot you, and I didn't tell you that I would not kill you. You were right; I wouldn't kill anyone unless I had to." She told the two women to go up to the house and call the police. Katie said, "I don't want to leave you here alone with that monster." Molly said, "No, it's okay, I'll be fine, he can't even stand up. Please just go up to the house with Hillary. Leave one of the four-wheelers down here so we can get back up." Katie said, "Okay Mom, but be careful." When both of the women were almost to the house, Molly said, "Why Charlie, please just tell me why. Why did you kill those woman, what drives you to do such a thing?" He answered, "You should ask Chase, he knows. He killed them, not me. He cuts them up and tortures them before he kills them. They were prostitutes or little rich bitches that didn't deserve to live". Molly said, "Charlie, you are so, so sick. You escaped some time ago. I know you have been without your medication". He said, "Yeah, and I feel better than I ever have. Molly, I would rape and torture you if I could". Molly knew what Charlie was doing and she said, "Charlie, I'm not going to kill you. I know that is what you are trying to get me to do, but you will have to go back to prison. You have to pay for your actions, just like everyone else. They will put you in a maximum-security mental ward." Charlie did not count on Molly knowing him so well. He lunged at her to try and get the gun. They wrestled for it and Charlie got the gun. He turned on Molly and said, "This is entirely your fault. All of you God damn women. You interrupt things just the way you always do. I am sorry Molly". He aimed the gun at Molly and she dropped to the ground holding the sides of her head and shutting her eyes. Molly heard, "Charlie, you mother fucker". Charlie fell over from the blow to the head that Chase gave him and Chase retrieved the gun Charlie was holding. Chase said, "Mother, I thought you went to the Rockies?" She said, "We did, I just felt the need to come home and check on things. It is a good thing I did, mother's intuition I guess. Your father stayed there in the hotel. I told him Katie was having some kind of meltdown and that I would come back to the hotel late tonight." Chase was surprised that she came home and his father did not come with her. I will stay here with Charlie until the police arrive. They all knew that living out in the country where they were, it could take up to an hour for an officer to respond, especially due to the fact that this town only had one Sheriff. There were only two officers on the whole force.

Chase was sitting down on the ground and holding a gun on Charlie. Chase told his mother, "Molly, take the four-wheeler on back up to the house, I'll be fine." She did and didn't waste any time in doing it. A few minutes later, Charlie came to. When his head cleared, he sat up and said, "Who hit me over the head? Was it you Chase? How did you get out of the closet?" Chase said, "So many questions to be answered, so little time. You don't tie knots worth a shit". Chase stood up but Charlie could not after being shot in both legs. Charlie said, "Hey man, put that thing away before you hurt somebody." Chase said, "You didn't mind hurting me. Leaving me tied up in a closet, watching my life's dreams die before my eyes." Charlie laughed and said, "Yeah, that was pretty cool, me making the Dr. eat whatever that was in the jar in the refrigerator, wasn't it? What was that stuff anyway?" Chase said, "Cancerous tissue I cut out of a man's brain." Charlie turned green and almost threw up. He did not mind doing something gross to a woman but that made him nauseous. Charlie said, "At least I let you watch me torture the Dr., I could have blind folded you, you know? I got to get out of here before the cops come". Chase said, "You aren't going anywhere Charlie except back to prison". Charlie responded with, "Oh come on Chase, I am your best friend, do not do this to me man. I cannot go back there". Chase said, "I didn't say you were going back there now did I?" Charlie said, "Common, we are best buds for life remember? You'll have to forgive me cause I'm your bro." Chase said, "Charlie, you did the unthinkable. You knew I had been planning the doctor's torture and death for years. The phone calls I made to her, breaking into her house. I had sent everyone away and I finally had her where I wanted her. I had a lot more I wanted to do to her before you got there. You ruined everything, all my hard work, you took away all of my expectations and excitement and don't say you didn't know how important this plan was to me because that is all I have talked about for years. I had killed all those young girls and prostitutes, practicing for the day that I took the Dr. You did nothing, nothing but waltz right in and steal her right from under my nose." Charlie said, "Because you knew they would catch me in time and that I would never have another chance to rape and torture another woman. You had the rest of your life to torture and kill any woman you wanted, just like you have been doing all along. You even have this farm to bury the women. Your one of the luckiest guys I know, do not begrudge me this one last torture. I would have killed her but I am not like you Chase, I got careless. I know you would not have let her get the best of you because you plan too well. Look at it this way, you still have a chance to take her later on when she forgets about what happened to her". Chase said, "You know I'll never get that chance again. You are a dead man Charlie, when you get to hell; tell the devil I said "Hello."

Charlie started to lunge for the gun and Chase fired point blank into his black heart. Chase dropped the smoking gun on the ground at his feet. He felt spent. It had been one hell of a day. He sat down away from Charlie for a minute to think about what he had done and what he would do now. He thought about his own sister, Katie. Of course, he knew that Charlie had hit and raped his sister the night he stayed over, but he did not care what Charlie did. Anything Charlie did at that time was okay with Chase. Chase was just glad to find someone like himself to be his friend. Charlie was his scapegoat. He would tell the police this was all Charlie's doing and that he had nothing to do with the abduction of Dr. Clark. A couple minutes later, he heard some rustling in the brush in front of him, on the other side of Charlie's body. His father came out of the brush, picking up the pistol as he walked towards Chase. The pistol was still warm. He took a seat on the ground a little behind and next to Chase. Chase looked surprised as he said, "Dad, what are you doing here? Mom said you stayed behind in the Rockies at the hotel". Caleb replied, "Chase, I heard the whole conversation between you and Charlie before you shot him in cold blood." Chase protested, "I didn't kill anybody, Charlie did it all". His father replied, "Chase, I got suspicious when your mother brought it up to me that she wondered if these girls around here that were dying were killed by you. She thought it might be you because every time we went away, one of the four-wheelers would be moved and have mud on it. Then, she would ride around out here looking for freshly turned earth and she did find some. She asked me what I thought, and even though I had already suspected you, I told your mother not to worry, it was probably just some animals digging. That night, she said she was going shopping but I knew she would go and confront you. She did not want me to know because she did not want you to look bad in my eyes or throw any more suspicion on you. When she had been gone a while, I came out here to find any freshly turned earth and, once I started looking, I would find a few spots that I never would have really noticed before. I started digging. I found the bones of someone who had been dead probably a hundred years but then I dug some more spots and I found a few of the missing women."

We were due to go to the Rockies soon and I wanted to see if I would find another new grave when I returned. When your mother said she had to come back home for an emergency with Katie, I knew she was lying. I knew she would come here to check on you. I could not let her do that alone so I came home right behind her, she just did not know". Chase no longer denied it but said, "Why didn't you turn me in when you found the girls then? Don't tell me it was because you loved me". His father said, "I won't tell you I loved you, not like a father should love his son. You were a very hard boy to love, although your mother loved you very much". Chase said, "What do you mean loved"? His father pointed the pistol that he had picked up into Chase ribs. He had checked to make sure there was a bullet in it while Chase was talking. His father replied, "You are just like my brother Henry, given the chance, you will never stop torturing and killing innocent people. Soon you will probably escalate to children. I cannot have that on my conscience and I will not put your mother through it. Sure, I could pretend I did not find those bodies; I could pretend that I did not hear yours and Charlie's conversation. I know you could blame this all on Charlie and get away with it except for the fact that some of the women were killed before Charlie even escaped from the prison van. I cannot let you do that. I cannot be responsible for letting you hurt innocent people and wrecking the lives of whole families just to satisfy some sexual need that you have. I do not trust the authorities to keep you locked up forever, just as they could not keep Charlie. Your mother and I can't keep looking over our shoulders all of our lives." Chase was thinking fast. He was trying to figure out where this was going and what to do about it. He did not really think that his own father would actually shoot him but he did not want to spend the rest of his life in a mental institution either. He would have to get that gun away from his father or change his mind on what his father was hell bent on doing. Chase knew that if had that gun now that he would have no problem shooting his own father. He said, "Dad, what are you going to do? I am your only son. I can get well I know I can. Think of what killing me would do to Mother!" His father said, "Chase, I know that you could torture and rape your own mother and not feel a thing. Do not even think of making a move to get this gun. I could shoot you before you even blinked. You leave me no choice. I am sorry for your mental illness, but I also know it is not your mother's fault or mine. What I do know is that I can put an end to this nightmare." Chase responded, "Oh, come on Dad, you'd never kill anyone." Caleb said, "I have. I killed my only brother Henry and for the same reason I am killing you." Chase said, "You killed your own brother? I always knew that you had your own evil side that is probably where I got it. Chase tried to make his dad feel guilty for his mental illness. Go ahead and shoot me Dad and get it over with." Chase really did not believe that his dad had the balls to kill him, his only son. Chase tried a different tactic. "What about Katie, your beloved daughter. You always loved her more than me. Think how she will feel if she ever finds out that you killed me. She will hate your forever and mom will divorce you, you know that don't you"? Chase was not ready to die but he also did not want to spend the rest of his life locked up. Caleb said, "Good-by son, I guess you'll get to tell the devil "Hello" for yourself".

Chase turned his head, looked his dad in the eyes and said, “Dad, you know if I had that gun, you would be a dead man right now”. His father pulled the trigger and Chase was dead before he hit the ground. Caleb wiped his prints off of the smoking gun. He put it in Chase’s hand. He would say he saw the whole thing. It was a murder suicide. Chase shot Charlie and then shot himself before he could talk him out of it. Caleb sat back down on the ground and wept. Chase was such a sweet little boy. He did love him. He loved the son that he thought he knew, not the son who raped and tortured women. He wept more for Molly. He knew that the women at the house had to have heard the shot and would soon be here to find out what had happened. He wiped his eyes and collected himself to tell his precious Molly that their only son was dead.

The women did not hear the first shot when Chase shot Charlie because the four-wheelers were running and drowned out the noise of the gun. They did hear the second shot. They got back on the four-wheelers and went back down the hill, cautiously, because Charlie could be the shooter.

As they got closer, they could see Charlie lying on the ground dead in the middle of the clearing. They saw Caleb standing there next to Charlie. When they were almost to the clearing, they saw Chases body slumped over near the brush. Molly became hysterical. She got off the four-wheeler before it even came to a full stop. She was screaming, “Chase!” She briefly looked at her husband, “Is my son dead?” She knew instantly by looking at her husband’s face that it was true. She quickly ran screaming over to Chase and she hugged Chase tight, she did not want to look on the ground. She did not want to see the blood spilling from his body. She did not want to look at Charlie's dead body either. Molly just held on tight to Chase and squeezed her eyes shut, wishing she was still in the Rockies and this was all just a really bad nightmare. She held Chase and rocked back and forth lamenting the death of her son. She was inconsolable. Katie obviously knew what had happened. The women called the police when they had gone up to the house the first time. Was Caleb the only one who noted at the time that Katie's eyes were dry? She didn't seem upset in the least that her brother was dead. Caleb knew that Katie and Chase never got along but he did not know how deep the hatred for each other ran. He didn't know what had happened between the two of them, and he guessed he would never know.

Caleb went over to his wife and pulled her up in his arms while she cried. She tried to pull away from her husband and she was pounding on his chest saying, "That was our son! How could he be dead? He isn't supposed to be dead!" After a couple of minutes, he said to Katie and the rest of the women, "Go on up to the house and take your mother. I will take care of this." Two officers' came and Caleb gave them a full report of what happened, calling it a murder suicide and he told them where they would find the bodies of the missing young women. The officers were amazed. The local news station had gotten word that something big had gone down on Caleb's farm. The media were there shortly after the officers, asking questions. It would be the biggest story this town had heard of in centuries. They solved a lot of their cases that night. The missing girls and Charlie's where a bouts. Chase was the town's hero for catching the killer, even if he did commit suicide afterwards.

The next day, when things had calmed down, Molly said to Caleb "What are you doing here? I told you I would meet you back at the hotel tomorrow. Caleb said, "You have been acting funny for a while now, especially wanting to ride the four-wheeler all the time and I noticed you always ride out to the same patch of woods. We had talked about whether Chase could have killed those women or not and then you told me you were going shopping, I knew you were going to see Chase. When you said, you had to leave the hotel in the Rockies for a night, and that Katie was having some kind of melt down and you had to go for at least a day, I knew something was up. I followed you right back here. No way was I going to let you come back here alone". Molly said, "I'm sorry I lied to you Caleb, about going shopping. I just didn't want to worry you, that is all." He said, "I know, its okay". She said, "Did you see Chase shoot himself; did you try to stop him?" He answered, "Of course I tried to stop him, but his mind had already been made up. I don't know why he did it". Molly replied, "I'm sorry Caleb, I didn't mean to imply that you would not have tried to stop him, of course you did. Someone is going to have to tell Megan. He said, "I will do it. I will call and tell her just in case she hears it on the news or something before we have a chance to talk to her." Molly said, "Those poor, poor women, no wonder Chase killed Charlie." Caleb knew there were girls missing long before Charlie had escaped from prison, but he did not say anything. He wanted to let her think that Charlie had killed all of the girls. He held her tight on the front porch swing while she sobbed and grieved for her only son.

"PART XI" "FINAL CHAPTER"

About three months later, after Marion had completely healed, Molly and Chase invited Marion and Hillary over to their house for dinner and told them that they had something important to tell them. Hillary asked Marion if she would go to Caleb and Molly's house with her for dinner, that they had something important to tell them. Hillary said, "Marion, I know how hard it will be for you to go back there after what happened, so if you do not want to go I understand. Marion replied, "Hillary, it's okay, I will go with you. Besides, nothing happened in the house, it happened at the funeral home and the processing barn. I will be okay with it, don't worry". Hillary kissed Marion on the cheek and said, "Thanks babe, I appreciate that. I do not know what is so important. It must be something big because Caleb or Molly had ever said that they had to talk to them about something important before. I wonder what is going on". After they were all seated at the table and had dinner and dessert, Molly poured coffee for everyone. Molly sat down and she said, "Caleb and I invited the both of you here to tell you that we have decided to move. We are selling the farm. We had originally intended to leave it to Chase and/or Katie, but Katie does not want anything to do with it. We wanted to offer it to you Hillary, since your family is buried here also, before we put it on the market." Both women looked surprised at this. Hillary said, "I thought you would never move from here". Caleb said, "In light of what has happened here, we have decided to move and get a new start". Hillary said, "Caleb, are you sure"? I mean, this is where you grew up, your childhood home. I do not want you to do anything rash. It's only been three months". Caleb and Molly looked at each other and smiled. They both thought that Hillary's concern was touching. Caleb looked at Molly and replied, "Hill, Molly and I have talked about this at length. We actually pretty much decided to move even before the incident because we want to do a lot of traveling and we would like to buy a condo or something smaller. This farm is just too much for the both of us. Besides, it's just an old farm with some good and a lot of bad memories. You don't live in your home, your home lives in your own mind. We are both ready to move on". Hillary said, "Well, it sounds like you have really thought everything out and are prepared to move on". Molly responded, "There are just too many bad memories here for us." Hillary said, "I understand. Can I talk this over with Marion first and let you know tomorrow?" Molly and Caleb both at the same time said, "That would be fine".

The next evening, Hillary dropped by and told Molly and Caleb that they would like the farm. They were more than willing to pay them what it was worth but Caleb would not hear of it. He said, "We have plenty of money and this is your heritage". Hillary said, "We decided that we just cannot leave this town because all of our clients are here and I did not want anyone else to live here where my brother, nephew, and grandmother were buried. I love this place, even with everything that has happened here." Caleb and Molly were so pleased that Hillary would take the farm. Hillary asked, "Do you know where you want to move to yet?" Molly said they were thinking about Arizona, where the weather was so much better. They had thought about Florida, But decided that it was too humid down there. They haven't made a concrete decision on where they were moving just yet but would soon.

Megan had taken the news of Chase's death pretty hard. She really loved him. Megan knew she was taking a chance with Chase anyway but she truly believed that their relationship could survive. She and Molly would always have that bond. Megan did not know why Chase would have killed himself either. She knew that with his diagnosis that Chase had, anything was possible. She still missed him terribly.

Molly called Katie and told her that Hillary and Marion were moving to the farm with the stipulation that they could tear down the pig processing barn and that was fine with her and Caleb. It was Hillary's farm now and she could do with it what she wanted.

Caleb asked Megan if she would like to have the funeral home and she said that she did not think she could afford to buy it. She also did not think she would if she could; knowing what went on in the embalming room with

Charlie, Chase, and Dr. Clark. Caleb got on the phone and said, "We would like for you to have the funeral home and if you would like to sell it and get a fresh start, you could do that also. We are giving it to you as a gift." Megan said, "I can't accept a gift like that." Molly replied, "Chase respected you and wanted to marry you and I think he would have liked that." Megan wasn't foolish, she said, "Thank you so much, you do not know what this means to me. I will sell it and get a fresh start." They talked a little more and then hung up.

The next day, Molly stopped over at Katie's and told her that Hillary had decided for certain to take the farm since she herself did not want it. Katie said, "That's great Mom, I know you will feel better about leaving, knowing that Hillary is there." Molly said, "We also gave the funeral home to Megan to keep or sell." Katie was a little jealous and said, "That's awfully generous of you and Dad. Looks like you have everything figured out". Molly replied, "Yes, it looks that way. Our moving was meant to be." Katie said, "I have some news also. We wanted to tell you and Dad earlier but there just never seemed like a good time to tell you lately." Molly said, "Well, what is it Katie?" Katie said, "I'm pregnant." Molly turned as white as a ghost. Katie looked at her intently and said, "Mom, what's wrong?" Molly gave her daughter a big smile and said, "Oh my God, a Baby! I'm going to be a Grandmother!" Katie said, "Yes, around Thanksgiving time. I also have something else to tell you Mom. We have decided to move away from here also. We are thinking about moving to Chicago where we can both get good jobs and we both love Chicago." Molly said,

"That's wonderful, what made you decide to move?" Katie said, "This town will never leave us alone or let us forget what happened that night at the farm. We have had enough and cannot see it getting much better around here. We still have news people following us around and asking for stories about Chase and Charlie when they were little, etc." Molly said, "I think that is an excellent idea. Would it be okay if Caleb and I moved to Chicago near you?" Katie said, "That would be wonderful. It would be nice to have my mother near when we have the baby." Molly looked excitedly at Katie and said, "Do you know if you are having a boy or a girl?" Katie said, "A boy. We are going to name him Drake Daniel, after Daniel and his father." Katie looked worried so Molly said, "What is it honey?" Katie said, "Mom, what if he is like Uncle Henry and Chase?" Molly held her and said, "Don't worry honey, that would be one chance in a million. Everything will be okay, don't worry." Molly said, "Caleb and I have been to Chicago a few times to see some special shows and we loved it there, even if it is a little cold. I can't wait to tell Caleb about the baby and where we will all be moving." Katie said, "That would be wonderful if we could all still be together somewhere, anywhere besides here. A baby needs his Grandparents." Molly had tears in their eyes contemplating a new life together somewhere besides this small town. A new start on life. She thought she may even get a part time position at one of the big decorating companies. They hugged and kissed each other good-bye and Molly left.

When Molly got home, she asked Caleb to sit down with her in the kitchen so that they could talk. Caleb was thinking, “Oh NO!” Molly took his hands and she asked, “Caleb, what would you think about moving to Chicago?” He said, “Chicago? It gets really cold there. Why Chicago?” She said, “That is where Katie and Daniel are moving to.” He said, “I didn’t know they were moving.” Molly said, “They are like us. They want to move and have a new start on life. It is just not the same here in this small town since the incident.” Caleb said, “We don’t have to move there just because Katie is, you know?” Molly got a big smile on her face and she said, “Yes, we do. Katie and Daniel are going to have a baby, a boy named Drake Daniel”. Caleb got a big smile on his face then as he said, “I’m going to be a Grandpa? Wow, that is good news. Of course, Katie will want us there, especially her mother. We can move to Chicago with them. I wouldn’t want to miss out on the babies first years.” They were both excited about moving to Chicago to be near their only daughter and new grand baby.”

When Molly left, Katie sat down on the couch and was contemplating her marriage to Daniel. She knew how much Daniel loved her. He told her so every single day. When they first got married, she thought that she was in love, wanted to be in love, tried to want what every other girl wanted. She failed miserably. Daniel was so easy to manipulate. She had learned how to manipulate men at a very young age, starting with her own father. Her and Daniel’s sex life was just okay; she just endured it and tried her best to act interested, but Daniel really just did not do it for her. She was really bi-sexual and she preferred to have sex with women. If he only knew what she fantasized about while they were having sex. If he only knew the real Katie, he would be very afraid. She knew she was only kidding herself if she thought that she could really be in love and live her life as women were supposed to. She also knew that she had known that she was really a lot like her brother Chase. She tried not to be like him. She hated him so much but she knew in her heart that she was as psycho as he was. She was able to hide it well from her parent's because they were so focused on her poor brother Chase. Katie knew that Daniel's life insurance was paid up and he was already fully vested in the company where he worked. Daniel would not have any problems moving to Chicago and working for the same company there. Even if she did not like being married, it looked good for her in her own career. She really didn't even like kids and wasn't very excited about it when she found out she was pregnant but Daniel was overjoyed. Katie knew between Daniel and her parents, they would take care of the little brat and she would not have to. If need be, she would hire a nanny. Katie decided that she would move to Chicago with Daniel but if she met a woman that she was really interested in, she would think of a way to get rid of Daniel to collect the life insurance money.

Lately, Daniel had been talking about having more than one child. He wanted her to get pregnant again soon after their son was born. That barefoot and pregnant sort of thing. Since she really did not like kids, she would just have this one but she would never tell Daniel that. She would just say, I'm not quite ready yet, let's wait another year" or, "I don't know why I can't get pregnant". She planned to have her tubes tied soon after the baby was born. She would not tell Daniel. She did not want to live in Chicago her whole life and she did not want to spend her whole life with him. She dreamed about living on a tropical island, lying on the beach with a drink in her hand, and of course, handsome men and beautiful women waiting on her hand and foot. Of course, Daniel could keep their son. Katie thought, "That damn Chase, he was so stupid getting caught the way he did. He was always doing something stupid. He was always drawing attention to himself with the help of his dorky, stupid friend Charlie. I am so much smarter than Chase ever was. He was always jealous of me because I never got caught at anything. "Katie hated him almost as much as he had hated her. Chase was always looking for anything she had done wrong, but he could never find anything and that really pissed him off. She knew that if Chase had not been shot to death that she would have surely killed him herself eventually. She knew that he thought about killing her more than once because he had told her so. She almost told him that she wanted to kill him but caught herself. She did not want him to know what she was capable of because then he would consider her competition. She thought, "I never drew attention to myself. I was the perfect actress, perfect child, student, and adult. I am a better planner. I know how to kill someone without getting caught at it, that is why I went into nursing in the first place. Look out Chicago here I come!

"THE END"

ACKNOWLEDGEMENT

Again, I'd like to acknowledge my husband. His support always carries me through to the end. I also want to thank him for spending so many nights without me, while I was on the computer and he was left alone on his own. My sister Sharon, for her help and patience in helping to read and edit my second book. I also thank her for being my person, for being there for me. I also thank her for listening to me even when she cannot figure out what I am talking about.

Most of all, a great big thank you to all of my family and friends who have supported me. Also a big thank you to all of my new fans!

AUTHOR BIOGRAPHY

J.C. Tolliver was born and raised in Cincinnati, Ohio during the 1960's and 1970's. She is a nurse, artist, and now a novelist. She has worked with many types of patients, families, and their relationships to each other. She feels she is more than qualified to write this type of book. Ms. Tolliver now lives in beautiful Indiana. She has raised four children and now has eight grandchildren. She and her husband still live in Indiana with their two dogs.

This is Ms. Tolliver's second novel, a sequel to Psycho Path I. She says, "I am very excited about this sequel and feel that it does the first book justice in further developing the story of Psycho Path. This is a dark and edgy thriller and written on the edge of what one's mind can comprehend." She hopes that you enjoy it as much as her first book, Psycho Path I.